Carmella McKenzie

BLOOMING GRAND

Acorn Independent Press

Contents

Acknowledgement

Thanks again to my sister Alison, for her unswerving
support and constructive criticism, or at least,
that is what she calls it.

Chapter One

SEEDLINGS

A young plant, raised from seed and not from a
cutting.

Very carefully, Lily lifted the small spindly plant out of
the tray, with the help of a lollipop stick. Concentrating,
her little tongue sticking out, she made a small hole with
her finger, nestled the seedling in and gently pressed the
soil around it. Her beloved Grandad, beside her to help
if necessary, smiled to himself. Beaming, she looked up
at him. 'That's it, Grandad, all finished.'

'Yes, Lily, and very well done too. You'll have a lovely
flower bed in the summer and it'll be all your own work.'

The eight-year-old Lily was bursting with pride.
Grandad had given her this small patch of earth in his
garden centre to encourage her. Mr and Mrs Overidge
had run the centre for all of their married lives and it
was their pride and joy. Building it up from a small
market garden attached to their ramshackle cottage, it
had grown in size as had the small village around them,
which now was more of a town. Their own son and
daughter-in-law had no interest in it, whatsoever. Robert
was the manager of the town's biggest supermarket and
his wife, Corrine, was the assistant manager of the hair
and beauty salon in the high street.

Lily loved everything about the place. To her eyes it
was a magical wonderland of greenery, with shoots

bursting through to the light, bringing forth flowers of every colour imaginable. Throughout the year, there was something new to be seen every day.

Grandma and Grandad had always looked after her at weekends, to give her mother a break and a chance to have a Saturday night out with Robert. She had her own bedroom in the cottage and helped Grandma make biscuits and cakes, something her mother never did. The rest of the time was spent in the centre. When she was a toddler, she was in a playpen, later, she followed them around with her tiny watering can and trowel, learning the names of plants and enchanting the customers. People asked her what she wanted to do when she grew up and very politely, she told them, 'I will work here.'

Lily's early years at school followed much the same pattern. She still stayed with her grandparents at weekends but learnt not to talk too much about flowers and gardening at home. Her parents weren't interested and her mother was always cross when she came home on Sundays with dirt under her nails.

* * *

On the outskirts of town, in the Park Homes, which used to be a caravan site many years ago and now upgraded, an eight-year-old boy was hiding under his bed. His parents were having another row and he lay, curled up, hungry and miserable with his hands over his ears. There had been no tea as yet, his dad had just got home from the scrapyard, where he worked, to find his partner waiting with her suitcase packed.

'I'm off,' she yelled. 'There's nothing for me here, my friend's got a job for me up North but I can't take the boy, so I'm leaving him with you. It's your turn to take responsibility. This isn't the life I thought it was going to be.'

'Are you daft, woman? I'm out to work, how can I look after him?'

'Looking after him might make you a bit more responsible and give you something else to think about apart from where your next drink's coming from.' There was a lot of shouting, the noise of china being broken and then finally, the sound of a slap. 'That's the last time you'll lay a finger on me, you great bully and I've told the Watkins to keep an eye on Murdoch. If you touch him, they'll call the social!'

There was a bit of a crowd gathering outside, so Brian had to hold his temper. Picking up the suitcase, he hurled it out of the door. 'Get out then and don't think you'll be seeing your son again. Call yourself a mother? Murdoch and I will be just fine!' She picked up the case and walked away, not looking at the faces of the Park inhabitants, most of whom, didn't give a damn what happened to her.

'What're you all looking at? Show's over.' Brian grabbed a beer from the fridge and sank down at the table

A short time later he saw a pale-faced Murdoch looking cautiously around the door. 'Ah, come here son. It's you and me now, so there'll be some changes around here. We'll go to the chippy and I need some more cans, then we'll talk about it.'

Not much was talked about that night. Murdoch was told that his mum had gone away to work, so he had to be a man now and help about the place. Evenings and Saturdays started with him helping in the scrapyard, but he must never tell anyone, or he'd be sorry. The Watkins family *did* keep a bit of a lookout for him and when his dad wasn't around or drunk, as he was most Sundays when not working, Murdoch would often be given a meal and helped Mr Watkins on his allotment behind the park site. That was where he learned, for the first time, how fruit and vegetables actually started out in life before ending up on a shelf or in a basket at the shop. Soon, he had a corner of the allotment to himself and grew firstly, potatoes, carrots and swede, which Mrs Watkins taught him to cook.

He attempted to keep up with his studies but trying to do homework was almost impossible and the state of his clothes and shoes made him the target of bullies. One thing his father *did* teach him, was how to look after himself and when he was ten and laid out the much bigger eleven-year-old bully in front of his followers, he was left alone. Alone and friendless.

* * *

By the time Lily was approaching sixteen, she had made a decision. Her parents had paid for her to be a day student at Greenfields School and the pupils there were expected to make the most of their abilities. That's when the arguments started. 'It doesn't matter what exams I do, I want to work at the garden centre. Grandad says I can run it one day.'

'Don't be ridiculous,' her mother looked pained. 'Robert, I have a headache, talk to her, will you?'

'That Garden Centre is a money pit. Far more modern ones are opening up out of town. The land will have to be sold for development, I've already made some enquiries.' Robert looked very pleased with himself.

'It doesn't belong to you!' shouted Lily, 'and my grandparents would *never* sell it. I know it's not doing very well, but I've got ideas. I've already talked to them and I know I could help to make it better.'

'Please Lily, this is laughable. You are a schoolgirl and you'll go to college or university. Your mother and I have made huge sacrifices to give you a decent education and you'll not waste it. I don't want to hear any more of this nonsense. Sort out your exams and then, you can think about your future.' *I shall have words with my fool parents and get rid of any ideas they have about keeping the place.*

Lily stormed off to her room, angry and upset. What a waste of time college would be. Or, would it? There were agricultural colleges, weren't there? Feeling a little more positive, she reached for her laptop and did some research. There were plenty of college courses on gardening and she could get a level 2 certificate in practical horticulture. A-levels were unnecessary unless she wanted a degree, that was a possibility of course. As long as she was in education, she wouldn't have to stay in school. She'd do some research and decide. It was her life and not her parent's decision to make.

Mr and Mrs Overidge listened in shock as their son, Robert, berated them about their encouragement of Lily's little hobby. 'This joke of a garden centre can't last much longer, I could get you a good price for it now. Houses need to be built and it'll give us all a better standard of living. You two shouldn't be working anymore,' he said, sounding very caring and sincere. 'A nice cruise, that would suit you both.'

A cruise? Mr Overidge didn't like the sound of that. Neither of them was inclined to give up, as their son was putting it. They both knew that Lily wanted nothing more than to manage the centre when they were good and ready to hand it over. She loved the place as much as they did.

They talked about it later that night. What if something happened before they were ready to retire? As things stood, it would go to Robert and they both now knew what *that* would mean. They wouldn't cut their son out of the will. Policies would be paid out and he could have those. Lily would get the cottage and the centre. They were agreed. An appointment would be made with the solicitor in the morning.

* * *

Brian Lawton couldn't believe what he was hearing. 'What do you mean, you can't leave school? You're nearly sixteen for feck's sake. Are you having a laugh?'

'No Dad, it's the law now. You have to stay at school till you're eighteen unless you can get a proper apprenticeship or, go on to further education.'

'Well, why didn't you say so? I can sort that. I'll have a word with Harry, at the scrapyard, leave it to me.'

Murdoch's heart sank. The scrapyard was not his idea of a future. He didn't fit in very well with the older men, who like his father, enjoyed a drink and spending time in the pub. Murdoch didn't object to the odd drink, but seeing his father spending money they could ill afford and passing Sundays in a stupor, seemed crazy to his way of thinking. Over the past few years he had learnt a lot more and managed to get his own allotment, albeit under his father's name. Brian had laughed but changed his tune when Murdoch produced roast potatoes and other vegetables he'd grown himself. Without saying anything, he also made up small boxes of fresh veg which he sold around the houses in town and used the money to get some clothes from the charity shops and also sorted some of the bills his father seemed to ignore.

* * *

At the scrapyard, Harry burst out laughing. 'An apprentice! Do you know what that means? *Paperwork* and busybodies sticking their noses into my business. Christ, you'll be expecting me to pay National *Insurance* next. I'm not having anything to do with that shite. Sorry mate, thanks for the joke though.'

Brian was determined the boy was going to earn some money. Staying at school till he was eighteen, no way was *that* happening. He made the point loud and clear. 'You earn or you're out. I can't support you all your life, you need to put into the pot now.'

'Into the pot! You've got no idea what I've been doing. We'd have no gas if I hadn't paid for the last bottles to be filled again, and the only money I get is from selling a few veg that *I* grow, while you drink it all away.'

'Don't you speak to me like that, boy. You do as I tell you.'

'Or what?' Murdoch drew himself up in front of his father, who hadn't realised how tall and muscular his son had become.

His own hand shook, he needed a drink. 'I just want a bit of respect in me own home, not too much to ask is it? What will you do then?' Brian was suddenly afraid, he couldn't manage this place on his own. Murdoch kept it nice, he had to admit, his clothes were laundered and he ate every night, not just from the chippy. 'Since your mother left, I lost heart,' he began to whine.

'I don't want to hear it, I lost a mother when I was *eight* and I had no childhood at all after that. You made me what I am, so don't complain when I go my own way. I'll find an apprenticeship myself.' Murdoch didn't want to stay on at school for a minute longer than he had too.

* * *

With only the solicitor's knowledge, the Overidge's will had been changed, making Lily the main beneficiary. However, they both realised that what their son had said was true. Roots garden centre was failing, badly. It needed an injection of cash and a new look. People were drifting away, attracted by the new, purpose-built, 'Garden Zone' several miles out of town. The tea rooms, gift shop, pet centre and outdoor furniture made it a family outing and apart from their loyal, older customers, Roots was losing out. They mentioned a few of their concerns to Lily.

'There's a lot of space that could be used for other things,' she said. 'You could have a bar-b-que area and a bit of a market garden maybe, there's a lot of call for fresh stuff now.'

'Your grandfather can't do all that work, we'd need some help. We want more staff, but I don't think we can afford it,' her grandmother said sadly.

'I'm sure you get financial help if you take trainees on, we can find out,' said Lily. 'I can't work here full time until I'm at least eighteen, I have to do A-levels or college, as I explained to you.'

'No, we don't want you to fall out with your parents, your education is important. If you're right and we get assistance, that would be a great help.' Her grandfather felt happier, he'd known for a long time that he needed help with the heavier work, but his pride had stopped him admitting it to anybody.

Lily smiled. 'They don't know what college it'll be, or what I'm doing, but it's my choice and they'll have to accept it. Mum would love me to go to the salon, especially as she's the manager now, I can't think of anything worse. She's making me condition my hair!'

'And very lovely it looks too,' her grandmother said.

Lily had inherited the best of Corrine's looks. Rich, chestnut hair that was thick and lustrous, kept at shoulder length, which she could manage, but never bothered to style. Hazel eyes, fringed by long lashes and a mouth that was almost permanently in a smile when she was working amongst the plants. A smattering of freckles and flawless skin, again thanks to her mother, but she was small for her age, which made her look younger than she was. 'We'll get somebody suitable and this place will get back to what it was before that modern monstrosity with its conveyor belt flowers took away all the custom.' Lily said firmly.

* * *

Murdoch was using a school computer to look up information on how to get an apprenticeship when the careers advisor came over to him. 'Can I help you with anything Murdoch?' The man had seen him at the allotments and also, his wife had mentioned a lad who came around selling veg. Putting two and two together, Mr Jarvis knew who it was.

Murdoch looked up, surprised. The staff never normally singled him out but had more or less given up on him. 'I'm... err, looking for an apprenticeship.'

'Is that so? Any particular line of work? Do you have a leaning towards anything?'

'I like being outdoors, using my hands, you know?' Murdoch felt daft trying to explain what he wanted, but Mr Jarvis seemed interested.

'Something in horticulture perhaps? The big new garden centre has just taken some people on, but I happen to know that there are still a few places. You can do day release courses as well; were you aware of that? And there're masterclass courses in such things as fencing and paving and soil nutrition, it's quite involved these days. Would you like me to check for you?'

Murdoch was about to say he'd do it himself, he wasn't used to kindness, apart from what the Watkins had done for him, but something in the way the man asked, changed his mind. He *knew* what Murdoch wanted, the only teacher who'd ever appeared to do that. 'Y-Yes, thanks, Mr Jarvis.'

'When are you sixteen, Murdoch?'

'Eighteenth of June, sir.'

'Leave it with me.'

* * *

Robert finished his evening meal and smiled indulgently at his daughter. 'Much homework tonight?'

'A fair bit, I've decided to do A-levels and then, I'll probably go to college or university.'

'Excellent. Any thoughts as to which direction? Business studies perhaps?'

'Oh Robert, that's boring.' Corrine was paying attention for a change. 'There are *so* many different therapy qualifications you can get now. I'm thinking of expanding the salon to allow for hot stone massages and wraps. Something along those lines dear, would be very useful.' Since Corrine had become the manager a few years ago, she was making her mark.

'Mmm, yes. I'm still thinking about it, looking at all my options you know?'

'Very wise,' said her father, 'No rush yet, let me know if you need any advice. Any cheese to finish off with, Corrine?'

He had already forgotten about her, thought Lily, with relief. Hot stone massage? It sounded more like a torture from the middle ages.

Up in her room, she made a start on her homework, then got her sketchbook out and doodled more designs for gardens. She had transformed the small area at the back of her house, not that her mum or dad had really taken much notice. A flower was a flower as far as they were concerned. All they wanted was a patio where they could sit, have a glass of wine and entertain occasionally. At least some of their visitors had commented on how beautiful it was. There was a vague, 'Oh our daughter is into all that,' but no actual thanks. Watching the flower shows on TV, she constantly made notes and drawings of the designs and show gardens that were displayed. How wonderful to create something like that? One day maybe, she could?

* * *

Murdoch turned up for an interview and looked at Garden Zone with a mixture of dismay and excitement. The site was enormous and very impersonal. It was certainly busy and they sold all sorts of things that had nothing to do with gardens but it would be a good start. They seemed happy and offered him a place.

He left school at the end of June and started along with two other apprentices. The manager soon had them run ragged, aware he lost a full day each week when they attended college, he liked to get his money's worth.

Murdoch was slightly perturbed when his father turned up one day being very loud and informing customers, 'That's my son'. He saw the supervisor looking in his direction and managed to persuade his dad to leave.

Over the next eighteen months, things seemed to fall into place. Murdoch enjoyed the work and was learning a lot, hands-on and through college. As long as his father stayed away and the manager thought he was being kept busy, everyone was happy.

Chapter Two

GERMINATION

The point when a seed undergoes physical changes and begins to grow.

It had taken two years of hard work but now, Lily was sitting the first of her A-levels and hoping to do well. She had not been at the garden centre quite so regularly, using her time for revision, but made sure she still spent weekends there, if not so many evenings. Her grandparents hadn't taken on any more staff and she worried about them because they only had Mr Taylor, who had been there for years and was almost as old as they were, along with Flora Harvey. She came most afternoons so that Grandma could do other things. She just wanted to talk about her neighbours and what they were all doing, they all seemed to lead a much more interesting life than herself, Flora grumbled.

Lily was nervously excited. She had told her parents about the choice of course being dependent upon her results. As neither of them had any clue how the education system worked these days, that satisfied them. She had already checked on the courses, she could go straight in and get her level 3, or, there was the possibility of a university, which would mean at least two years, but the qualifications she would get would stand her in good stead for running the centre in the future.

Another thing to look forward to, was the Prom, a great excuse to dress up and have a party. No drink of course, she was only seventeen like many of the others, but it was a major event for this time in her life. As Lily was still the shortest girl in the class she had bought shoes with ridiculously high heels and was practising walking in them. The Prom dress was something her mother had taken an interest in and did have an eye for. The girls were all wearing pastel colours and Lily's was a pale peach which made her chestnut hair look even richer. Her mother had promised to give her a light spray tan at the salon, nothing obvious, just an enhancement for her pale skin. As some of the other girls had already said they were having one, she agreed. A few of them were going to be partnered. Lily hadn't actually gone out with anybody yet, she hadn't been asked and wasn't really too keen on the idea. She didn't seem as physically developed as her friends and didn't attract the attention that they did. Having said that, her body had begun to change and she had breasts at last. Although she wore a bra, there hadn't really been the need. But now, as she studied herself in the mirror that morning, there was definitely more shape there. She would never be tall, that was for certain. A slight growth spurt had given her a couple more centimetres, but she had to wonder if that was her lot.

Her first exam was English, which she felt confident about. The biggest battles were yet to come.

* * *

Murdoch cleared the detritus of his father's latest binge and emptied it into the dustbin. Empty cans and the remains of a pizza had lain strewn across the table and the smell of stale beer and unwashed body hung heavy in the house. Theirs was not one of the more modern Park homes but at least it had a decent bathroom. He showered after cleaning up and also had to shave, just a bit, but it still pleased him, before he dressed for work.

His father had recently been laid off from the scrapyard. Harry had received one too many visits from the Old Bill and had to temper his activities for a bit, so there wasn't the work. Brian's answer to this was to drink a bit more and complain about how unfair his lot was.

One thing that had come their way, was a small, green, ancient van. Somehow, it had passed an MOT and was now in Murdoch's name, under the proviso he asked no questions, but he still needed to pass a test and up until now, didn't have the money to spare. He was quite excited about the van, he could use it to sell more of his veg and maybe advertise as, man and van, to earn a bit extra. He'd had an unexpected windfall, however. His mother had sent him £100 for his eighteenth birthday which was in a month's time. There had been little communication since she'd left, but there had been the odd birthday or Christmas card with a few pounds. This time, there was a letter.

She was sorry, he read, for what had happened and hoped he was okay. She was getting married, Murdoch was a man now and she wanted to mark his special birthday. She and her new husband were moving abroad and she wished him well.

No invitation to the wedding, no forwarding address, nothing. He almost didn't want to take the money but had to be practical. He could make that go a long way to help to set himself up. Hiding it in an old piece of drainpipe, he went off to work, leaving his father sleeping it off.

Garden Zone had expanded over the last two years. Murdoch had got his level 1 and 2 in practical horticulture, but they still used him mostly for routine work and heaving slabs and cement around in the patio area. He had walked past the small Roots nursery a few times and thought it would be a much nicer place to work. Looking around on one of his days' off, he liked what he saw. It needed a make-over, but there was room for expansion and he began to think what he would do with it, given the chance. Leaving his name and number for the owners in case of a vacancy, he had heard nothing as yet.

As he walked across the park, past all the now permanent homes, a voice called out to him. 'Hiya Murdoch, how're you doing?' It was Megan, a rather striking looking girl who was the eldest in a family of six.

He'd seen her around and knew she was interested in him, but up till now, hadn't encouraged her. Why not? It was about time he had a bit of fun, he thought. 'I'm okay, just off to work, what about you?'

'Same here, it was the only way I could get out of school at sixteen. Actually, wait for me, will you?' She dashed inside, grabbed her bag and jacket and joined him. *Yes, I can get to talk to him for a bit.* 'I had to train for something or go to college, so I got a place in that beauty salon? I'm a trainee hairdresser and nail technician. It's not so bad, the manager's a bit up herself and bosses me around.'

'Oh right. Are you busy?' He studied her a bit more closely while they talked. *Nice boobs.*

'Run off my feet. I don't see you go out much of an evening?' She was fishing. 'Everybody walks past us to go out, so I notice. Would you fancy a drink one night?'

Murdoch was about to say he didn't drink and wasn't even eighteen, but he realised how lame that sounded. 'I don't have an ID,' he mumbled, 'not for another few weeks anyway.'

'I can sort that,' she laughed and then thought he may feel happier in a group, the first time. 'There's a crowd of us going out Saturday. A burger and then a few at the Goose and Gander, they're not so fussy in there. Why don't you come?' She batted heavily mascaraed eyelashes at him.

He thought of the money he was trying to save and then, looked at her boobs again. 'I can't splash the cash, I don't get paid till the end of the month.'

'None of us are flush,' she said. 'We make a few drinks last a long time, come on, it'll be fun. No need to dress up or anything, it's all casual.' She'd noticed that when he didn't work, he still seemed to wear the same clothes and guessed he didn't earn much. 'You do gardening stuff, don't you?'

'Yeah, that would cover it.'

'Have a word with my dad, he tarmacs people's drives and things, they're always looking for extra workers. They do jobs on Sundays as well. It's cash in hand, no questions, you know what I mean?'

Murdoch did know what she meant. He'd heard stories about home owners being persuaded to have a drive tarmacked and weren't always happy with it, especially when they had to pay cash up front. But her father *had* been doing it a long time. 'Perhaps I will, but I already work some Sundays, I could use a bit extra though.' *Especially if I start taking you out.*

* * *

The exams were finished, Lily had the rest of the day free and needing a break, she headed off to the garden centre. It was bedding plant time and at least their regulars still came to stock up on lobelia, antirrhinums, begonias, geraniums and petunias. Those were the most popular ones that always sold and Lily had painstakingly brought most of them up from seed and transplanted them into the little plug trays that were favoured now. When she got there it was quiet, but Grandad said they'd had a few people in during the morning. She found a note on his, very untidy, desk. Murdoch Lawton was the name written on it, with a phone number, interested in working at Roots, with details of his qualifications and experience. If he was at Garden Zone, why would he want to work here, she wondered? But, they desperately needed more help so, picking up the note, she went to find Grandad.

Murdoch got a call and had an interview on his next day off. He liked Mr Overidge right away and the older man seemed impressed by his knowledge of some of the more unusual plants.

'So why do you want to leave the new place then, and come here?' The old man's eyes twinkled.

'I've learnt a lot.' Murdoch said carefully, 'but Garden Zone's very big and I have to get involved with cards and books and stuff when I just want to be outside. My interest is more with growing things and garden planning. I do understand what people want these days, but sometimes it seems like a bit of a theme park. I had to hold rabbits for petting last week.' He wondered if he'd said too much.

'Rabbits eh? Well, we don't have *them* here, not by invitation anyway.' He chuckled. 'I can only pay a bit over minimum wage I'm afraid.'

That's all he was getting now. 'That would be fine, Sir.'

'Ah, here's my granddaughter, Lily, she's the one you need to thank, prompted me with your note that you left.'

'Err, thanks, Lily.' He saw a young girl with an earth smudged face, carrying a box of plants to the tray displays. He wondered why she wasn't at school.

'Are you going to be working here?' She smiled at him.

'Umm?'

'If he wants to, the job's his. When could you start?' Stuart asked.

'I'll check my notice time and let you know, thanks.'

* * *

As it happened, the notice time was not an issue. The next day when he was at work and hadn't had a chance to speak to his manager, his heart sank when he saw his dad.

'Son,' Brian weaved through the plant displays, knocking several trays onto the floor. 'I'm just after a bit of cash, you haven't got twenty quid, have you?'

The lady that Murdoch was assisting, moved away as this large, obviously drunken man, almost bumped into her.

Murdoch wished his father to Hell. 'Dad, go *away*. I'm working.'

'Aw, Son, just twenty, I've had this tip...'

'I've not got any, *do* one, will you?' *Christ, the manager's coming over.*

'Murdoch, is there a problem here?' Mr Heavers asked.

'I'm talking to my son, is *that* a problem?' Brian said belligerently, instantly taking a dislike to anyone who chose to wear a suit to work.

'It is rather, sir, would you mind leaving the premises?'

'Don't tell *me* what to do you little ass wipe.' Brian shoved the manager who, arms, flailing, fell backwards into the petunia display.

Things moved quickly on. Murdoch hustled his father away and threatened never to come home again if he didn't buck himself up. Mr Heavers, after cleaning himself down, while glaring at the staff and customers who found the sight very amusing, hauled Murdoch into the office.

After a 'chat', Murdoch agreed to leave by the end of the week. The deputy manager, who felt a bit sorry for him, wished him well and suggested he keep his next place of work a secret from his father. 'I've noticed he's been in a few times, he's dragging you down, Murdoch.'

* * *

Saturday night, Murdoch put on his best top and jeans, from the charity shop. They were a bit scruffy-looking, but that wasn't too out of place. He fretted about how much money to take. Would twenty be enough? A burger and a few drinks, Megan had said. Should he pay for hers? It wasn't really a date, as such. Feeling sick, he stuck another twenty in his pocket and hoped he'd be bringing that home again.

As it happened, the Goose and Gander was being checked up on, so they weren't served. One of the older looking lads got some cans from the off-licence and they all went to the park, sat around, drank and smoked. Murdoch didn't smoke, but Megan did and that put him off a bit. He didn't particularly like the beer either and made his can last ages. She did sit very close to him though and he could see right down the front of her top. *Jeez,* he wondered what they would feel like. Apart from the view, he was pretty bored with the crap they were talking about.

One of the boys stood up. 'Let's get some more booze, got any more money?' he stared at Murdoch.

The other twenty was still safe. 'No, sorry mate. I'm skint. I'm going to head back, Megan, you want to come?'

'Just a minute,' said one of the others. 'You're working, you can't be *that* skint, you come out with us, you pay your way.'

'I've paid more than my way,' he said calmly. 'I've had one can to your three or four.'

'He can count!' the first one shouted and they all laughed.

'Leave it out, Ryan.' Megan moved beside Murdoch who in turn, gently moved her away from him. This wasn't good, there were three of them along with the girls who were watching.

'Look. Thanks for including me, but I'm going now, okay?'

'What if I say it's *not* okay?' sneered Ryan.

Murdoch sighed. 'I don't want trouble, let's just go our different ways and agree to differ.'

'Eh?' said the weasel-faced one called Davy. 'Wassat posh word mean, is he taking the piss?'

'Guess he is,' said Ryan and launched an attack. The girls started screaming and in a second, Ryan was flat on his back, with a bleeding nose and the other two leapt on Murdoch. One girl held Ryan's head and wailed, Megan grabbed a handful of Davy's hair and pulled with all her might. A siren was heard.

'The cops! We're out of here.' The two boys hauled Ryan to his feet and made off with the girls. Megan pulled a dazed Murdoch up as a policeman arrived.

'What's happened here, are you alright Miss?'

'I'm perfectly fine, it was just an argument, got out of hand, no harm was done. Thank you for your concern.' Megan smiled at him.

'Is that right sir? You look hurt.'

'It's nothing, really, we don't want to make a fuss. It's as my friend said, just a bit of an argument.'

'Well, if you say so, get that eye seen to, you'll have a shiner tomorrow.'

They walked away in silence, Murdoch took Megan's hand, waiting until they were clear of the copper. 'Sorry, I spoilt your evening but thank God, he didn't spot the cans.'

'S'alright. That lot can be tosspots as times. Are you okay? Shall I kiss it better?'

'Umm...'

She kissed it better and *even* better, let him have a feel and suggested they go out again, just the two of them.

* * *

Murdoch started at Roots on Monday and loved it immediately. Mr Overidge asked him if he was up to clearing an area down the end. 'I'm not quite sure what we're going to do with it yet but it's a bit of a mess.'

'Have you thought about maybe some specialised varieties of vegetables? If we treat the soil properly, it could be a healthy fresh line and you could sell them?'

'Specialised you say?'

'Yeah, things like those coloured carrots, the supermarket sells them and people like the look of anything that's a bit different.' Murdoch had taken note of some of the comments he'd got from people who bought his veg.

Flora had come back one day from shopping, exclaiming about purple carrots and how she'd seen that chef on TV using them. Mr Overidge looked thoughtful. 'I'll leave it up to you Murdoch, you make this your project and if it's successful, you can have a share in the profits, how's that?'

'That's great, thanks, I'll make this work.'

Stuart Overidge wondered about the bruised eye, but young men would be young men he thought and let it lie.

The next day, Murdoch saw Lily arrive and wondered why she was off school again. Maybe it was one of those training days? When he went up to the coffee hut she was there, with the tray.

'Hi, I saw you down the bottom, I've made you a coffee.' She smiled at him.

'Ta, you've got a free day then?'

'Free day? Oh, school, you mean. No, I don't have to go in now after my exams.'

'Exams?'

'Yeah, my A-levels.' She looked puzzled. 'You took them, didn't you?'

'Not those, only GCSE's... but, how old are you, are you taking them early or something?'

'What? No, I'm seventeen. Oh, I get it. I'm so damned small you probably thought I was about fourteen!'

'Not quite that young,' he grinned. 'But I am surprised.'

Lily couldn't remember if she'd seen him smile before. It totally transformed him from his usual serious self into somebody who looked like he'd be good fun. He was much nicer than any of the boys in her year, but he'd probably had loads of girlfriends, no wonder he thought she was still a kid. 'I'll be leaving school soon and I won't be going to college until September, so I can be here most days. I have to go on holiday with my parents,' she pulled a face. 'Two weeks in August, when they sun themselves in Majorca and I'll be bored stiff. Are you going away?'

Murdoch had never had a holiday in his life. He liked swimming and walking, if he got the chance, but sitting in the sun all day? That was his idea of hell. 'No, nothing planned. I'm happy working.'

'Me too,' she said happily. 'This will be the last year I have to go, hopefully. They probably won't be speaking to me anyway.'

'Why ever not?' He couldn't imagine Lily doing anything to upset anybody, let alone her parents.

'They think I'm going to college to do something they'll approve of. They don't know I'm doing horticulture. That is, as long as I get my grades of course. I want to run this place when it gets too much for Grandma and Grandad, but that should be a few years away yet, I hope. But if I get good grades then I may do a university course, it depends.' She shrugged.

It was the longest proper conversation he'd ever had with a girl. Murdoch was enjoying talking to her, she wasn't the kid that he'd thought she was, but she was still young and there was no way he could see her running this, without a few years' experience behind her. But to have an ambition like that, was good. Where was his path? He did like it here, but he didn't think it had a long-term future. Maybe, he could help to develop it. 'I hope I'll be around to give you a hand with it. There's so much could be done here and things you could diversify into.'

'Oh, I know, we'll talk about it some time. Look, there are customers, I'll take the old gent, you take the ladies, they'll like you.'

What was that supposed to mean, he wondered?

* * *

It was the night of the prom. Lily hadn't worked that day, her mother insisting that the time was needed for preparation. The spray tan had been done two nights ago and it was, as promised, subtle. One of the girls in class had taken to social media, moaning that she was *orange* and praying it would fade slightly by the evening. Lily knew there were a few hours to be spent in the salon to have her hair and make-up done. First, a long soak in the bath and the legs de-fuzzed. She tried the shoes again, they were a bit of a problem. She felt quite unnerved being so tall and was still unsteady, but the dress wasn't right with her normal flats and she had no intention of being the shortest in the photos.

She had been dreading the salon, but when her mother was nearly finished, Lily was staring at the mirror in amazement. The makeup was very understated but really accentuated her eyes and made her skin glow. One side of her hair was pinned up and the other had a few trailing ringlets.

There was a girl in the salon, sweeping up, changing towels and serving drinks to customers.

'Megan, get me a new spray, this one's running out and be quick about it please.'

'Yes, Mrs Overidge.'

Lily felt sorry for her and smiled her thanks. Megan rolled her eyes when Corrine wasn't looking and then was absolutely horrified that Lily had seen it.

There was a quick, 'Don't worry, I know what she's like,' from Lily, while her mother was busy for a moment.

A final spray and Corrine admired her handiwork. 'Doesn't she look stunning, Megan?'

'She looks beautiful, Mrs Overidge,' Megan replied truthfully. As soon as they were both out of sight, Megan moussed and sprayed her hair, ready for tonight's date with Murdoch. They'd been out a few times since the disastrous crowd night and now she was prepared to move it along a bit. He was different to other boys she'd been out with. He didn't really drink, which was a bit of a pain, but he was more of a man than she was used to and she liked it.

Lily had been dropped at the house of one of her friends, where they had all planned to meet. There were screams of delight at every new arrival, with dresses and hair being admired and photos taken. Lily took it slowly with the shoes and in a carpeted house, it wasn't too difficult. The street was a different matter. Luckily it was only across the road to the two limos, which took six girls each to the hotel in town, hosting the buffet spread and disco. Unbeknown to the parents, they had all had a couple of drinks and as Lily hadn't eaten much all day and was not used to it, her head was already swimming a bit. She made it into the hotel safely, drank some water and had something to eat. As there were no more drinks there, she began to slowly sober up.

Murdoch had taken Megan for a meal. She appreciated he couldn't afford much and had suggested a place that she knew was fairly inexpensive, only having a main course, saying she was watching her figure. He spent the meal watching her figure alright, her top was *very* low and he didn't like the way the waiter leered at her. He nearly choked when he felt her foot rubbing the inside of his thigh and moving upwards to his crotch. She had another glass of wine while he had a coffee and then pointedly looked at her watch.

'It's getting late, shall we make a move? I... don't suppose your dad's out tonight, is he?'

'Probably not,' sighed Murdoch. 'With no work, he can't really afford it. Your father doesn't need *him* for tarmac work, does he?'

'Umm... if he cut back on the drink a bit. Sorry, Murdoch, I don't know how else to say it.'

'It's okay, come on, let's go.' He was angry with his father, angry that other people obviously talked about their problems and fell into a brooding silence as they walked along the street.

'Look at that crowd, all dressed up really smart, it's one of those school proms.' Megan pointed to a group further down the street.

Murdoch glanced up without much interest, just youngsters making a lot of noise. There were some girls coming towards them.

'Oh Murdoch, see that one in the peach dress, that's my boss's daughter, somebody Overidge?'

He did look then. *Lily?* She looked so tall and... pretty. She was wobbling a bit, had she been drinking?

'She can't walk in those shoes,' tittered Megan.

'Hi, umm Murdoch and, err... Megan, isn't it?' Lily felt a bit awkward after only having seen him a couple of times.

'Lily, come *on,*' a voice called from up ahead.

'Coming, bye then.' She turned quickly, there was a loud crack and as her heel came away from the shoe her ankle twisted, causing her to fall against Murdoch, who caught her and held her upright.

'Have you been drinking?' He sounded very cross.

'No, I have *not*, well, just a tiny bit but my heel broke and my ankle *really* hurts.' She put her foot down and gave a shriek of pain.

'Murdoch, leave her with her friends, how do you know her anyway?' Megan hadn't factored this into her equation.

'Can you walk?' he asked.

'Noooo, it *hurts.*'

'Where are they all going?'

'Just to the coffee shop at the end of the road, if I could get there I can phone my dad.'

'You should go to the hospital, it could be a bad sprain.' He was a bit concerned, her eyes were full of tears.

'Murdoch, what about us?' Megan whined.

'It's just twisted, if it's still bad I'll get Dad to take me, I promise.' Lily was as white as a sheet.

'Megan, I'm going to help her to the coffee shop, it won't take long, you can wait here or come.'

'You bet I'm coming.' She wasn't going to let him out of her sight.

'If you lean against me can you walk? and take off that other ridiculous shoe!'

She only came up to his shoulder. 'I don't think I can walk.'

'Okay, sorry, but I'll have to do this.' She felt his arm go behind her legs and then she was being carried down the street. It was no strain at all for him and he looked down and winked at her. She thought she would die of embarrassment.

Megan was fuming and even more so, when he swept into the coffee shop to thunderous applause as he sat her down.

'T-Thanks Murdoch, sorry if I messed up your evening.'

'No problem, hope your ankle's alright.'

She'd looked so pretty, he thought, as Megan took his arm and pulled him away.

Chapter Three

PILEA LIBANENSIS

Better known as Silver Sprinkles plant. A tender
and evergreen perennial

Lily had a bad sprain. Upon seeing the swollen ankle
and bruising, her father had taken her straight to A&E.
Ordered to keep the weight off her foot, she had the use
of crutches for a few weeks. When she pictured what
had happened, she cringed. Murdoch must have seen a
little girl, *dressing up,* not even able to walk in heels
and what must his girlfriend have thought? The memory
of being picked up and carried down the street made
her burn with shame, but another feeling as well, which
made her breathless. She actually fancied him. It was no
good. He had a girlfriend and anyway, he wouldn't be
interested in her at all. It was a non-starter, but it didn't
stop her thinking about him.

Lily wasn't stupid, although she hadn't had a
boyfriend of her own yet, she'd seen some of her friends
fixating on certain boys at school, only to then see it all
fizzle out before it got started. She was going to have to
see Murdoch though, all through the summer until she
started college or went to university. He would never,
never know how she felt. The only thing she had to
concentrate on now was her future and to put him out
of her mind. At least she didn't have to see him *right*
away, her ankle took care of that problem.

* * *

Megan had clung to Murdoch after he had sat Lily down in the coffee shop. With all her friends whistling and cheering, he couldn't get out of there quickly enough. Telling Megan about how he knew Lily, and that when he'd first met her, he thought she was much younger, seemed to appease her, and even made a few remarks about, kids with more money than sense, which had made her even happier.

Murdoch remembered Lily's white face, strained with pain and knew how embarrassed she was about being picked up, which was why he had winked at her, to make it all a bit of a joke. When they got back, the lights were on in his home. 'Dad's in.' *And probably drunk.*

'Oh, that's a shame. We can't go to mine, it's always crowded. I wanted us to spend a bit of time together, you know?'

Damn. 'I'll see if I can get him out one night.' Murdoch would have to give him a bit of money, it was the only way. 'I've messed up another night out, haven't I?'

'It's not your fault, I can wait. But let's not make it too long?'

The next morning, it was only just light when there was a hammering on the door of the Park home. 'Open up, it's the police!'

Murdoch, who was awake, instantly thought that Ryan had finally made a complaint of assault and that the police had caught up with him. Going to the door with resignation he heard his father mumbling, 'What the feck do they want?' and opened the door to see six policemen, one with a piece of paper in his hand.

'Brian Lawton?'

'That's my father, I'm his son, Murdoch, what's the problem?'

'Step outside please sir, we have a warrant.'

'What the bleeding 'ell's going on?' Brian staggered out of his bedroom, wearing saggy jogging bottoms and looking much the worse for wear.

'Brian Lawton? We have a warrant to search these premises. You can step out or sit at the table. But you don't interfere.'

'Warrant fer what? It's a disgrace, disturbing folks at this time of the day. Feck off the lot of you.'

'Don't make trouble Mr Lawton. We have reason to believe there are stolen goods on these premises.'

'What?' Murdoch paled. 'Dad, you haven't...'

'Shut your mouth boy.'

'Sit down Mr Lawton, or I'll have to restrain you. Murdoch, wasn't it? Wait outside please.' He nodded to one of the officers outside, who stood beside Murdoch, but was not intimidating.

'My dad's not a thief, you won't find anything here.' Murdoch's face was now reddening with anger. Surely his father wasn't mixed up in anything like that? He *was* desperate though, with no job. 'What is it you're looking for anyway?'

'Can't tell you that, son, sorry. Hopefully, it won't take too long.'

'I've got to work and I need stuff from inside.'

'As I said, hopefully, it won't take too long.'

It didn't. To Murdoch's dismay, two of the officers were poking around outside and went to the back of the home. There was a shout from inside almost at the same time as one from the back. He could see through the open door. The officer in charge had what looked like jewellery in a plastic bag and was showing it to his father.

'Ain't never seen that before,' Brian said, sounding flustered.

'Shall I ask your son about it, sir?'

'No!' then more quietly, 'No, it's nothing to do with him. I didn't know it was stolen, I just bought it from a guy in the pub.'

An officer came from the back with Murdoch's money in another plastic bag.

'That's mine.' Shouted Murdoch. 'That's my money.'

The officer in charge stood in the doorway. 'Where was it?'

'In a drainpipe,' both Murdoch and the officer who had found it, answered. 'I was going to use it for driving lessons, my mother sent it to me,' Murdoch continued.

'How much is there?'

'A hundred pounds.'

The officer with the money gave a nod of affirmation.

'A hundred feckin pounds! That bitch sent you a hundred quid and you kept it a secret?' His father's furious voice came from inside.

'I didn't want it drunk away,' shouted Murdoch, ashamed of having to say it aloud. The usual gaggle of neighbours, also disturbed by the early morning noise, had come over to see what was happening and Murdoch for one, was grateful to the policeman who asked them all to, 'move away, there's nothing to see'.

'If you make a statement and can prove it's your money, you'll get it back. I suggest you put it in a bank and not a drainpipe,' the officer said kindly.

'Yeah, right.' Murdoch hoped he still had the letter from his mother. His father was brought out, better dressed, cautioned and handcuffed. 'What's going to happen to my dad?'

'He'll be held for questioning, you can find out more if you come down later to make that statement.'

Megan had come over to join the crowd, he heard her call his name and went to join her. 'They've arrested Dad. Apparently, he's got some stolen goods. He may be many things, but he's not a thief. I've got to look for something, get to work and then I'm going down the station.'

'Ma's making stew tonight, I'll keep you a plate. Give me a text when you're back and I'll bring it down.' *And have you to myself with a bit of luck.*

* * *

Lily had a visit from two of her friends. In the back room which had extra windows, so that Corrine could call it a conservatory, she sat with her foot up on a cushion while they all ate bowls of ice-cream.

'We never did get a chance to ask you the other night, but that boy, you knew him. You called him Murdoch, I can see why you kept *him* quiet. So, tell all.' Amy fixed her with a *come clean* look and Laura was also looking very interested.

'It's nothing like that,' Lily protested. 'I just met him a few weeks ago, when he came for a job at Roots. Grandad introduced us, that's it.' She hoped her face wasn't red.

'He's working at your garden centre? We'll have to come by and check out his err, suitability for the job, eh Laura?'

'Definitely, he's obviously got muscles, he carried you with no effort.'

'I couldn't walk and it wasn't *that* far,' Lily replied crossly. 'He happened to be there when I broke my heel and fell.'

'Alright for some, nothing exciting like that ever happens to me,' Amy pouted.

'He's well fit, I'd fall into him anytime.' Laura wondered if she could think of an excuse to buy some plants. 'Who was the girl with him?'

Lily didn't want to admit she knew *her* as well. 'Dunno, his girlfriend, obviously.'

'One of many I expect, they're not engaged or anything are they?'

'How should I know?' Lily snapped.

'Alright, calm down.' Laura smirked. 'What's the matter, do *you* want him?'

'No, I do *not*. That's just silly.'

'Is it, why's that?' Amy piped up, enjoying this immensely,

'Well, I-I have to see him at work and... and he's too old.'

'Too old!' Laura burst out laughing, 'What are you on? He's only about eighteen for God's sake, same as you.'

'Oh, shut up, let's talk about something else. What are you both doing for the summer?'

Giggling and finishing their ice cream, they talked about holiday plans and summer jobs. Lily was quite envious to hear that Amy was going with her cousin to a campsite in Wales on their own. No way would her parents let her do that, she thought.

Having finished her exams, Lily didn't really have to go into school for the rest of the term. Her results would be the deciding factor as to what she did. Sitting around with a bad ankle had given her some thinking time. College was all well and good, but Grandma and Grandad wouldn't be around forever and if she was going to take over the garden centre she would have to have a head for business, as well as a love for the product. It was a daunting thought but Lily knew what she wanted and had to prove to everybody that she was capable of taking it on.

* * *

Murdoch spent the day venting his anger on the ground he was organising for the vegetables. There was a large area to be completely turned over and all weeds eradicated. Luckily, the Overidge's had always done things the old-fashioned way and that meant months of soil preparation would be avoided and planting could begin very soon. It would take a while before any produce worth-while would appear, but there were some quick crops to get it started and establish the concept of fresh, tasty alternatives to the mass-produced choice in the supermarket.

Mr Overidge wandered down to see how he was getting on. 'About time you had a cuppa isn't it? You've been digging like a man possessed for over two hours.'

Murdoch straightened his aching back. 'I just wanted to get on with it, Sir.'

'Eh, don't be calling me sir. You can call me Stuart, and my wife is Marigold, but she can't abide that, so she's Madge, to most folks.'

'Err… Stuart?' Murdoch was puzzled. The name on the paperwork had been F and M Overidge. 'Who is F Overidge then?'

The old man smiled. 'That's me, Frederick, but I didn't want to be Fred to all and sundry so I use my middle name. Shall I put the kettle on then?'

'I'd rather get on… Stuart, if you don't mind.'

'I don't mind, but I want you able to move tomorrow. You've got something bothering you I can see that, I'm a good listener if you want to get it off your chest.'

Murdoch would dearly love to talk to this man who looked so kindly at him but couldn't bring himself to say how ashamed he felt of his own father and the circumstances they lived in. 'I'm fine, really and I will stop soon for coffee, I promise.'

'As you like Son, I'm always around, remember that.' Disappointed, he moved away. He didn't like to see the boy upset and he obviously was, about something. He went to pick a punnet of raspberries for Lily. She was laid up with a twisted ankle or some such, twisted it on her night out, he'd been told. Perhaps he'd ask Murdoch to drop them over on his way home, she'd probably like to see a younger person and have a chat.

Over by the fruit canes an elderly woman, rather strangely dressed, looked as if she was picking the fruit. As he got nearer he saw, to his astonishment, that she had a bee on the end of her finger and seemed to be talking to it! She saw him and smiled.

'Lovely day isn't it?'

'Yes, can I help you at all?'

'Oh, I'm just browsing, that's a lot of hard work going on down there,' she gestured to where Murdoch had started digging again.

'The new vegetable patch, the boy has just started here, a good worker.'

'A young man with the weight of the world on his shoulders. Still, I'm sure things will work out for him. Good day to you.'

'Err, yes, and to you.' What a strange woman he thought. The raspberries shimmered in the sunlight and the sound of tinkling laughter faded as he watched her walk away. Glancing back to Murdoch, he decided to take a coffee down to him and turning back, wondered where the old lady had gone. She just seemed to have disappeared.

The garden centre and particularly the boy Murdoch, were on Fae Dorothy Grimm's mind. So much so, that as soon as she got back she looked out the briefing papers to see which one of them had been given the task. It took a moment to find the name and then a large satisfied smile spread across her face. Perfect, she thought. Absolutely perfect, I couldn't have chosen better myself. You, my fine lad, are in very good hands indeed.

* * *

Lily was delighted to see her grandparents with a large punnet of raspberries still warm from the sun.

'How are you?' Grandma asked. 'Your poor ankle, what exactly happened?'

'Stupid high heels, didn't Murdoch say anything?'

'Murdoch, what's he got to do with it? I asked him if he'd like to drop these over for you, but he mumbled something about an appointment and rushed off.' Grandad said.

'It's just that he happened to be in town when I had m-my accident and he helped me to the coffee shop because I couldn't walk.'

'Did he now? Your knight in shining armour.' Grandad beamed. Two young people with the same interest, what could be better?

'Hardly that, he was with a girlfriend, it was very embarrassing. I'm glad he didn't come with the raspberries, it's awkward.'

'Oh, a girlfriend.' Grandad shrugged. 'Well, he's been hard at it today, worked up quite a sweat turning over that ground.'

Lily tried hard not to imagine Murdoch, with no shirt, skin glistening with sweat. 'It was a good idea, the vegetables, I've been looking some up, some unusual varieties.'

'Don't worry about it now, get yourself better for the summer. Eat these before your parents get back, there's not enough for three, so you enjoy them.' Said Grandma.

* * *

Murdoch produced the letter from his mother and told his story of the hundred pounds found in the drainpipe, signing the statement when it was all done. The policeman seemed happy with it and said he could collect his money from the desk, shortly.

'What's happening with my dad, can I see him?'

'He's still being held for questioning, but I expect he'll be released in the morning. I can't tell you anymore at the moment, sorry.'

'Released, so he hasn't done anything?'

'I didn't say that. Just wait until the morning, go home now and don't be putting any more money in drainpipes.'

Murdoch took his money and left. What on earth had his father done? Texting Megan, he made his way home. Only back for ten minutes, she appeared with a bottle of wine, a casserole dish and a very skimpy outfit.

'On your own tonight? We can eat and then relax.'

'I've had a pig of a day, I *need* to relax. Do we *have* to eat?'

'It won't take long and you ought to shower, aren't you hungry?'

He was, but seeing her in that dress, gave him an appetite for other things. 'We've got all night I suppose. Okay, I'll shower.' It also gave him the opportunity to make sure his room was presentable. Not having much in the way of personal items, it didn't take long.

In the main room, she'd pulled all the curtains, poured two large glasses of wine and was dishing up a plateful of stew that smelt delicious. He hadn't eaten a meal like it for ages, not counting the one they'd had out. The soft light filtering through the gap in poorly fitting curtains was flattering, the wine made him feel very at ease and comfortable and when she took his hand, he led her into his room and watched, mesmerised, while she undressed and then unbuttoned his shirt.

'Come on, I've been waiting long enough for you Murdoch.'

He needed no further encouragement.

* * *

Brian Lawton was released on bail after being charged with handling stolen goods, adamant that he'd bought the bracelets from a guy in the pub and didn't suspect a thing. He was to appear at the magistrates' court in four weeks' time. It was a first offence and likely he'd get a suspended sentence. The police were frustrated. The bracelets were part of a much larger haul that had been stolen from a jeweller's in the city several miles away. They had been hoping to get a lead on the fence they suspected was working in their area but they got nothing from the arrest.

Brian, knowing they'd be keeping an eye on him, would keep well away from the scrapyard, but Harry now owed him and he'd call in that favour when things quietened down. A celebration was in order, so he headed for his local.

Murdoch, having asked for the morning off, was at the police station. 'What do you mean he's gone, didn't he know I was coming?'

'We did tell him, but he wanted to leave, sorry.'

'Is he free then?'

'Not exactly, you'd better speak to him yourself.'

Suffering slightly from so much wine to which he was unaccustomed, but still on a high from his night with Megan, Murdoch had a good idea where his father would be. Well, if he couldn't be bothered to wait for his son, hard luck. He went straight to the driving school he'd had his eye on and asked how many lessons would be covered by a hundred pounds. When he found out he felt sick. He could never afford to learn to drive, there had to be another way. In the meantime, there was more digging to be done and he headed back to work.

* * *

Fae sat in her rocking chair and waited until the twittering colourful butterfly creature in front of her, quietened and settled. 'That's better, you make me feel quite giddy you know. Now listen to me carefully, it's time for you to go out and take on your first challenge.' The butterfly beat its wings furiously and the little face was animated. Fae sighed. 'Do behave. I have told you that you need to calm down and try and curb this over-exuberance that you have about everything. However, don't get too excited, you will be dealing with young people and you are the best candidate to fit into their way of thinking. We've all discussed it and we agree that it is your time.'

The twittering reached a crescendo and then, with the look on Fae's face, it subsided.

'Yes, I understand you need some help. There is a selection of magazines on the table which you can read, all about the sort of fashions and music that are popular at the moment. I haven't paid too much attention, it's of no interest to me, but you need to study them. Your main point of contact is a young man, very troubled, with a difficult home life. He needs no help in the romance department, don't look so disappointed, he probably will later on. What he needs now is a friend and gentle guidance on how to follow the right path. There is a young girl in his spectrum as well, but she will come and go in and out of his life for the time being. There is a lot for you to do. Their place of work will come under attack.' The butterfly looked shocked. 'Not that sort of attack! Unwanted interest, which you'll need to monitor.

I will leave you to your own devices, but you know you can come to me if you need help or advice. Have you decided on a name?'

The creature flew up towards Fae, leaving a trail of silver sparkles and twittered quietly in her ear.

'Yes, very nice, that will do, I'll leave you to study these magazines and get some ideas.'

As Fae disappeared, the butterfly hovered over some of the glossy pictures and stories. Fae had just picked a selection from where she had seen young people browsing without, as she had said, paying them much attention. An article on the latest catwalk trends caught the creature's eye. Bizarre clothing and interestingly coloured hair. Humans she had observed up to this point were fairly boring, these were much more exciting. A plethora of possibilities went through her mind. This was going to be fun.

* * *

Lily was talking to her father. 'I've decided to take your advice and do some sort of business studies, but I'll do it with something else as well, maybe at university?'

'A very good decision, what else were you thinking of? I'm glad you've got that garden nonsense out of your head.'

'Mmm, something to tie in with it, management, retail of some sort maybe?'

'I'm sure all those overpaid careers advisors can help. Your mother will be delighted as well. There's no future you understand, with Roots? It won't be there forever, but it'll benefit us all in our standard of living.'

Lily was furious. There *was* a future for Roots and she would make sure of it. If her grandparents wanted the money, they could have sold it a long time ago, it was their hope that she would carry it on, that's what they'd always said to her. She smiled sweetly. 'Well, that's all supposition, isn't it? They're doing all right at the moment and they enjoy it, it isn't a burden to them.'

'Huh, they're not getting any younger, should be putting their feet up, a cruise, I suggested. Suit them down to the ground.'

Lily knew they liked to keep busy and that might be a nice holiday but neither of them wanted to stop working, not yet, anyway. 'To get back to what I was saying, depending on my results, I may be away in term time, but I'll still help Grandma and Grandad as well while I'm here.'

'Your mother would be pleased if you did some work at the salon, a much better use of your time.'

'No thanks, I hate the smell of all the hair stuff and the tanning. I'll do what I enjoy, while I can.' It made it sound as if she was resigned to giving it up.

'If you must fiddle around with a few plants I suppose it won't hurt, if you're moving on later, I'm very pleased and I'm sure your results will be fine.' Whistling to himself, her father went to see what was for tea.

I'll talk to Grandma and Grandad in a few days and see how they still feel about the future. Maybe it was getting too much for them? Lily wondered. But all she could see was the pleasure on their faces when they were working, if somebody spent even just a few pounds on a plant they had nurtured, or asked advice about what to grow in a certain area. The personal touch, that was what they offered. That's what they needed to build on. Ideas began to sprout in Lily's head.

Chapter Four

TOXICODENDRON
RADICANS

Commonly known as poison ivy recognised by
its three-leaf stem

Three weeks passed before Lily was on her feet again.
Tentatively at first, with a bandage around her ankle
for extra support, she was soon confident that it wasn't
suddenly going to give way and cause her to fall. It had
been a grade two sprain, which was why it took longer
than usual before she could walk on it. The school term
would end in just over a weeks' time and she'd agreed to
go in with her friends and collect any personal bits still
in her locker or classroom. Apart from that, her time
was her own and it was now waiting for results and
the dreaded holiday with her parents to look forward
to. In the meantime, she could go back to the garden
centre, on the promise that she'd be careful, still used the
crutches if needed and not put undue strain on her foot.

Not having been there for a few weeks, she was surprised
but pleased to see large hanging baskets, with a mix of
glorious colour and trailing plants on either side of the
gate.

'Murdoch's idea,' Grandad said. 'Don't know why we
never did it before. He planted some up for us and they

flew off the shelf. We've always done pots, as you know, but never bothered with baskets.'

'I've noticed a lot more people putting them up, has the town entered for any competition?'

'The council has got something going, best garden, best vegetable plot and best planters or baskets. Of course, they're supposed to start the basket off themselves, not just buy them, but it makes the place look much better.'

'If it's successful, that's something we could get more involved with for next year. Perhaps a few classes on how to plan and prepare a basket or planter, lists of plants that are suitable and a discount if they buy half a dozen or so.' Lily's mind was a whirl.

'Slow down.' Laughed Grandad. 'It *is* a good idea, though. Hey Murdoch,' he waved to the figure coming up the path and Lily took a deep breath.

'Hey Lily, how's the foot?'

'A lot better thanks and umm... thanks again for helping me.'

'No worries, you wanted me, Stuart?'

Stuart? Grandad must like him.

Mr Overidge repeated what Lily had said. 'She was very impressed with the baskets.'

'Just so long as you don't expect *me* to do any classes, that's not my bag at all. We've got the first batch of cut and come again produce ready, I was just going to pick some and make up batches to put by the till.'

'What's that, salad stuff?' Lily asked.

'Yeah, come and have a look.' Murdoch saw her crutches. 'Are you okay?'

'Just being careful, I'd love to see what you've done.' She picked her way carefully down the path and was delighted when she saw the results of his hard work. 'Right, I can see coriander, lettuce and spinach. What else is ready?'

'There's chard, mustard and radicchio, another week or so and there'll be pak choi, red kale, basil and leaf celery.'

'You know, some of the restaurants might be interested, especially with the unusual variety angle.'

'I thought that but it's a bit too soon, a couple of months and we'll have a steady supply of herbs and leaves. I've already got dwarf beans and beetroot planted. Carrots are going in today and I'm going to try some Kohl Rabi, that might grab people's attention.'

'You seem to know a lot about vegetables, did you learn that at Garden Zone?'

'Some,' he looked at the patch. 'I helped on an allotment when I was young, and I've got my own now. I grow quite a bit.'

'Your family must enjoy that.'

'Yeah, I better get on.'

He closed off and obviously didn't want to talk any more. Lily wondered what she had said to upset him. The mention of his family? It must be a touchy subject and she felt bad about making him feel awkward, so stayed out of his way for the rest of the day.

Murdoch cursed himself for being cold towards her, but her remark had thrown him. Family, something he didn't have. A father yes, but not much of one. One who had rolled in, the evening of his release, drunk out of his skull and muttered in the morning, about a court date and it all being a *stitch up*. Court was coming up next week and Murdoch had to ask for another day off, at the end of the day it *was* his father and he should be there to support him.

In one of his sober moments, Brian had admitted to holding the stuff for Harry, with a view to finding a buyer. The boy was to keep his mouth shut about it, Brian ordered. It was difficult times for him, with no job, he had to make a living the best way he knew how. Murdoch didn't even bother to mention how much money was spent on booze, he'd done that once, when he was younger and got a clip around the ear for his trouble. He could hold his own against his father now, but it wasn't worth the aggro. He was aware of Lily, hobbling around, but thought the best thing was to stay out of her way for the day.

* * *

Robert Overidge was at the golf club, having a drink and waiting for the people he had arranged to meet. He didn't actually play golf, it was an expense he couldn't stretch to at the moment but was very much part of his future plans. The clubhouse however, was open to non-members for food and drink and, as a committee member of the town's Chamber of Commerce, he was known to many of the clientele and it wouldn't hurt at all, he thought, to have some of them acknowledge him during this business meeting.

A large out of town development consortium. He'd done his homework and knew what sort of sites appealed to them. The fact that the garden centre had originally been land attached to a cottage, still lived in, made it possible, through his enquiries, for housing development, there were endless possibilities. At least ten, superior detached houses with ample parking and garages, a mixture of one, two and three-bedroom town houses or, even apartments, which could be vast in number. It was a valuable site, whatever option they chose.

A group of 'suits' arrived, three of them, looking as if they belonged in the mafia. Robert thought if they took him as a nobody hoping to make a few quid, they could think again.

'Mr Overidge? I'm Peter Simmons. May I introduce my associates? Jeremy Cole, our architect and Martin Jones, a planning consultant.'

'Gentleman, please take a seat. What can I get you to drink?' Robert called a waiter to the table.

After pleasantries and a polite, stilted conversation, Peter Simmons leaned forward on the table. 'Okay Robert, you got our interest with your initial contact. Let's cut to the chase, what have you got for us, can we see the footprint?'

Knowing full well they'd have already done some homework, Robert took a map from his briefcase and spread it on the table. It showed the boundary outline of the garden centre, along with the small private garden and cottage attached. An access road ran alongside and other houses were already established nearby. 'A prime site.' Robert announced.

'I can see how you would think that,' Peter said slowly. 'But it's not that simple. There's the question of drainage and possible contamination. Heaven knows what chemicals have gone into that ground over the years.'

They must think I came up in the last bucket. 'Don't come all that with me. There's no drainage issue and it's been cultivated in an old-fashioned way for at least forty-five years, before that it was just shrubbery. The *only* problem with it, is, that it belongs to my parents, but they're elderly and can't keep it going for much longer. No-one would buy it as a going concern, it can't compete with what people want these days.'

'Are they any covenants on it?' asked Martin.

'Eh? Covenants, what do you mean?'

'Have you actually seen the deeds?' Peter narrowed his eyes. 'A lot of places like this could have us tied up in knots for years, getting nowhere with stipulations about what can and can't be built.'

'Is there a chance there're any rare plants or bats, anything like that?' The crooked planning consultant was already spending the money in his head. Any problems like those he'd mentioned, he could deal with, *if* he knew about them before it was public knowledge.

'I'm sure there isn't.' Robert began to sweat. Covenants? Surely, he would know about that?

'So, who would we actually be buying it from?' Peter persisted. 'It belongs to your parents, you say?'

'I'm working on them, but there's always the possibility of power of attorney, one never knows what's around the corner.'

'What sort of deal did you have in mind?' Peter relaxed slightly.

'Cash up front, what you build is up to you, but I know what *could* go there, so don't waste my time. I realise it's subject to you getting the permission of course, but as soon as you do, I want the money paid.'

'That's a big investment, we don't have cash like that on tap *and* have it available for development as well,' said Peter.

'You've just built houses near this golf course, three-quarters of a million plus, one of those could be included. There are several still for sale.' Robert smirked. 'You put together an offer and get back to me, no rush, I have work to do on my side yet.'

'Finished wiv these drinks, 'ave you?'

Robert glared at the figure by the table. A girl with the most terrible hair he'd ever seen. Blonde and spiky with bright blue tips. Looking like she had two black eyes with her makeup, she wasn't even wearing the golf club waiters' uniform, but a black t-shirt with some skull design in glitter and *jeans*. The members weren't even allowed to wear jeans. She was staring at him and he had the awful feeling that she'd overheard part of the conversation. 'Yes, take the tray, we've finished,' he snapped. As she leant down to pick it up, glitter fell all over his suit. 'For God's sake!' Jumping up, he brushed his suit furiously, sending the glitter in all directions, and was that somebody *laughing* at him? He turned to call the maître d', to complain, but the waitress was then nowhere to be seen.

After the consortium left, he found the manager who protested loudly that there was no such person working there and Mr Overidge must be mistaken.

'I know what I saw, this place is going downhill. I shall hold my business meetings elsewhere in future.' Robert left, his bad mood gradually dissipating when he thought of the potential money coming his way.

* * *

Lily was at the centre, a little more confident on her feet now, when she saw a mature man studying the colourful display of bedding plants and pots. 'Can I help at all, or are you just looking?' She had learnt not to pester people too quickly but he seemed a little unsure, she thought.

'That's very kind of you, I'm looking for some flowers for my wife.'

'Do you mean cut flowers, a bouquet?' Lily was disappointed but would rather send him to the florist so that he got what he wanted.

'Oh no, they don't last very long, do they? I want three or four pots to go on a window sill. My wife's not well and her bed is by the window.'

'Oh, I see, I'm sorry. Do you know what she likes?'

'The garden is her pride and joy, it upsets her that she can't get outside. Yes, to your question, I have a list.' He pulled out a piece of crumpled paper and his glasses. 'They have to be sweet-smelling, she prefers the scent in most cases.'

'Okay, let's see what we can find. When do you think she'll be up and about?'

The man looked away and then, took a deep breath. 'That's not going to happen, I'm afraid. S-she won't be getting out of bed again. I want to make her last months as pleasant as possible. Please don't say anything my dear, tragedy touches all of us at some time in our lives, you look young enough for it not to have affected you yet, at least, I hope it hasn't. Now, the first one on my list is...' He put on his glasses and studied it.

Lily was glad he had told her not to say anything, she wouldn't know where to start. How sad, but what a lovely thought he had about the pots. She was determined to find the best possible selection for him and re-pot if necessary. 'Do you have a car, they may be quite heavy?'

'Do I look that old? Perhaps I do to you, I can still drive, we live quite a way out of town,' he chuckled. 'Roses, they're her favourite, but they don't all smell strongly, do they, and what is your name?'

'I'm Lily. We have a lovely old-fashioned one, called "Mr Lincoln" it's a beautiful red with a fantastic scent. Let me show you.' Lily spent a good hour with Mr Wavish, as he introduced himself, and she potted up the rose, along with some sweet alyssum and dianthus. He was delighted. She put the pots in a trolley and walked with him to the car. 'I do hope your wife likes them and... and'

'It's alright,' said Mr Wavish, 'I understand. You have been very helpful and I won't forget it. You know, my wife, Rosemary and I used to come here, maybe forty years or so ago when we married and were setting up our garden. It's really lovely. I can't be doing with that new place, it serves a purpose I suppose and if it gets people interested in their gardens, all well and good. But I find it... soulless, I think the word is, with no personal touch. Let me give you my card, I'm semi-retired now, but still have contacts in the business. If you ever need any advice, please don't hesitate to contact me.'

Lily took the card which read, *Alexander Wavish, Barrister-at-law, Wavish and Pearce Law Firm.*

'Thank you, but I don't think I'd ever need to take up your time.'

'You never know what'll happen in the future, you're young and it looks rosy. Have you left school?'

'I've just done A-levels, waiting for results and then, after that maybe I'll go to university.'

'With a view to doing what?'

He looked interested and Lily didn't mind talking to him, they weren't busy in the centre, unfortunately, which was just as well, seeing Murdoch had a day off. 'My grandparents own this and they've always wanted me to run it, so in addition to more horticultural knowledge, I need to do something like business studies as well. Much as I'd love to just be up to my arms in potting compost, there's a lot more to it.'

'There certainly is and university is never a bad thing, gives you a lot more options, that's important. I wish you the best of luck with your results and it's been a great pleasure talking to you, Lily. I hope we meet again. You remind me of my daughter, she was about your age when... never mind.' He opened the boot of his car. The pots safely wedged in, he raised his hat and drove away. Lily went back to make herself a coffee.

'You were a long time with that gentleman,' Grandma said. 'Stuart and I left you to it, you seemed to be coping with what he wanted.'

'Yes, it was sad though,' Lily recounted the story.

'They came here before, what were the names?' Grandma had a very good memory.

'Alexander and... Rosemary, I think it was, Wavish. He said it was years ago.'

'Wavish, I think I remember them. They had a daughter, yes, that's right, the rumours were that she ran away with some travellers and they never traced her. It was in the local paper. She would be about your mother's age now, maybe a bit older. Broke their hearts it did, they may have grandchildren they know nothing about. What a shame.'

'He *said* I reminded him of his daughter, he couldn't finish what he was going to say. That poor man, and now he's losing his wife as well, I'm so glad he was happy with the selection.' Lily sipped her coffee, watching the plants on the trellis create dancing patterns on the pathway with the sunlight and thinking how unfair life could be sometimes.

* * *

Brian Lawton walked out of court, rubbing his hands. 'A free man, how about a drink to celebrate, son?'

'A suspended sentence means you can't get into trouble for two years. I'm taking you for a breakfast and coffee, you and I are going to have a serious talk, Dad, and if you walk away from me now, we *are* finished.'

'You can't lay the law down like that.'

'Can't I? Do you want a breakfast or not?'

Breakfast won and Brian, chastened and somewhat quieter than usual, suggested the East-side café, cheap and cheerful and back street, where at least he was on nodding terms with some of the 'faces' around the town. They were all small time, anybody worth their salt wouldn't give Brian Lawton the time of day, he was bad news, a drunk couldn't be trusted to keep silent. With food in his belly, along with several cups of coffee, he mellowed and had the grace to apologise to Murdoch for it getting as far as court. 'It was all your mother's fault, up and leaving me in the shite...'

'Don't start on that, she left *me* as well, we have to work together, not just me bringing money in. I *know* you lost your job,' Murdoch stopped his father before he went off on one. 'I'm not earning much, but I end up paying all the bills. You need to stop drinking, at least during the week and get down to the job centre.'

'I'm not crawling to them, I've got my pride.'

'Pride doesn't put food on the table or pay the bills. I can't even afford to have driving lessons. What's the point of that van sat there, if I can't use it? I could sell more veg if I could go further.'

Brian scratched his chin thoughtfully. The boy was right, what *was* the point of the van? If Murdoch could drive perhaps he could help with some *other* sort of deliveries? First things first. 'You're right, Son, I've let you down and I'm sorry. Let's see what's to do at this job centre and I'll put the word out about some driving lessons. I'm owed favours, you won't have to pay for them, get your... whatever it's called, licence and we'll go from there.'

'Provisional licence, you mean. Are you being upfront with me, you won't start drinking all the money away again?'

'I'm no saint, boy, but I'll do me best. Friday and Saturday nights are mine though, you understand?'

It was a start. Murdoch agreed and prayed his father would keep his word.

'Of course, when you can drive, you'll be taking that Megan out and about I guess?' Brian asked slyly and grinned at his son's surprised look. 'I ain't blind, Son, I was young once. Her father's in a good trade.'

'The tarmacking, yes I know. It's not for me though.'

'You want to spend your life being a gardener! What future is there in that, unless you get yerself on the telly like those other ponces.'

'It's what I enjoy, Dad, just let me do my own thing alright?'

'Alright, Son, how about another bit of toast before we go?'

* * *

Corrine eyed her husband suspiciously. 'You're in a very good mood, what are you up to?'

'Don't fret, pour us a glass of wine, things are going to get better for us very soon.'

'You've said that before.' She came back with two glasses. 'Are you going to tell me what it's all about?'

'Not just yet, I have a bit of... sorting to do, but I'm so confident, I've booked us two weeks in Barbados instead of Majorca. Lily will be impressed with that as well.'

'Barbados, really Robert? I'll need some new swimwear and a couple of good evening dresses. How hot is it over there in August? I have to protect my skin.'

'I don't know, in the thirties I think, nice to tell your friends though, eh?'

'Yes, you know it's a shame we can't go on our own, Lily never seems to enjoy a holiday, not since she was little.'

'This will be the last holiday she'll have with us I expect. She'll be eighteen while we're there and won't want to go away with her parents anymore. I promise you something *really* special next year, a month-long cruise, I had in mind.'

'A *cruise*?' Corrine's mind went wild with the thought of all the evening dresses and invites to sit at the Captain's table. Her friend had put on a stone on the last minute cheap deal cruise *she* went on. The food would have to be carefully monitored, Robert's in particular, he was getting a bit of a paunch but they had gyms and things on these cruise liners, didn't they? It would be wonderful. 'Not one with *children,* Robert, but I don't mean one of those *old* peoples' deals. A select cruise, I know they do them, for people like us.'

'It'll be the best, I promise you.' He looked at his wife, still very attractive and she looked after herself of course. He guiltily compared her with the new checkout lady that he'd just taken on at the supermarket. A single mother, whose children were now at school. A wonderful *curvy* body with a cleavage he'd spotted when helping her change the till roll. Hints of a black lace bra, Corrine never wore black underwear, she said it was common and she kept her figure trim, it could hardly be described as curvy.

'You're looking a bit flushed Robert, slow down on the wine. That won't be a good look on holiday.'

'Quite right dear, perhaps I'll sit outside for a while.' He looked at her questioningly, holding open the door to the garden.

'Too many midges at this time of the year. The flowers Lily put in are lovely, but they attract all sorts of *insects*. I'll sit here and read my magazine.'

Robert nipped to the kitchen, selecting a packet of nuts, two chocolate biscuits, topped up his wine and grabbed his 'Supermarket Monthly' which had another select magazine inside, then strolled out to the garden.

Chapter Five

HIPPEASTRUM PUNICEUM

One common name – Barbados Lily

The idea of a holiday in Barbados did not impress Lily. 'Isn't that well expensive, Dad? You've always been happy in Majorca, why spend all that money when I'm not fussed anyway? You don't have to take me.'

Robert didn't say that was what her mother had suggested. 'You'll have this holiday with us, it's what we both want, after that, you can do as you please. It's booked now and I don't want to hear any more about it. I'm sure your friends would give their eye teeth to go, you sound very ungrateful.'

'I'm sorry, I don't mean to, but you know I hate the heat and spend all my time in the shade with a book.'

'Your mother doesn't sit in the sun either, set your mind to enjoying it, you may surprise yourself. What a wonderful place to have your eighteenth birthday celebration.'

Laura and Amy were *very* envious. 'Wow, Barbados, that's fantastic,' Laura gushed. 'You are sooo lucky.'

'I don't feel lucky, I mean, the first few days will be okay, just lying about and reading, but then I get so *bored* and I'll have my birthday there with no friends.' Lily looked glum.

'Well to be fair, most of your friends aren't around when you have your birthday, we always celebrate later,

that's the problem with being an August baby.' Laura
pointed out

'There'll be all sorts of water sports with some
really hot instructors, I'll bet. Swap you for Wales? It'll
probably rain.' Sighed Amy.

'I've got to make the best of it. Dad more or less said
this is the last family holiday, thank God. What are you
doing Laura, you haven't said?'

'Nothing much, can't afford it and my parents won't
cough up for anything. I've been trying for some part-
time work but no luck yet. Hey! Does your gardener
need some help while you're away?'

Lily threw a cushion at her. 'They can't afford
anybody else and don't call him *my* gardener.'

'Oooh, touchy, aren't we?' Laura snickered. 'Don't
worry, gardening's not for me thanks, although, *he* could
run his green fingers over me any time.' She laughed and
the other two joined in, Lily hoping it was all a joke.
Even if *she* couldn't have him, she didn't want to see her
friend trying it on.

* * *

If Megan had known of the interest in her boyfriend,
she'd have been livid. Having set her sights firmly on him,
there was no room for anyone else in his circle and once
she'd given herself to him she had no intention of letting
go. Megan was not an innocent, having been, around
a bit, but Murdoch was different. Okay, he wasn't in
the best of jobs, but he had ambition and a purpose to
his life and would look after her. One thing nagged her,
when she and Murdoch hadn't had the opportunity to be
as physical as she would have liked, having no privacy
anywhere, she'd met up with Ryan, had a few too many
beers and one thing led to another. That was only a week
before she'd finally got Murdoch into bed and it was an

episode she bitterly regretted and had no intention of repeating. Thankfully, Ryan's recollection of the night was vague and she wasn't going to join any dots for him. It was all best forgotten.

A secret, guilty thought had been, that Murdoch's father might have been given a short, custodial sentence, but that hadn't happened and now he was around again all the time. Apparently, he was trying to find some work, although that wouldn't help if he was there in the evenings, in their way, as she saw it. It wouldn't be so bad if they lived in proper houses, but the Park homes were small with hardly any privacy. Hers wasn't even a possibility. It was a larger home, but a larger family, which filled it to the brim.

At work, Megan looked up to see Mrs Overidge's daughter come in. 'Hello, it's err, Lily, isn't it? How's your foot?' she asked politely.

'A lot better thanks, I-I'm sorry to have messed up your evening.'

'You didn't. Murdoch would help *anybody* and it was only a few minutes. He's just like that, it was nothing special.' Megan sounded very sure and possessive. *He's mine, I know him.* Even though she didn't see Lily as a threat, subconsciously, she was warning her off.

'That's okay then, is my mother around?'

'She's just doing a treatment; do you want to wait? She should be through in about fifteen minutes.'

'Thanks, I will.'

While Lily flicked through the magazines she wasn't interested in at all, Megan studied her covertly. Nothing special and quite small, she *did* look young. With no make-up, she appeared quite insipid and uninteresting. When she'd been done up for the prom, she *had* looked good, but obviously didn't worry the rest of the time. Megan looked at her own carefully manicured French nails and smiled. Murdoch would never see her looking less than her best.

Corrine came through just as her daughter was getting fed up. 'Mrs Gleason will be through in a moment to pay her bill, Megan. Oh, Lily, I do wish you wouldn't come in looking like that, you're not a good advertisement for the place.'

'I did wash my hands, I didn't come covered in earth.'

'There's no need to be insolent. You're not a child anymore, you're a young lady and you should start to look like one. Let me…'

'No thanks Mum, you wanted to take me to buy some beach wear?'

'Oh yes. I'm finished now, Megan, stay on reception. Bryony will lock up tonight, I'll see you tomorrow.'

'Goodnight, Mrs Overidge.' Megan was thrilled, she'd have a chance to use some of the products while the other girls were busy and wax her bikini line, always difficult to do at home with nosy younger brothers and sisters and not much private bathroom time.

* * *

Murdoch got home to find his father sober and in a good mood.

'Right, I've got you some lessons with Joe Simpson, Harry's mate. They owe me a favour so it'll cost nothing, he'll get you up to test level, the rest is up to you, and, I've got a bit of night-watchman work, only three nights a week, Tuesdays, Wednesdays and Thursdays, but it's something. Give you the place to yourself as well fer a bit.'

'Oh, err, great, thanks, and well done for the job. Shall I get us some fish and chips to celebrate?'

'You do that, Son, I'll make a pot of tea.'

'T-tea?'

'First night's work tomorrow. I'm trying Murdoch, I said I would, didn't I?'

'Yes, Dad.' Murdoch hoped it would last. His father had had good intentions in the past and it came to nothing but, he would encourage him as much as possible. While he walked to the chippie, he rang Megan and told her the news. 'Three nights a week, you can come over and we'll be on our own.'

'That's fantastic, and maybe we could have a few people over, have a party, you know?'

'I don't know about that…'

'Don't be so lame, it'll be fun. Not right away, we'll have some time on our own first, I'll see you tomorrow then.'

Murdoch didn't like the sound of a party at all if her friends he'd met before were anything to go by. Hoping he could talk her out of it, he was beginning to realise she could be quite determined when her mind was made up about something. He had to smile, maybe she was worth it?

Fish and chips finished, Murdoch noticed the signs of restlessness in his Father. 'Dad, I've got to go and do some work on the allotment, it's still light for a couple of hours, I could do with some help?'

'Help, with the garden stuff? I wouldn't be any use there.' Brian was wondering if he could allow himself one pint, that wouldn't hurt.

'I need a bit of muscle, there's a tree stump I have to get up, I can't do it on my own.' He'd planned to leave the stump alone, but it was the perfect excuse to stop his father wandering in the direction of the pub.

'Oh, well that's different, why didn't you say so? Come on then.' It was nice to feel wanted.

Surprisingly, Brian enjoyed himself and the thought of a pint went from his head as he levered the stump back and forward with his son. Not knowing anything about growing vegetables, the allotment looked full to his eye. 'Peas! I used to pinch those from a neighbour when I was a kid, they tasted handsome, straight from the pod.'

Murdoch picked a handful. 'They're not pinched but should taste just as good, the plants are taller, it's a variety called "Aldermans" I'm really pleased with them.'

Mr Watkins was walking over, getting on a bit now, he still pottered around but had given half his allotment over to Murdoch, in exchange for some of the heavy digging needed. 'Evening, Mr Lawton, nice to see you down here.'

'What?' Brian was instantly suspicious of any friendly overtures but saw nothing untoward in the man's expression. 'Oh yes, just helping my boy out.'

'He does a good job here, made it very productive.'

'He has too, I never realised.' Brian was actually feeling proud of his son. They worked for an hour or so, with a few more peas being consumed and for the first time since he could remember, he went to bed tired, but happy without a drop of alcohol passing his lips all day.

* * *

In the morning, Lily came to say goodbye to her grandparents. 'It's only two weeks but it'll seem like a lifetime to me.'

'Get away with you,' said Grandma. 'You deserve a break after your exams. You make sure you enjoy it.'

Murdoch brought out a tray of tea. He'd listened to Megan moaning about how her boss was going on a fantastic sun-filled holiday and taking Lily. 'Everything will be alright here, it won't disappear because you're away for two weeks.'

She smiled weakly. 'I know, I'm being daft and I'll be back for bank holiday weekend when it's really busy.'

Mr and Mrs Overidge hoped it *would* be busy, they were just about keeping their heads above water and had discussed an annuity they would be receiving soon when it matured and what they would do with it.

'I don't know if we're doing the right thing,' Stuart had said. 'Are we leaving Lily with just a big problem, maybe we *should* sell?'

'It would break her heart, you know that. There must be something we can do. That boy, Murdoch, has a lot of good ideas.'

'Yes, he does, but is it too little too late, Duckie?' Stuart looked at his wife affectionately as he used his pet name for her. 'We're struggling and we need more help.'

'Then we'll use the money to take somebody else on. Now we can't do so much, we have to take a step back. All of this fresh vegetable stuff may be the centre's saving grace, we owe it to Lily to try.'

'At least we agree, September, we'll get the money, so we'll advertise then.'

They were both thinking about this conversation while watching Lily and Murdoch talking animatedly about the bulb rush that would come at the end of summer.

'You need to get people thinking about it now,' Lily said, trying to forget she was about to go on holiday.

'You know, in all the seed catalogues, there are always pictures. Could we get some big ones and put them up on the fence with, I don't know, plan early for the best out of your bulbs, or something like that?'

'That' a *great* idea, I'll get onto it as soon as I get back. If we deal exclusively with one of them, they may do us a special deal and help with a display. I'll tell Grandad.'

Murdoch grinned as she rushed off, Lily got over excited about things but it was quite refreshing to see a girl like that so enthusiastic about gardening, especially when she had a mother who ran a beauty salon.

When Lily got home, she immediately slipped her drawing book and notebooks into her suitcase. Her mind was already working on the bulb promotion. Everything from the early snowdrops, through to tulips.

* * *

Alexander Wavish took a cup of tea to his wife and was pleased to see her awake and looking at her plants. Although Lily had told him how to look after them, Rosemary was still capable of giving instructions.

She was pale and looked tired, but smiled as he came in. 'The rose has another bud coming, which will be open soon.' She didn't add that at least she'd see that one. Every day, she wondered what she *wouldn't* see again. The holly berries? And then her thoughts went to her drift of snowdrops, the scattering of daffodils and her favourite spring plant, the beautifully scented, lily of the valley. She had accepted it was her time, people didn't go on forever, it was just a lot sooner than she would have liked. Her eyes flicked to the picture of their eighteen-year-old daughter, the last one taken before she had run away. 'I've been thinking about Caroline today.'

'You think about her every day, as do I, especially, since I mentioned the girl in the garden centre. I think it was just the age, it brought her to mind, that was all.'

'It's the not knowing, that's always been the worst thing, where she went, what happened, if she's even still alive.'

'*Stop*. Don't distress yourself. We've gone over this time and time again, all we can hope is, that she is happy and found what she couldn't find with us.'

'I hope so, I only wish I knew before… before.'

Alexander put his finger to her lips. 'Don't say it. We were blessed with her for eighteen years before it fell apart. Remember the happy times.' He also looked at the photo that showed a girl with dark hair and brown eyes, which, in a certain light showed hints of green.

Travellers had been camped nearby for a few days, her parents had seen her talking to them and what had started off as a cautious warning turned into a row. She'd screamed at them, saying she was treated like one of her mother's precious greenhouse plants, kept in a prison and not allowed out. In the morning the travellers had gone and so had Caroline. All she left was a note saying, Goodbye, she was off to 'get a life'.

She was never found. All leads led nowhere, sightings came to nothing and there had not been a word from her since. Her parents were broken, but they got through it. Over the years, Alexander had paid thousands in private investigators' bills, never telling his wife, not wanting to get her hopes up. Once or twice, there appeared to be a breakthrough, but then, again, nothing.

Now, after all the years of heartbreak, Rosemary was slipping away and he would lose her as well.

* * *

After a long flight, Lily wanted nothing more than to sink into bed, but her parents insisted they get into the time zone straight away. She spent the afternoon, zombie-like, exploring the hotel with her mother, who booked in for several massages and other treatments. Lily allowed herself to be booked in for a massage later in the week, it was something to do, after all. Then they had to study the activities board. All the usual options were on offer, team sports, archery, painting, she might do that, she thought, but not the line dancing. Moving along to the excursions, she was pleasantly surprised to see such a choice and there were a lot of gardens. Yes, it was hot outside, but the gardens would be shady, from the pictures, there were many trees. 'I wouldn't mind doing some of these, Mum, how about you?'

'Oh no, I can't stand day trips, so exhausting, ask your father, or if it's with a guide, I'm sure you could go on your own if you stay with everybody else. You might make some friends, there's a very good class of clientele at this hotel and there may be some young people.'

Anything to keep me out of your hair. 'Maybe, can I go and book some?'

'Of course, whatever you like, your father's paying for everything. He's promised things are going to be a lot better for us soon.'

'Really, I didn't think the supermarket was doing that well?'

'I don't know, I'm sure your father knows what he's doing. Actually, I am feeling quite tired myself now and the rooms are ready. So perhaps a lie down before dinner might be in order. Meet us at the bar no later than eight.'

Lily escaped and after setting her alarm, drifted off in the cool, air-conditioned room for a couple of hours much-needed sleep.

Three days later, she went on her first excursion. As she thought, her father had no interest in going either, so she joined the group of fifty plus somethings, for the garden delight full day tour. A tall man, lighter-skinned than most she had seen so far with a smile showing gleaming white teeth came into the foyer with a clipboard. Lily had got used to some of the Bajan dialect but it was still difficult to know exactly what he was saying.

'Hiya, all-a-wanna go de Garden trip? I am man for de day. My name Tobias, like in de song.' He started saying something about being a captain on coconut airways and all the older people started to laugh and join in with 'Whoa, I'm going to Barbados'. Lily was quite bemused, he noticed and gave her an even bigger grin. 'Girl, wuh wrong wid you? You no know dis fine tune? It was big hit in your country, before you born I tink.' All the older people laughed again and Lily, feeling even younger and very self-conscious, followed them out to the minibus.

As everybody else were in couples, she ended up in the single seat next to Tobias. He winked at her and passed over a booklet which explained the trip. 'I can speak proper English,' he said quietly, 'but people love the Bajan dialect.' He turned around to face them all. 'Okay, every man and woman, dis is whahappen today. One, we go Andromeda Botanical Garden. Dis started in 1954 and woman give to Barbados National Trust. De sun is hot hot hot today, hope you all got hat? We don' want nobody drop-down,' Tobias chattered on in this vein all the way to their first stop and Lily could hardly stop herself laughing at the other people's puzzled expressions at some of the phrases he used.

'We here, stop two hour and I thirsty, so all de talk stop now, all-a-wanna be back for bus at eleven.'

People started to wander off and Lily studied her map.

'Why you 'lone, sorry I mean, why is a lovely girl like you by yourself on this trip?' Tobias was at her side, smiling.

'Isn't it hard work, keeping up that talk all the time?' Lily grinned, it was infectious.

'It's fun and it's what they pay for, I was born here and everybody speaks like that, but I have spent time in England, we have family there. My mother came from England, that is why I am not so dark skinned. If you like, I can show you the best parts of the tour, what you should see in the time you have?'

'Don't you want to have a rest? I'm not so interested in the touristy bits, I like the plants,'

'It's a nice walk in the shade, you like plants?'

Lily gave him a brief story of the garden centre and what she hoped to do. 'I'm here with my parents, they're not interested in the trips. I was surprised to find how many gardens were here.'

'You will enjoy them all, especially Hunte's, it's on the site of an old sugar cane plantation. Girl, yuh like liquor bile over.' Tobias flashed his white teeth again in a wide grin.

'Maybe I shouldn't ask, but what does that mean?'

'A girl is so beautiful she looks like sugar-cane liquor which has boiled over the rim of the container. One of our local expressions, and no, I have never seen the liquor boil over the rim.'

She laughed and enjoyed the next ninety minutes admiring exotic plants, some she knew, others she had no knowledge of. She insisted on buying them both a drink at the shop where most of their party were already spending money on souvenirs and postcards. It seemed natural they spent the rest of the day together and he had been right about Hunte's garden. Towering trees gave welcome shade and statues and other ornamentations were a constant surprise and delight. At the end of the day, he presented her with an orange bloom.

'We call this the, Barbados Lily, it seemed appropriate,' he said, tucking it behind her ear.

'It looks like what we call an Easter Lily, thank you,' she blushed slightly.

'I hope I will see you again, my English Lily. We are having a party down on the beach tonight if you would like to come? Just as friends,' he added quickly. 'There will be music and dancing, come and lime with us, have some fun.'

'Lime?'

'Hang out, chill. You mus' learn de Bajun speak, girl.'

'Thank you, maybe I will.' It was only the beach, fifty metres from the hotel that should be safe enough and he was… very nice.

'Any time from sundown, you will see the fire.'

After enduring a boring meal with her parents, who didn't really want to hear about the garden trip, Lily thought she would walk down. Paths were lit all the way to the beach and there were many people around. It was still very warm and quite unnecessary for a fire, apart from the light it gave. She soon saw it and could hear a lot of laughter and guitar music. There was also a smell she recognised as she got closer. She didn't smoke, so it would be easy to say no, if it was that sort of gathering, she didn't want to know.

Tobias soon spotted her, 'Lily, over here.' He passed her a bottle which she noted was unopened.

It was like he could read her mind. 'Don't worry Lily, I said, just friends. There is weed here.'

'I know, I smelt it, not for me thanks.'

He nodded and there was no pressure. She was quite pleased to see he didn't partake and she began to relax. The music was good, the conversation, although difficult to follow, flowed and people included her as best they could. She told them where she came from and that's really all they wanted to know. Most of them were very dark-skinned but there were a few like Tobias, with one white parent, she guessed. Careful what she drank, it was still the most fun she'd had since arriving.

Tobias walked her back to the hotel entrance. 'Are you going on any more trips?'

'I quite liked the look of the "best of Barbados" it's seven hours, do you do that one?'

'I do sometimes, but not this week. Would you trust me to take you on our own? I'll understand if you say no, but you know who I am now and we can inform the hotel if you are unsure.'

'Umm, my mother would have a fit.'

'Why, cos I is black?' the customary grin.

'Of course not,' she laughed. 'Because I hardly know you and I'm in a foreign country.'

'Let me reassure you.' He took her to the desk and spoke to one of the women, who greeted him effusively.

'I am Lola, his sister, you will be most safe with him Miss Overidge.'

'In that case, yes please, I'd love it.'

'Can you snorkel?' he asked.

'Not very well, is this for the turtles?'

'Yes, I will help you. I am free on Monday?'

That was her birthday. 'That would be perfect Tobias, I'll err, sort things with my parents, they were going to spend the day with me Monday, I'll say there was no other choice for this trip.'

'If you are sure?'

'Very sure.'

'Monday, but that's your birthday, can't you go another day?' Her father spluttered.

'It's the only day I can do that particular trip, I'm so sorry, but I will be back by eight, we can celebrate in the evening? Unless you want to come too, we leave at six in the morning.' She held her breath.

'No, no that's fine. We'll have a meal in the evening, you enjoy yourself.'

On Monday morning, swim gear and towel packed she was waiting outside when Tobias pulled up in a jeep. 'This is so kind of you,' she said as she jumped in. 'I insist on buying you lunch.'

'We'll see, now relax. Our first stop is the East coast and Bathsheba beach, then to the Gully where you will see the rainforest and hopefully, the green monkeys.'

The first part of the day was wonderful, they did indeed see the monkeys and everywhere they stopped, people knew Tobias and welcomed her as a friend because she was with him. After a bar stop where they had rum and coconut water, they headed inland for Harrison's cave. There was quite a queue, but Tobias had a chat with someone and they were taken past the waiting tourists to a few 'tuts' and went on the mile-long driveway to see a fantastic limestone cavern with waterfalls, stalagmites and stalactites. Then it was off to Pirates Cove where they argued, and Lily won, about who would pay for lunch. They stayed on the beach for a while.

'Are you enjoying yourself Lily?' Tobias brushed her hair back from her face.

'Yes. Umm...'

'What?'

'D-do you take many women out like this, I mean, you must have a lot of holiday romances?' He looked at her and she thought she saw disappointment on his face.

'Is that what you want, what you are looking for?' He was staring out over the sea.

'Well, no, not really. I'm sorry, if that's what you...'

'No, Lily. You are sweet and I like you, that is all. Is that enough?'

'That's plenty. I like you too.'

'Good, come along then.' He stood and held out a hand which she took and he pulled her up. She didn't let go and they walked back together to the jeep. 'Now we will meet my cousin who is a tour guide for the turtle swimming, he will explain it all to you, they are very strict.'

His cousin, Joseph, told her that there was no contact or interaction with the turtles at all, so there was no disturbance to their natural environment. It was one of the most exhilarating experiences of her life.

'Oh,' she said, as they came back. 'That was the best birthday present ever. *Damn*, I didn't mean to say that, I didn't want you to know.'

'It is your birthday, why shouldn't I know?'

'I didn't want you to think you had to get me something, this has been the best day ever Tobias, really it has.'

'How old are you?'

'Eighteen,' she mumbled, feeling embarrassed, but he said no more.

He got her back to the hotel in time for her meal. 'Will you meet me at the beach bar later, please Lily?'

'I'll try, if my parents have had enough of me.'

In the jeep, she had left a bag of shells from Pirates Cove. Smiling, he took them to the beach bar.

Her parents gave her a laptop and new mobile phone. 'You'll need it with the studying you're going to do,' said Robert.

'Thank you, it's a great present.'

'*I* got this for you,' her mother handed over a vanity case filled with expensive lotions and skin creams. 'You need to start now Lily, to have good skin in middle age.'

'Thanks, Mum, I promise I'll try and get into the habit.'

They had a meal and after a drink or two, they were quite happy when she said she wanted a last bit of air. Slipping down to the beach she found Tobias waiting.

'Happy birthday my little Barbados Lily.' He slipped a necklace of shells over her head.

'Oh, Tobias, thank you, I left them behind.'

'Now you have them as a memory of a wonderful day, walk with me.' Walking along the wet sand he held her hand. 'I will not give you a holiday fling, you are worth more than that, but I would like to give you one memory.' Taking her in his arms, he kissed her gently. 'Have many men kissed you, Lily?'

'No-one,' she said, 'Is that awful, at eighteen?'

'No, but it is time.' She felt a deeper kiss, her heart fluttered, just a little bit and she wrapped her arms around him as the sea lapped gently around their ankles.

Chapter Six

CREEPERS

A plant which can be decorative but also grow
around another, sometimes choking it.

Peter Simmons looked approvingly at the drawings in front of him. That Overidge chap had it pretty well sussed. The architect had sketched twelve executive houses. Four or five bedrooms with additional office space, saunas, double garages with neat gardens geared for entertaining. A gated, exclusive development, worth a small fortune. One of the houses that Robert wanted near the golf course, plus some cash, would be tempting enough for him. He smiled, they would find enough difficulties with the site to beat him down on what he expected, but they still had the problem of actually buying it. Surely, the old folks would give into their son, the place must be a constant drain on their resources. Peter wasn't in an enormous rush, they were still working on another project which would take at least a year, but he liked to landbank and have sites ready for when he wanted them. Martin Jones, the planning consultant, had gone to sniff around Roots and suss it out.

* * *

Stuart had mentioned that the family were back from holiday and Lily would be in the next day. Murdoch was surprised at how much he'd missed seeing her around.

For the two or three weeks before she went away, she'd been there most days and he'd got used to chatting to her, aware of what she was doing and her general cheery manner brightening the place up.

He was exhausted. His father had seemed to have got through the first two weeks of his part-time job with no problems, but for three nights in a row, both weeks, Megan had been over. He wasn't exactly complaining, but he did need *some* sleep and couldn't understand how she seemed so wide awake and upbeat the next night, after a day at work. She was now pressuring him to have a party and he was dreading it. They both had Thursday off next week and there was no getting out of it, Wednesday night was booked as far as she was concerned. He hoped the weather would hold so that at least they could be outside and not all squashed in the home. He'd stipulated a limit of twelve and she'd smiled, which worried him. He also had to make sure there would be no bottles or cans laying around anywhere afterwards, for his dad to pick up, he had already gone to the pub a couple of nights when he wasn't working and had got drunk, but not quite as badly as before. Murdoch was now in charge of all the bills and as his dad was paid his wages in cash, he made him hand over at least half if of it straight away.

Going to make a coffee to wake himself up a bit, he saw a man standing and staring across the rows of summer bedding plants, towards the Overidge's cottage. 'Can I help you with anything, Sir?'

The man, startled, turned and closed a notebook he'd been scribbling in. 'No, not really, I'm, err, looking for some plants for my wife's garden, just a small patch that's a bit bare, you know?'

'I see. Did you want perennials or just some bedding, for instant colour?'

The man's eyes glazed over. 'I'm not quite sure, ha-ha obviously I didn't take proper instruction, I'll just look around for a bit and report back. I won't bother you now.'

'Okay, I'll be here if you want to ask anything.' Murdoch thought he was a bit odd and would have been more than happy to offer some advice.

Martin frowned, he could have done with more time. This setting was perfect as far as he could see, but he might need to introduce a few problems that would discourage customers. He swatted away a few wasps that were beginning to buzz around his head.

A short distance away, behind the sweet peas, stood a young woman, a hat pulled down to conceal her blue-spiked hair. She was dressed in fairly subdued clothing and nobody had seen her, but she wasn't taking any chances at this stage. She glared at Martin. So, he thought he might drive customers away, did he? He was the one who needed to be driven away. She made a swirling motion with her finger and on a post just behind him, there appeared a wasps' nest and its inhabitants were *not* happy. They came streaming out of the nest with a vengeance.

Martin was about to write some more notes when a large wasp landed on his hand and promptly stung him. 'Blast and damn!' He slapped his hand down as the wasp flew off. He looked around, glaring at the laughing noise he heard, *children!* but there were none to be seen. He felt another sting on the back of his neck, then another right on his nose and gave a howl which was heard from quite a distance.

Looking out of the hut, Murdoch saw the man, arms waving furiously, beating at the air and cursing loudly, as he started running up the path. He stepped out. 'Are you alright, what's the matter?'

Martin's face was now covered in angry red spots and he kept slapping himself. 'Damn wasps! There's a nest down there, get rid of it, they're pests.'

'A wasps' nest?' He hadn't seen it, neither could he see any around the man, who was still dancing about and slapping himself. Murdoch thought he heard children laughing but couldn't see them either. 'Would you like some vinegar for the stings, Mrs Overidge would have some?'

'Don't be stupid! I'm going to A&E, I'm plastered with them, it's a disgrace.' He stomped out, still swatting madly and screeching every few seconds.

Murdoch walked down and saw no wasps, no nest, just some very colourful butterflies, most unusual ones and traces of glitter, on the ground, where that had come from, he had no idea. Still hearing the faint laughter, he didn't see the hatted figure leave, chuckling and very pleased with herself.

The start of the Bank Holiday weekend, Lily was back. A bit pink rather than tanned and with her freckles more noticeable. She had a woven basket filled with a bottle of rum, some hot pepper sauce, seasonings and some bags of sweets for her grandparents and handed one of the bags to Murdoch. 'Just a little thing,' she said shyly, 'they're tamarind balls, quite sweet, but very nice.'

'You shouldn't have, but thanks. That's nice.' He pointed to her shell necklace.'

'Oh, yeah, it was a... it's a souvenir.'

He noticed that she went a bit red, what had she been going to say? 'So, did you get your results?'

'My A-levels, yep.' Glad to change the subject, she smiled. 'I did well, I guess I'll be going off to uni. Actually, it's not the most convenient, but the best thing for me to do is a two-year foundation degree at the Eden Centre in Cornwall.'

'Eden, that's that domed place isn't it? It was used in a Bond film.'

'Was it? I wouldn't know, I've never watched one of them.'

'Lily, you haven't lived,' he grinned. 'Your education is sadly lacking.'

'Never mind that, I've done some ideas for the bulb thing, have a look while you have your coffee.' She left her notebook and took the basket of goodies to the cottage. *Bond films?*

* * *

Martin Jones knocked on the door of Peter Simmons' house and when it was opened by his wife, she gave a scream which caused Peter to rush out of his office.

'What the hell! *Martin?* What in God's name have you done to your face?'

'Wasps,' he mumbled through swollen lips. His whole face was an angry looking red colour and covered with pustules. 'I've had some sort of allergic reaction. A-a nest of the varmints at that garden centre. I want a damned bonus for this.'

'For heaven's sake, Natalie, pull yourself together and get this poor sod a cup of coffee, you can drink, can't you?' Peter directed the question to his colleague.

'Just about, something stronger wouldn't go amiss.'

'Of course, come through and have a brandy. Wasps, you say, did you make them angry?'

'Came from nowhere, it was like a horror film, I had to go to hospital and was there for hours. Look at the state of me!'

Peter *was* looking with a morbid fascination and hoped none of his neighbours had noticed his visitor. 'Tell me about the site.'

'Let me drink my brandy first.' He slurped rather than drank, encumbered as he was with lips looking like they belonged on a puffer fish.

Natalie brought in coffee, staring with a mixture of terror and disgust, put down the tray and scuttled out.

'Christ, do I look that bad?'

'Yes mate, you do. Now, what did you see?'

'The place is going nowhere. Ticking over, but that's about it. I didn't see the old people, just a boy and the blasted wasps. There may be a few things we could do to... help put customers off? I'll give it some thought when I feel better.'

'A wasp invasion perhaps?' chortled Peter.

'Not funny, not at all damned funny.'

'Sorry mate.'

* * *

Lily got home and knew she was going to have to talk to her parents, she'd already asked them to have tea with her and listen to her plans.

Her father was effusive in his praise for her results. 'Always knew you had a brain love, I hope you're putting it to good use now.'

'I'm going to do a foundation degree.'

'Oh Lily, I'm so pleased you took my advice to go into the beauty line.'

'What? No Mum, for God's sake, not *that* sort of foundation. I've made a decision, it's two years down in Cornwall.'

Robert looked shocked. 'Cornwall? That's the back of beyond. What can you do down there that you can't do closer to home?'

Lily took a deep breath and prepared for the explosion. 'I'm going to the Eden project to do a degree in horticulture.'

'I don't understand, what's a foundation degree if it's not to do with cosmetics?' Corrine looked totally baffled.

'Shut *up* Corrine.' Her father was furious and rounded on his daughter. 'I thought you were over this gardening nonsense. There's no future in it and certainly not in that compost heap of my parents'.'

'Don't tell me to shut up...'

'Stop it, both of you! It's my life and it's what I want to do. How dare you call it a compost heap Dad, you have no idea of its potential.'

'And you do I suppose, at the grand age of *just* eighteen. I don't want you thinking about any future there, there is none, it won't be around for much longer.'

'What do you mean by that?'

'I-I mean, it's failing and a worry for my parents, something they don't need at their time of life. Surely you can see that?'

'That's why they need me. I'm sorry you're not happy, but it's *my* future and I think I'm entitled to decide what I want to do.'

'Indeed, you are,' said her father, 'but as *we* don't agree, don't expect much support. We won't see you starve of course, but don't think you can come running to us every five minutes for money. Where are you going to live eh, have you thought about that?'

'Oh Robert, we don't want to see her on the news as one of those... those *rough* sleepers, let her get it out of her system for goodness sake. She'll soon see it's a mistake.'

'Dad, she's right. I have to find my own path, if it doesn't work, I *promise* I'll go in another direction, but please, give me this chance for a couple of years. You know I don't waste money.'

Robert glowered. Money down the drain, that's all he saw, but then, there was Garden Zone, that was making money, perhaps she could find a niche there? 'Eden, you say, wasn't that in some film?'

'A Bond film, yes how clever of you to have remembered that.'

'Don't push your luck, Lily. Alright, get your damned degree if it makes you happy, but I'll be telling you "I told you so".'

'Oh Dad, thank you, *thank* you.' She hugged him and her mother, who still seemed rather confused.

'So, you will... live somewhere then?' Corrine asked anxiously.

'Yes, there're rooms in student houses. Maybe you and Dad would drive me down with my stuff, then you can see it.'

'You'll come home in-between?' Her father still wasn't happy.

'Yes Dad, of course. I-I'll miss you both.'

'Humph, I *said*, don't push your luck.'

* * *

On Sunday, Murdoch noticed that Lily was still wearing her shell necklace. Her fingers went to it, often, playing with the shells, a dreamy look in her eye. *She was given that, I knew there was something about it. She met some boy in Barbados, I wonder if she...*

'Murdoch, I told my parents last night, it was grim, but they came around. So, I'll be off to Cornwall in a couple of weeks and won't be back till the end of October, unless I can afford the train to come up for a weekend, but I won't have a lot to spare. I'm really going to miss being here.'

'Don't worry, I'm not going anywhere. I'll help as much as I can and you're doing the right thing. At least you've got the opportunity, don't waste it.'

'I won't. Oh, my friends are here, what do they want?' Laura and Amy were strolling down the path and Laura was smirking.

'Hi Lily, thought we ought to have a catch up about your holiday, are you busy?' Amy asked.

'We will be soon, Sundays can be a bit rushed and its Bank Holiday of course. How was your trip, Amy?'

'Oh boring, nobody of interest,' *not like here.*

'It's Murdoch, isn't it? Hi, I'm Laura, we sort of met in the coffee shop when you carried Lily in.' She gave him the once-over quite blatantly.

'Did we? I'm sorry, I don't really remember, would you mind? I have stuff to do.' He turned and walked down the path, leaving Laura fuming, Amy disappointed and Lily, amused.

'Just tell us a little bit,' said Amy. 'Were there any gorgeous boys on your holiday?'

Murdoch was still in listening distance, he stopped and although feeling a bit guilty, was interested in hearing her reply.

'Not... exactly, there was a guy, a guide, called Tobias. He was very nice, we went out for the day.'

'What? Did you actually... like, *do* anything?' Laura was instantly jealous.

'Nothing like that. He did, well, kiss me.'

'Hey,' shrieked Amy. 'Lily's had her first snog.'

'Oh Amy, shut *up*, I don't want everybody to know. It would be better if we met tonight, do you want to come over, we can cook some burgers or pizza?' Lily pointedly picked up a trowel.

'I suppose so, there's nothing here, is there Amy?' They said goodbye and Lily heard Laura muttering, 'just rude', as they left.

Murdoch was a little surprised. Her first snog? *It's none of my business, who cares.*

She caught Murdoch later. 'Thanks for that, they can be a bit, you know, full on, especially Laura.'

'It's alright, I didn't remember her at all, I didn't take any notice of anybody, I was just worried about you.' He realised how that must have sounded and busied himself with the salad crops.

'Yeah, well, thanks anyway.'

'It's cool.' He carried on and more or less ignored her. As she turned away he did add… 'Bank Holidays at Garden Zone were awful, are they busy here?'

'The August one is, see you tomorrow then.'

He didn't answer.

* * *

Murdoch had always hated Bank Holidays. They were never anything special to him as a child, no traditional family outings to the seaside or visits to the fair or circus, the sort of things all the other children in his class seemed to do. Being at Garden Zone and seeing the people who were coming in now, it was full of what he called, *poser gardeners*. People who watched the flower shows on television or admired the pubs' hanging baskets. The *let's go and buy a few plants* brigade. However, it was extra money that was desperately needed, so he smiled and agreed with everybody's suggestions, trying to explain that they would need more than one bag of decorative stones to replace the lawn.

He had just spent nearly half an hour with a lady who wanted to start a perennial border and, could he explain what that was? And another satisfied customer with a trolley full of plants had left him exhausted. On his way to grab a coke, he was spotted by a middle-aged couple. The man looked bored but resigned to the plant shopping. The woman, sour-faced and thin-lipped, brushed past the bedding plants as if they were something nasty.

'You, young man, are you serving or watching the plants grow?'

What a bitch. 'How can I help?'

'We've just had a forty-metre long fence put up at the bottom of our garden because, I can't stand to see the family who has just moved into the house behind us, can I, Hugh?' She turned to, 'Mr bored', who nodded. 'Five children, *five* and a trampoline, can you imagine? It seems we're only allowed two metres in height, so I've had some wire put along the top because if its covered in flowers that doesn't count. Does it?'

'Err?'

'It doesn't, I'm telling you. I need something quick growing and attractive to cover it all up, what shall I buy?'

'Well, there are lots...'

'Flowers, it must have *flowers*, I don't just want green, do I, Hugh?'

'No dear, let's see what the young man suggests.'

'Well! I'm waiting.' The thin lips got even thinner.

Murdoch scanned the climbers and creepers quickly. 'Montana Rubens, that would be best.'

She stared at him, open-mouthed. '*Rubens*? He was the man who painted all those naked women. How dare you, do you think I want *that* all over my fence, what sort of garden centre is this?' She was turning a shade of purple when she saw Lily. 'You girl, come here, you do actually work here, don't you?'

'Yes, I do, what's the problem Madam?'

She pointed a bony finger at Murdoch, who was looking stony-faced. 'He is, he's the problem,' the woman shrieked. 'I asked him for something attractive to cover my fence and he wants me to adorn it with outdoor murals of curvaceous nudes. We don't want that, do we, Hugh?'

Hugh was looking perkier. 'Oh, I don't mind really, it would make cutting the grass more interesting.'

'Be quiet, you fool! What do *you* have to say about it, eh?' She poked the bony finger into Lily's chest.

Lily was completely flummoxed and looked pleadingly at Murdoch who was now glowering at the woman.

'Montana Rubens, the *clematis*.' He muttered.

'Ah, I... see.' Lily tried not to laugh. *Rubens, the artist*. 'It's a simple misunderstanding, let me show you.' From the row, she grabbed a tall, straggly plant tied to a bamboo cane with a photo showing a profusion of pink flowers. 'It's a very popular choice for clematis and its name is Montana Rubens, or mountain clematis.'

The woman looked as if she'd swallowed a lemon and glared at Murdoch. 'Why didn't you say so, instead of making a fool of yourself? Get me enough plants to cover forty metres and bring them to the car park. Hugh will put them in our 4x4. I shall get a taxi home, I can feel a migraine coming on, sort out the money Hugh.'

'Yes dear. I think the nudes would have been more fun,' he winked at Lily, who was now laughing.

'I'll help you, Murdoch, we've got more plants in the nursery section. I hope you don't mind if I tell my grandparents later, it'll make their day.'

'Silly cow,' he muttered, '*her*, I mean, not you.'

They all had a good laugh later at the end of the day, over tea and Madge's homemade scones with jam and cream. Even the dour Mr Taylor chuckled. It had been a good day and for the first time in ages, the till was full.

Chapter Seven

WEEDING

To remove unwanted plants,
making sure to kill the root

It was Wednesday, Murdoch's day off and the night of the dreaded party. He told his father he and Megan were having a few people around, but they'd mostly be outside as it was a lovely summer's evening.

'Be nice for you to have some of your friends here,' Brian had said.

Murdoch didn't bother to correct him and say that none of them were *his* friends and then he realised with a bit of a jolt that he didn't actually have anyone he could call a *friend*. Fleetingly he thought of Lily, but just because he found it easy to talk to her, didn't mean she was one. They worked together and got on well, that was it and she was off to university where she'd make even more of her *own* friends, he didn't fit into her life outside of work at all.

He bought a load of sausages, burgers and bread rolls. Megan said people would bring booze so he needn't worry about that. However, he didn't want to appear a cheapskate, so also got some cans and large bottles of cider which weren't too expensive, even though he didn't want to drink the stuff. Megan was excited about it, so, making an effort, he put nightlights into jars and scattered them around the small area that passed as their garden. He'd also got a bundle of blankets from a charity shop and spread them out for people to sit on. Megan was bringing her mp3 and a speaker for music, she said his ancient iPod was an embarrassment and not fit to be seen. She had a good iPhone as well and he wondered how she could afford it all. She'd laughed when he asked and said everybody had them, it was no big deal. She came over in the afternoon, making sure they had time in the bedroom, then showered and changed into a crop top and tight jeans.

She felt a little bloated and struggled with the button. Her period was due, she reckoned. Not always very regular, it did seem a bit of while since she'd had one. About...? *Oh shit*. It must be at least two months, it was now the end of August, she hadn't had one since... since, before that mistake of a night with Ryan. No! no, it wasn't possible, she was on the pill. She did drink a lot sometimes and was often sick after a binge night, but that didn't matter did it? *Did it?* She slumped back down onto the bed. This couldn't be happening, it wasn't in her plans at all. She had the makings of a good job with lots of perks and free samples, meant for the customers, that she sold on to her friends. A *baby*, no thanks. Was it Murdoch's? It had to be, the number of times they'd done it, it stood to reason. That one time with Ryan didn't count. Her mother's words rang in her ears, *it only takes the once, my girl*, of course, as with most of the things her mother said, she hadn't listened. Should she tell him? Not tonight, that was for sure. *If* she told him, what would he say? He wouldn't want a baby, they were far too young and even though she wanted *him*, she wasn't sure about forever, he may be the best-looking boy around, but his future prospects weren't great and even so it wouldn't be a good start. Money would be short and it was a responsibility she didn't want. After having to help raise her siblings, babies were no novelty to her. Murdoch may well think differently though, he was the sort that would want to accept what had happened and make it right. Taking a deep breath, she put on a smile and joined him outside.

'Alright? What time do you think people will come?' He tried to look enthusiastic.

'Not before nine, I'm going to have a beer, join me?'

'Not just yet, I'll sort the food first.'

Megan opened a can, hesitated, then started drinking. It wouldn't matter, she'd get this sorted as soon as possible.

Ryan, Danny and three girls arrived first. Murdoch's path had crossed with them once or twice since the first night out, but only in passing and the atmosphere quickly became tense.

'Hi,' Murdoch said, a bit too brightly, 'help yourself to a drink.'

'I'll do that.' Ryan smirked and grabbed a four pack, looking disappointed when Murdoch didn't take the bait.

'What have you brought along then?' Megan stood in front of him and he silently handed over a carrier with cans and another couple of bottles of cider wondering if she'd mentioned meeting up with him for a drink. Quite a few drinks actually, he remembered that, but the later part of the evening, he wasn't very clear about. Pretty sure something *had* happened, he now was *un*sure as she seemed cool. If she hadn't mentioned it to Murdoch, it would be a nice big stick to poke the stuck-up shit with. Thinking he was better than them, what did he have going for him anyway? Not much of a job, bloody flowers and stuff and here he was, living in a glorified caravan.

Another four arrived who all knew Megan, Murdoch hadn't seen any of them before. 'Are there many more to come?' he asked her quietly.

'A few, don't fuss it'll be fine, they've brought plenty of booze, that's the main thing. Have some yourself and relax a bit.' He took the beer she offered and stopped himself from saying she was having enough for the both of them. She seemed a bit hyped-up, but maybe that was the drink.

By eleven o'clock, there were at least twenty people, the burgers and sausages had been consumed and they were all drinking heavily. Nobody made much effort to include him in the conversation, Megan was drunk and laughing loudly with a group of her friends and Ryan who was glowering at him in between drinks, sauntered over. 'Life and soul of the party, ain't she?'

'She likes to enjoy herself.' Murdoch said. Maybe a bit *too* much at times he thought.

'She certainly does,' Ryan gave him a knowing look.

'What do you mean by that?'

'Nothing mate, just saying. She's a fun sort of girl.' He turned away, grinning. This could be spun out for quite a while, it would be fun.

Murdoch watched him suspiciously, what had he been inferring? The guy was a knobhead troublemaker and, so it would seem, were a lot of the people here. He was getting a bit anxious about the noise, it *was* a weekday and some of his neighbours worked. Perhaps they had better go inside, if they did, it would be very squashed and hopefully, some of them would leave. One or two had wandered in already he'd noticed, so taking some plates, he went to see where they were.

Two fell out of the door as he got there, laughing and with their clothes in a mess. Inside, there was another couple on the rug, he avoided looking too closely and a noise coming from his bedroom. Opening the door, he saw the weaselly Davy, stripped naked, with a girl bouncing about on top of him. 'What the hell do you think you're doing?'

'What does it look like, don't mind, do you?'

'Yes! I bloody well *do* mind. This is *my* room.' Picking up the clothes nearest him, he took them to the door and threw them outside. 'Party's over,' he shouted. 'Piss off, the lot of you. Megan, I need to talk to you.'

'The party's over?' she looked puzzled, swaying on her feet.

Ryan lurched beside her. 'He's boring, do you really want to shack up with that nerd?'

Weasel-face appeared in the door, a trainer, covering his nakedness. 'Oi, where's me bastard clothes and why are you in such a snit? We weren't doing any harm?'

'Murdoch doesn't want anyone to enjoy themselves.' Ryan stirred the pot to nearly boiling point.

'I'm not being taken advantage of and you've pushed your luck so, as I said, piss off.' Murdoch folded his arms and stared down Ryan.

Remembering how he came off last time, Ryan shrugged. 'No fun here anyway. C'mon guys, we'll take our booze and go somewhere that *is*. Coming Megan?'

'No, she is not.' Murdoch took a step forward. Davy was scrabbling on the ground for his clothes and the girl who'd been with him was weaving unsteadily across the grass.

'Murdoch, what happened, why is everybody leaving?' Megan whined.

'C'mon babe, come with us,' Ryan persisted.

'Megan, if you go with them, we're finished.' Murdoch was furious with her for getting so drunk and inviting these... losers.

'It's alright, I don't want her. Not *again* if you know what I mean?' Ryan smiled.

He's just winding me up. She wouldn't, not with him. 'Megan?'

'All *right*, see you guys later.' What had Ryan said? Her head was spinning and she vomited all over the grass.

'Gross,' muttered one of the girls as they wandered away, Ryan giving Murdoch the finger when he was well out of reach.

Megan felt herself being steered into the house. 'Black coffee for you and orange juice, then we're going to have a talk.' Murdoch sat her on the couch, where she promptly passed out.

In the early hours of the morning, she felt awful. Mumbling an apology and saying they'd talk later, she went home. He was so mad but afraid she might be sick again, walked silently with her until she was at her door. 'Leave it for a few days,' he said tersely. 'We're going to be busy at work with a promotion to get ready. I'll see you next week.'

She just made it inside before she was sick again.

* * *

Before she left for Cornwall, Lily helped to get the bulb promotion ready. It was a little bit soon to put the pictures on the fences, but she'd done a deal with one of the larger bulb suppliers, who was sending them in the next week, along with display cases and gift packs for a special promotion. 'You'll have to let me know how it goes and, I was going to ask if you'd keep an eye on my Grandparents and keep me up to date with everything. Have you got my number?' She asked Murdoch, who'd been a bit quiet for a few days.

'No, I've never had reason to. But yeah, I'll let you know if there's anything to worry about. Here, give me your phone.' He put the number in, alongside his name. 'Just send me a quick text, then I'll have yours.'

Lily couldn't help but notice that he hardly had any contacts in his phone and that it was old and rather basic. She was conscious of her brand-new model and what it cost. 'Is... is everything okay? You seem a bit, I dunno, not your usual self?'

'I'm fine. Sorry if I'm not the life and soul of the party. I need a break.' He started to walk away when he felt her hand on his arm.

'I'm sorry, it's not my business, I just thought you were worried about something, that's all. I didn't mean to upset you.'

He took a deep breath. She was only being... well, being Lily. 'You didn't. *I'm* sorry. I don't want to talk about it, okay? Show me the list of bulbs that they're sending and then I'll make us coffee as an apology.'

Watching what she said for the next half hour or so, they looked through the lists and discussed the best way to entice people to buy some more unusual varieties along with their old favourites.

'The pictures will help,' he said. 'I don't suppose your Grandparents could stretch to a newspaper advert?'

'I don't think so, but maybe, there could be an angle for a story, a competition or something along those lines?'

'What about one for children? The best crocus pot or biggest hyacinth? There're a load of plant pots down the bottom, if we supplied different colours, they could paint a pot and have that free, then choose their bulbs?'

Lily stared at him. 'You're a genius, that's a brilliant idea. You get the pots cleaned up and ready, I'll sort some paint, Grandad's got loads in his outhouse and I'll get onto the local paper. Oh, I wish I wasn't going away, this'll be great.'

'*I* wish you weren't going away,' he said wryly. 'All those kids, it'll be a nightmare. Actually, I've just thought of something. If the pots are going to be outside, they'll need to be painted in gloss which doesn't dry quickly. What we could do, is they come in and paint a pot, with a prize for the best-decorated one the next Saturday or whatever and then take it with the bulbs they've already chosen and paid for. It'll get the parents in a second week as well.'

'Umm, children and gloss paint? Not a good idea.' grinned Lily.

'Perhaps not, I didn't think of that, okay, ordinary paint and I'll varnish them afterwards.'

'What's all this excitement?' Stuart and Madge had both walked down to see what the chattering was all about.

Lily explained, praising Murdoch for his brilliant idea. 'I won't be here though, can you manage?'

'Of course, we can manage Lily, you're not to worry. Grandma and I have a policy that's matured and we're going to invest a bit here. There's also an advert going in the paper today for an assistant as we'll be able to afford another salary. If young Murdoch keeps coming up with these ideas we'll be well away.'

'I'll supply some refreshments for the painting contest and Flora will give me a hand, as long as we don't charge, it's not a problem.' Said Grandma. 'We *have* thought about a café, but it's a lot of admin and fuss to get it going.'

'We could look into that later,' said Lily. 'People would spend more time here if we had one and we could promote our produce with some recipes. We want local, freshly made stuff. I wish the two years was up now and we could get on with it.'

'All in good time,' Grandad said, smiling. 'This place is in good hands, I can see. Now, break time, there's some nice fresh bread Madge made, come on, you two.'

'Grandad, can I have a quick word?' When Murdoch was out of earshot, Lily explained about her phone and what she had in mind.

He chuckled, 'you leave it with me.'

* * *

The girl with the spiky blue hair had been directed to a newspaper advert. *Assistant wanted, full-time for Roots Garden Centre,* she read further. CV? That wouldn't be necessary, or the application form. She would just turn up in a few days. Perfect, enough time to swot up on plant names and soil conditions and all the things she'd need to impress them. The boy was heading for a bad time, she could see that, he would need a friend which he wouldn't want of course, but she'd sort that out, Lily would be some help to him, coming and going, as she would be for a time. There would be problems for the centre too and as she was here, and it was connected to Murdoch's future, it could justify a little of her input. She didn't think about whether or not her peers would view things in the same way. Now, should she stick to the blue hair, or something different? This was such fun. Picking up a pile of the catwalk magazines she'd taken a great liking to, she lost herself in the pages. Mauve was making a comeback apparently, a comeback? She'd always liked it. That could be in her hair, there were all sorts of pastel shades that looked nice. She did like the blue tips, perhaps she could grade it from mauve. Through to pink and then blue, why not? Swirling glitter around her head, she created the desired effect.

* * *

Megan turned up at Murdoch's in a very subdued mood. 'I'm really sorry, I had too much to drink and I didn't know they were going to do that.'

'What did Ryan mean?'

She paled. 'W-what did he say?'

'He *implied* that you and he had... you know.'

'We're just mates, he pushed for it once and I made it quite clear. Don't let him get to you, he's jealous.'

'Look, I realise you may have had other relationships, but I don't want them waved in my face, alright?'

'There wasn't any relationship.' That was true she told herself. Did Ryan actually remember or was he just stirring it? She'd taken a pregnancy test which was positive and not wanting to see the doctor, made an appointment at a clinic further away. Needing to finance it, without anybody knowing, she'd watched Mrs Overidge putting some money from the safe into her bag, and then Megan took it without anybody noticing. Corrine hadn't realised until the evening, when she was home and got very upset, thinking she must have lost it when she'd stopped at the mall. Megan was in the clear, for the moment.

'I don't like him and I don't want him around us again and I *don't* like you drinking so much, I've seen what's happened with my Dad.' Murdoch said firmly.

'For God's sake, I'm not an alcoholic like him, I enjoy a drink, what's wrong with that? You can be such a prude sometimes.'

'I didn't say you were, but it's easy to forget how much you're drinking and what's the point of making yourself sick? Where's the fun in that?'

Megan didn't want to argue with him, she felt nauseous again and couldn't wait to rid herself of the cause. 'I'm sorry, I did go a bit over the top and I'll make it clear to Ryan he was out of order, okay?'

'Well, okay, but I still don't to see him around. Do you want to come over tonight?' he softened slightly.

'Umm, do you mind if I don't? I'm err, going on a course tomorrow, a brow and lash thing and it's over in Southwitch, I've got to get the train early.'

'Oh, okay, sorry I can't drive you to the station, but hopefully, it won't be too long before I pass my test.'

'Oh yeah, great.' *Shame it's that horrible little green van.*

* * *

Lily had come to say goodbye as she was leaving the next day and also to meet the reporter who wanted a look around before he covered the story. She showed him the long table with all the pots and explained what they wanted to do. 'I'm going to drop some posters into the local primary schools and see if they'd like to get involved as well. We can take pots and bulbs to them and they can make it a school thing.'

The man was taking pictures on his iPad.

'No pencil and notebook anymore then?'

'He laughed. 'Went out with the ark love. I'll write up a piece and we'll send a photographer around on the day. Kids sell papers; the families want to see the little darlings in the news. Might be worth letting the local TV know, they're always looking for a, *and finally*, nice little safe story.'

Lily wasn't sure whether to be insulted or not, but there was no harm in it. Before she left, she contacted them and gave them Grandad's name. 'Or you can speak to Murdoch Lawton,' she added. Better not mention it to him, he'd get all uptight about something like that. If they turned up, he'd just have to deal with it. She caught up with him later.

'Best of luck with your course Lily, you'll do fine. Might see you end of October then?'

He was looking a little happier, she thought. 'Yep, definitely, Dad even said he'd come and pick me up, so that'll save me one train fare.'

'You wouldn't be tempted to hitch or anything like that would you?'

'Oh God no, I might be able to get a coach, that could be cheaper. I'll look into it all when I get there.'

'Well, look after yourself and I'll let you know how it's going.'

'Thanks.'

They both stood there, a little awkwardly and then Lily stuck her hand out. Rather amused, Murdoch shook it, looking very serious. 'Bye then.'

'Bye Murdoch.'

* * *

Megan had been to the local clinic two days earlier for the first tablet. Southwitch had another clinic where she was going to have the pessaries that would uproot and flush out the 'thing', as she thought of it. She was praying that it wouldn't take too long, but she knew it could be about six hours. Due to work at the salon the next day, what would happen if they wanted to keep her in, she didn't want to think about. Megan felt nothing, no regrets, it was an inconvenience, in a few years' time she would feel differently, for sure, this would be something to forget. It never happened.

It was a most unpleasant experience, having the tablet-sized pessaries inserted and she tried to think about other things. Having been warned what followed was uncomfortable and could be painful, she was grateful for the gas and air that was offered along with painkillers. Her lower half was covered, so she didn't see anything, not that she wanted to look, being more concerned about the time. Murdoch had texted her around midday, asking how it was going? If only he knew, she thought and messaged him back with a *Gr8 thx, tell u all later.* Already having talked to the girls at the salon about brows and lashes, she knew the basics, enough to make it sound as if she had been on a course at least.

Eight hours later she was ready. Padded up and with a leaflet explaining possible side effects she couldn't get out of there quickly enough. Waiting an hour for a train, she texted Murdoch, *going home, V tired and got stomach ache. Time of month*. That would cover her for a few days.

* * *

Stuart went to find Murdoch, who was busy on his patch. Although the crops were limited at the moment, people were interested and most picked up a selection when they bought other things. 'I need a bit of advice if you've got a minute.'

'Sure, what about?'

'Our Lily had one of those new fancy phones for her birthday and she's given me her old one, she said something about it needing a sim card, but I can't make head or tail of it. To tell you the truth, I'm more than happy with the one I've got. I know it's old-fashioned, but it suits me. I just want to make a call, I don't want to take photos, or talk to it. It seems criminal to leave it in the drawer, I don't suppose you could make use of it, could you? I'll explain if she asks.'

Murdoch looked at it sitting in Stuart's hand. He'd love a phone of that type. 'I can't take that, you could sell it if you wanted, she gave it to you.'

'It wouldn't feel right to sell it and as I said, I can't use it, I'm far too long in the teeth, if I still had my own of course,' he winked. 'Come on, lad, you'd be doing me a favour. As long as it goes to someone who appreciates it, I'll be happy. Please, I don't want the thing, it scares me, that great screen looking at me.'

Murdoch laughed. 'Well, okay. Thanks very much, but if Lily's not happy, I'll give it right back.'

'Am I right in thinking you can send pictures on it?' Stuart knew very well what it was capable of. 'You can keep her right up to date with the goings-on here, can't you?'

'That's true, I can. In that case, I feel happier about it, thanks, Stuart. Have you had any decent applicants for the job yet?'

'One or two promising ones, a lot just wanting any job they can get, not that I blame them, but it would be useful if they knew a flower from a weed. We'll see.'

Murdoch looked at the weeds sprouting in the veg patch and sighed. It was a constant battle.

Chapter Eight

TRANSPLANTING

Moving a plant to another location.
Allow time to recover from the move.

Robert and Corrine drove their daughter down to Cornwall in the estate car which was jammed full. Lily was squashed in the back with her duvet and pillows that she said *had* to go, or she'd never sleep. Having checked the size of her room and the storage, she had packed accordingly, but knowing she'd be outside quite a bit, had included a selection of waterproofs, some warm jumpers and two sets of wellington boots with thick socks. Along with a large box of foodstuffs for herself and another for the communal kitchen, that took up most of the space. She tried to talk about all sorts of things except gardening on the way there, mindful of her father's disappointment in what she had chosen to do. She was surprised, however, that he did make an effort and seemed to be quite encouraging.

'Listen Lily, you appreciate I'm not over the moon about your choice, but I know you'll work hard and just remember, even if Roots doesn't make it,' *which it won't if I have my way,* 'There's Garden Zone, or other places, if that's what your heart's set on. Who knows? You may end up on one of the makeover programmes, you could be quite the TV star like, what's her name, a few years ago? The one who never wore a...'

'Robert!' Corrine's voice was shrill. 'I didn't think you paid that much attention to gardening programmes.'

'Just happened to be scrolling through the channels,' he muttered. *Made it worth watching.*

They stopped in Plymouth for lunch and went around the historic Barbican and onto the Hoe. It was a perfect day and the sun sparkled on the sea. 'Oh Robert, how wonderful to have a view like this,' Corrine enthused, 'and to have one of those nice little ships, just imagine.'

'You mean a boat, not a *ship,* and yes, the weather's very nice today, but I wonder how many times you could actually use it? Expensive hobby, boating.'

'As expensive as golf?' She asked pointedly. 'Bobbing around out there is something we could do *together,* I can just picture us, in the right outfits, of course, navy and white, with a few friends and a bottle of champagne.'

'Hmm, yes. We'd better get on if we're to get Lily to St Austell and be home again by tonight.'

St Austell was where Lily was going to house-share. Although the school holidays had ended, there were still a lot of motorhomes and caravans on the road, which Robert tutted about continually and then cursed the satnav which didn't seem to recognise the postcode Lily had given him. 'Are you *sure* it was correct?' he said through gritted teeth, as he had to reverse *again*, in a narrow lane.

'It's on headed paper, it must be, but it is quite a new house. I think, if we get to the general area, we could ask somebody.' When they did, Lily was convinced that the first person they asked, was actually paid to dress like a yokel and speak with an accent they could hardly make head or tail of.

'You'm going the wrong way.' The man said, after thinking about it for a few minutes.

'Could you possibly tell me the *right* way?' Robert tried to be patient.

'Reckon I could like.'

Robert waited for thirty seconds. 'So, that might be… where?'

'Oh yeah, you'm need to turn around like, go down past the 'ill covered in furze then turn left… or is it right? No, no tis left, by Tregantle farm. Bout ten minutes and you'll see a load of noo ouses. Tis there, you'm need to be.'

'Thank you,' shouted Lily as her father struggled to turn the car in the small gateway to a field while the man just watched them, shaking his head and muttering to himself. 'Actually, Dad, put in Crofter's Lane, that's close to it and not part of the new estate so it should register on the satnav.' She hadn't really trusted the local's directions and was afraid her father was about to combust if they went wrong again.

Within minutes, they found themselves on a proper road and the satnav sprang into life. "*After a quarter of a mile, you will reach your destination*".

'Now she tells me,' Robert grumbled.

At the house, Corrine stepped carefully between boxes of girls' belongings and let Robert and Lily unload everything. The room that had been allocated was on the third floor, under a pitched roof with a dormer window, looking towards the sea that could just be seen in the distance. A wardrobe, some drawers, a bed, a desk and a small TV became homelier once Lily had put some of her personal belongings in place.

'There's good Wi-Fi at least,' she said, setting up her laptop.

Corrine was looking around as if there was a bad smell under her nose. 'It's very small, are you sure you're going to be alright here?'

'Of course.' Lily was carefully unpacking her pots of herbs. 'I'll take these down to the kitchen later, we can all use them.'

'All? How many of you are there and where's your bathroom, do you have to share that?' Her voice was strained.

Lily had a quick look at the landing. 'There's one other room up here and a small shower room and toilet. I know there're three other girls and one boy, I think.'

'How very... modern,' Corrine sniffed, 'Robert, I don't think I want to see the kitchen, we ought to be making a move.'

Before they left, Robert pressed one hundred pounds into Lily's hand. 'For emergencies,' he said gruffly. Knowing he was going to break his daughter's heart with the selling of the garden centre, he felt guilty but believed it would be best for them all in the long run and felt it was now his due to reap something from his parents.

* * *

Stuart Overidge was looking at the dilapidated greenhouses at the back of the centre as Murdoch came up beside him, with the post that had arrived that morning. 'Looks like some more job applications.'

'Yes, thanks my boy. I'm just wondering if we've enough money left to do some repairs on these glasshouses, we could do so much more with indoor plants and displays.' They were already used to bring seedlings on before repotting but were not in a safe state to allow public access.

'It's a shame, they're really wasted. I think what we need to do, is get rid of all the broken or loose glass first. We could cover it with some sort of plastic as a temporary measure. Once it was all cleaned up it would be safe and we'd have a lot more space.'

'We *will* have a new assistant within a week, hopefully if it's another strong lad maybe we could?'

'I don't mind staying on an extra hour for a week or so, not for pay,' Murdoch added quickly. He knew they weren't rolling in money. 'Perhaps I could take it as a day off later? I need to fit in some more driving lessons and hopefully take my test soon.'

'Have you got the use of a car then?'

'I was… given an old van by a friend of my dad, it's just about roadworthy. I sell some vegetables from my own allotment and it would mean I could go out further, maybe increase my customers a little.'

Stuart looked approvingly at him, *enterprising young fellow*. 'A van you say? You know, my Madge doesn't like me driving so much these days, daft she is, but I have to humour her. *If* you could drive, we could make use of that. Tell you what, rather than give you time off, which I'd do anyway, I'll help pay for some of your lessons and you can drive for us, how about that?'

Murdoch had a feeling he was being manoeuvred into accepting, not exactly charity, but a favour, Stuart was very kind to him and he didn't want to take advantage. 'That's a very generous offer, I don't know…'

'Think about it, it would help us out and you can always pay me back in overtime.' Stuart puffed on his pipe. 'Have to do this outside, Madge won't let me have it in the house.' He took the mail and went up to his office.

Four applications, he'd expected more, but the money wasn't that good and people didn't like hard work. Two of them he could tell right away wouldn't be suitable. One from a man who was semi-retired, looking for part-time and the other, a woman with children at school who was already pointing out she would have to leave early every day to pick them up. The other two were possibilities, he would ring them later and arrange interviews.

As he came out of the office, a most extraordinary sight greeted him. A young woman in a glittery top, jeans and what looked like hobnail boots. But it was the hair that was rather disconcerting. It seemed to change from a light purple, then pink and blue spiky bits on the ends. She was blowing a large pink bubble which popped and disappeared back into her mouth.

'Oh, hi there,' she spotted him. 'I'm Merry.'

Merry? Was she on something? 'Err, jolly good, can I help you?'

'It's me who can help *you*. I've come about the job.'

'T-the job? do you have an application form?'

'Hasn't it come yet? Rubbish, the post these days. Oh well, I'm here now and I'm ready to start if you like? Oh my,' She darted over to a small tray of plants. 'Scabious atropurpurea, I can see you've been dead-heading this one, it has a lot of blooms and the bees and butterflies love these, but I'm sure you know that?' She weaved down the pathway, graceful in her boots with Stuart following, in a daze, listening to her babbling about the plants, their Latin names slipping off her tongue as if it were her natural language. 'Tropaelum majus, I just love nasturtiums, so cheery and not fussy at all. They'll flower in the poorest soils with no feeding, all they want is the light, a bit like myself.' A tinkling laugh accompanied this remark as she picked a leaf and popped it in her mouth. 'Perfect, nice and peppery, you could suggest that with your salad bits up by the till. Specialised, weren't they?'

'Err yes, t-that's the responsibility of young Murdoch down there.' Stuart pointed to a figure further down.

'Would you know if he's got any peppers on the go? I just love crunching into an Antoni Romanian.'

'Do you? I think he was a bit too late for the sowing of those, m-maybe next year. Umm, where did you acquire your knowledge, it seems quite exten...?'

'Here and there you know. All my family are well into plants and especially flowers, we're at one with them you could say. Now, have I got the job?'

'I know it's a bit sexist or whatever the word is but we do need someone with a bit of muscle, some of the work is quite heavy.' Stuart found it difficult to picture this... creature working here.

'I'm stronger than I look,' she spotted the bags of compost and skipping over, lifted two and moved them to another pile, then swung a bag of bark chippings up on top.

'Well, that was impressive I must say, there were two ladies here the other day, couldn't lift it between them. P-perhaps you'd better come up to the office and fill in some details Miss...?'

'Merry, I told you, Merry Faith Good, to be exact. I'm going to fit right in here I just know it.'

* * *

Megan was feeling dreadful. Using the excuse of a bad time of the month, she had avoided Murdoch for several days. She also still had nausea and a headache which, according to her leaflets, were common side effects. There was no way she wanted to indulge in any physical relationship with him at the moment. Phoning work and telling them she had the flu gave her a few more days. Texting Murdoch with the same message, he told her to hurry up and get better. It wasn't fair, she thought, having to suffer like this as he went on as normal. It was always women who had the short straw in life.

Her mother took one look at her. 'You're not swinging the lead, are you? Another hangover?'

'No Mum, I feel awful.'
'Well alright, I'll believe you this time.'

Murdoch was at home on his own, his dad had gone to work and he quite enjoyed the peace. Texting Megan, he hoped she was feeling better. Back came a sad-faced emoji and, "A few more days in bed", with lots of x's. Lily's name was above Megan's and he wondered whether or not to send her a message. In the end, he sent a short one.

Hi, hope ur settling in. Not much 2 say except a new girl started. V odd looking with coloured hair but seems to know her stuff. Ur Grandad was impressed x.

Suddenly realising he'd put an x, quickly deleted it and sent it with a smiley. Force of habit with Megan, *not* appropriate for Lily. An answer came back almost immediately.

Hi urself. Just met all my housemates. Last 1 arrived today. I've got an attic room which is gr8. Not much of a garden here but Eden will make up for that. Send me a foto of the hair, sounds fun. Looking forward to my 1st day. Good luck with the bulbs.

She had also sent a smiley. Another ping came almost immediately. *PS It's pouring down.* This was sent with an umbrella emoji which made him smile. He played around with the phone for a while, it had a lot more features than his old one. Take a photo, she'd said, so he needed to practice a bit. After taking several around the house he decided to delete them all. When he worked out how to do that, he knew he had to empty them from somewhere else, like on the computer. Finding the, recently deleted, folder he checked it. There were his photos along with a load of Lily's that looked like her holiday. She'd forgotten to remove them when she cleared her phone before giving it to Stuart. Immediately, he clicked off it, he should delete them for her, but he'd read up a bit about the model and they would go after thirty days. Curiosity got the better of him and he sneaked a look. Lots of pictures of flowers and gardens, how like her, he thought. Then a picture of a very good looking black man, was that the one she had meant when she talked to her friends? A selfie of them together and she was wearing the shell necklace. The man's arm around her shoulder with her smiling. He deleted them all, it wasn't his place to look. So that was her first kiss? Good for her. He felt... what did he feel? Pleased that it had meant something and wasn't a drunken fumble she may have regretted? Jealous? No! why should he be, she was a kid. *She's your age, she's not a kid.*

It's not my business, he told himself, but couldn't quite stop wondering what it would feel like to kiss her. Feeling like a complete shit for being disloyal, he watched some TV and tried to think about Megan.

* * *

Robert had returned to an email, from Peter Simmons, suggesting another meeting, so a few days later, he was back at the golf club. Glaring as he looked around, he saw no sign of the dreadful waitress, for which he was thankful. Peter was on his own this time, already waiting, so Robert strolled over. 'Peter, good to see you, have you come with an offer?'

'Let's not be hasty, have a drink first.'

Robert drummed his fingers on the table while Peter talked about everything except a possible arrangement. Eventually, the man leaned back, a smile on his face. 'So, the garden centre?' Robert knew he had jumped the gun earlier so tried not to appear so eager and just listened. Peter's smile turned into more of a smirk. 'We can certainly do something there, but we're not prepared to spend money on detailed drawings or planning enquires until we have a more definite word on a purchase.' He thought of the drawings he had at home, he could be ruthless when he wanted something and he wanted this little goldmine.

'It's only a matter of time,' spluttered Robert, 'I've just got to work on them a bit.'

Peter had his own ideas of how they could be worked on but kept *that* to himself. 'Well, we're not in a rush, we couldn't do anything for a year anyway, something else may come along though.'

'A y-year? It won't take that long, give me six months. The winter isn't a good time for garden things, is it? They'll be struggling come the spring and probably be grateful for the offer, you could get it cheap.'

I intend to. 'Well, I suppose six months won't make too much difference. Alright then. Keep me posted on any developments and we'll meet up in the future.'

Robert was feeling quite deflated after Peter left, he'd have to have a serious talk with his parents and that would be easier without Lily around. He may have to persuade Corrine to do a Sunday lunch, they didn't warrant a meal out. He knew who he'd *like* to take out for a meal. Szarlota, the new checkout lady with the delightful curves. She was Polish and, it appeared, no partner on the scene. It would be impossible of course, too many people knew him, but a man could dream, couldn't he?

* * *

Merry had been at Roots for a few days without having the opportunity for much conversation with Murdoch. He'd had a day off in that time and when he *was* there, he busied himself down the veg end. She had been the recipient of a few sideways glances from customers, but her friendly manner and knowledge soon won over the ones who looked askance as she approached them. Madge had been rather taken aback at her first meeting with the girl.

'Are you sure this was a good idea? She does seem rather strange.'

'Don't worry Duckie, I wasn't convinced when I saw her, but there isn't anything yet I've found that she doesn't know about plants and she's a worker for sure.'

'Where does she live? I've never yet seen her at the bus stop or being picked up. It's like she walks out of the gate and disappears.'

'That's the strange thing, I asked her for all her details, for pay and national insurance, all that stuff and she gave her address as, Bumble Cottage in Lower Puddlecombe. I've never heard of it, have you?'

'Can't say I have, but that doesn't mean anything. She seems to be happy here and she brought some delicious looking ginger cake in this morning. Heavens!' she exclaimed as she reached for a piece. 'It's still warm, how can that be?' Madge brushed some glitter off the table as she put a piece on a plate for Stuart. 'Our Lily would like this cake, I hope she's getting on alright.'

Lily was on Murdoch's mind as well. There had been a piece in the local paper that morning, reporting on the bulb competition and promoting the pot painting competition for the weekend in two weeks' time. They'd decided to do it over two days in case it was busy. Murdoch had gone around to all the allotment owners asking for any spare pots and one lady had come that morning with a boot full, saying she needed to get rid of them and would the children like them? He took a photo of them to send to Lily and then, surreptitiously, managed to get one of Merry's hair. He smiled, thinking of her opening it and her reaction.

'Hiya Murdoch, we've not had much chance to chat, I brought you a coffee, milk two sugars, that's right isn't it?'

He jumped guiltily, stuffing the phone back in his pocket. 'Err, yeah, thanks. Merry, that's a strange name.'

She cocked her head. 'Is it, don't you think it suits me? I try to be merry all the time.' She looked fierce and then burst into the most musical, tinkling laughter he'd ever heard.

'I didn't mean to sound rude, sorry, I've just never heard it before, as a name, I mean.'

'I've never met a Murdoch before either, so that makes us quits. Tell me about Lily.'

'L-Lily, what do you mean?'

'People talk about her. That Mr Taylor who helps out looked at me as if I was the devil incarnate, shook his head and said "I'd never replace Lily", Flora Harvey said I'd turned the milk sour, so what was so special about her?'

'She's the Overidge's granddaughter and gone to university now, the Eden project. I thought it was a tourist thing until she told me it's connected to Cornwall college.'

'She'll have a great time there, it's wonderful, have you ever been?'

'No, I've never really been anywhere, I have to be honest.'

'That's a shame, but you're still young.'

'You talk like Madge,' he grinned, 'you're not so old yourself.'

'Oh no, of course, I'm not, what a silly thing to say.' Her pink face matched the colour in her hair for a moment, 'I'd better get on with the watering. Are you sowing spring cabbage now?'

'I was going to, yes why?'

'Precoce de Louviers is a good one, fast growing and people like things with a French name, especially restaurants when you're ready to supply them.'

'How did you know that's what we wanted to...'

Merry had disappeared again.

Chapter Nine

BIENNIALS

The classic biennial, in its first growing season,
produces only foliage. The second year,
it will flower

Alexander brought over the pile of photo albums. 'Do you really want to look at these now, you should rest.'

'I do nothing but rest,' Rosemary said weakly. 'It'll be the last time I see them, see our daughter. Please, look at them with me.'

'Alright, it *is* a long time since I saw them. Let me help you sit up a bit.' Moving the cushions, he helped his frail wife carefully into a comfortable position and was able to spread the albums in front of them both.

There was Caroline through the years and they paused at her fifth birthday, one of their favourite pictures. An angelic looking little girl with beautiful big eyes staring at the camera. Brown, with a slight reflection of green, when they turned to the light. Lots of pictures and happy memories up until the time she was nearing sixteen, then she didn't like having her photo taken and when they *did* manage to include her, she looked sullen, almost angry.

'What did we do wrong?' Rosemary's anguished voice broke Alex's heart, again.

'We did nothing wrong, she was a teenager and we lost her before we could weather the storm. She took a long time to grow up and when she did, it was too late, I've told you, don't torture yourself. I'm putting these

117

away now, here, have the local paper, you can read all the nonsense that goes on and the latest council rows, that should cheer you up.'

Rosemary closed her eyes for a moment, composing herself, picked up the paper and leafed through it, without too much interest. None of these events would make any difference to the life she had left. An article caught her eye. 'Alex, look at this. The garden centre where we used to go and you bought me those plants, they're doing a competition for children, it's such a good idea.'

He read the story. 'They all have to paint a pot for their bulbs. It *is* good because they'll be keen to bring them back in the spring with the bulbs in flower. It's such a nice little place, I'd like to see it getting more custom.' He studied the photo more closely. 'The girl who served me, Lily, isn't there but she did say she might be going to university, that would be now, I suppose. There's a young man and another girl, can't tell in black and white, but her hair looks a bit strange.'

'Different colours I think. A good-looking boy, he reminds me how handsome you were when we were young.'

'You mean I'm not now?' he asked with a smile. Gently, he lifted her hand, the skin now paper-thin and kissed it. 'You are as beautiful to me as the day we met.'

'Alex, please take all my plant pots for the children. I'd feel a part of me will carry on if they're used for growing things, does that sound crazy?'

'No, I understand. I'll do it first thing tomorrow.'

* * *

Lily was standing cross-legged waiting for the bathroom, her mother would have been horrified, she hadn't liked the idea of bathroom sharing at all. The shower was still running and it wasn't helping her bladder, listening to it. Running down to the next level, thankfully that one was free. There was chatter coming from the kitchen and she went down to join whoever was there. Her housemates, who had all arrived in the last few days, seemed a nice bunch. Two of the girls were doing the same foundation course as she was, the other three were doing three-year BSc (Hons) one specialising in plant science and Rupert, the boy, whose name had made them all chuckle, was doing garden and landscape design. When he had introduced himself, he'd told them to have a good laugh and get over it, he'd suffered all his life. He turned out to be an excellent cook and made a huge chilli for everybody that night, so was forgiven and they all started calling him, Roo.

Lily shared her attic floor with Kate, a down to earth girl from Newcastle, who called everyone *pet* and drank copious amounts of fizzy drinks while eating crisps and chocolate bars and was a size eight by Lily's reckoning. *Not fair.* They were all catching the bus together for their first day and trying to get ready, which put a strain on the bathrooms. The others had been down previously, to an open day and Lily was looking forward to seeing the famous biodomes for real and not just through pictures.

Kate joined them, smelling of green tea shower gel. 'Sorry pet, you can have first dibs tomorrow, I didn't realise I was taking so long.'

'No worries,' said Lily. 'If we're all catching the same bus every day, we'll have to share out bathroom time.'

Rupert sat smirking. There was one bedroom on the ground floor with an en-suite and because he was the only boy, it made sense for him to have it. 'If any of you lovely ladies want to use mine, I'm sure we can come to some arrangement.'

'Yuck, no thanks,' said Becky, one of the first-floor girls. 'I come from a house with two brothers, I hate seeing the loo seat up all the time.'

'Your loss,' he grinned. 'Who's eating in tonight?'

'Are you cooking again pet? I will if *you* are.' Kate was very lazy regarding proper eating, but if it was put in front of her, she'd enjoy it.

'I don't mind cooking if everybody else does the cleaning and stuff. We'll sort out a kitty and make a list of what we all like. I just need to know how many.'

'If we're having a kitty, it should be used for when we're *all* eating together,' Zoe said primly. Lily guessed that she was already drawing up a rota for household duties.

'I guess that's fair,' he said. 'I think we should all try and eat here at least twice a week and be sociable, what are we doing about booze?'

'We'll buy our own,' Zoe said very quickly. 'We won't all drink the same amount, and I only drink white wine.' All the others looked at each other and smiled, which went unnoticed as she carried on. 'We *must* be organised with all the bottles and cans, fridge room is limited and we don't want lots of empties cluttering up the place, straight into re-cycle, agreed?'

They nodded, trying not to laugh.

'That told us,' Rupert muttered to Lily as they filed out for the bus. He was over six foot and she felt even smaller than usual beside him.

'She's obviously our house-mother,' Lily smiled.

The bus arrived, he stepped back to let her on, then sat beside her. 'So, what's your story, then Lily, why Eden?'

She told him about her grandparents and Roots, also her father's opposition. 'What about you?'

'Always loved plants and visiting gardens. Everybody at school thought I was a complete nerd and what with my name, it was horrendous.'

'Were you bullied?'

'A bit, but they got bored and I did have *some* friends. It wasn't as bad as some people suffered, at least I was good at football, that saved me. Anyway, enough of that, are you going to go out for a drink with me one night?' he asked abruptly.

'I... it's a bit soon, maybe in a while?'

'You want to do the, get to know me first, do you? What you see is what you get, there's nothing strange about me and I don't have any peculiar habits or anything.'

She laughed. 'Neither do I, I don't think, but I'd still like to settle in a bit first, sorry.'

'That's okay, it wasn't your only chance, I will ask again.'

I don't think I'd mind him asking again.

* * *

Robert Overidge sipped his coffee and thought how nice Szarlota had looked this morning. While he was overseeing the distribution of the till floats, he noticed her very short skirt and shapely thighs. The flirtatious look she'd given him, also did not go unnoticed. Unconsciously, he sucked in his stomach, perhaps he should shape up a bit, give her something better to look at? Idly, he flicked through the local paper, mainly to see what his rivals were up to. A minute later, he almost spat out his coffee. *Bloody hell!* The wretched garden centre was in the news, along with a photo and write up. It was as good as a free advertisement. Some children's stupid pot-painting competition and bulb promotion. That would mean footfall and *money* coming in. *Dammit*. His parents were coming for lunch this Sunday, now they'd be all fired up about this daft idea and not so easily open to persuasion.

How could he salvage something? Lily was their weakness, always had been, he thought sourly. He was their *son,* they should be more concerned with his future, still a relatively young man, he could have years of work ahead of him, what a depressing thought, so he would have to make them see that it was far too much responsibility for their granddaughter to take on which, given their ages, he'd have to put tactfully, could be sooner than they wished. As her father and beneficiary, he would have to make sure it was in her best interests and sadly, it may not be. That should do it.

Corrine had moaned about doing lunch and now he had this to contend with. Hopefully, he could still talk them around. A few children, that's probably all it would amount to, he was getting upset about nothing, in the scheme of things, any extra money they made would be a drop in the ocean. He looked again at the picture and frowned, two young people on the staff, he hadn't known about that, where had the money to hire them come from? Still, they couldn't be *that* experienced and if left on their own, as they would be on Sunday, they may make a real mess of things, which would do no harm at all. Finishing his coffee, he decided to check the shop floor and have a friendly word with Szarlota.

* * *

Peter Simmons had also seen the article. Let them have their fun, it wouldn't last long, he didn't really want to cause upset while children were involved but soon they would start turning the screw. He hoped to by-pass Robert Overidge completely and let the old folks sell to him directly. There was a field nearby which would fit in very nicely with the plans and he'd already put in an offer, it used to be riding stables, so had established buildings and a courtyard. Once he had the field, the rest of it, somebody else could buy, there could be all sorts of groundworks being done, involving large tipper lorries that would block the small road leading to the garden centre, on a regular basis. If people couldn't get to it, they'd go elsewhere and if the sellers accepted his offer, that could start in about two months' time. It would be bought by one of his subsidiary companies, so if Robert *did* start nosing around, there would be no connection to the people he thought he was dealing with. Studying his drawings again he marked one of the houses with a cross. It was the five-bedroomed exclusively private one that would stand on the site of the current owners' cottage. Gated, within a gated development, it would be a bespoke, top of the range dwelling, one he fancied for himself.

* * *

Murdoch had not seen Megan all week. Although she told him she had crawled back to work, being so exhausted at the end of the day, she just wanted to have some early nights, obviously, the flu had knackered her and she was really sorry.

It was okay, he was staying on at work a bit longer and once Merry found out what it was all about, she also volunteered.

'Got nothing better to do,' she said cheerily when Stuart had protested about her giving her time up. 'We need to make use of the evening light while it's still here.' So, the last couple of evenings had seen her and Murdoch slowly and carefully removing the broken glass and stacking it in boxes for the tip.

He was puzzled. When he had first looked, there had seemed an awful lot that needed removing, but now, most of the panes seemed to be okay, perhaps a little extra putty here and there to be on the safe side. He knew absolutely that when he moved his ladder, there were three cracked panes, now he was here, there was only one. He said something to Merry about not understanding it.

'Must be a trick of the light,' she said, blowing out her bubble gum with a loud pop. 'A reflection making it look like a crack. Those electrical wires perhaps?' As he looked, black lines danced across the roofs of the glasshouses.

'You could be right, anyway, it's made our job much easier.'

'Sweet. Shall we grab a burger when we've finished, I'm starving.'

Murdoch wondered where she put it all. Cake was consumed daily and she never turned down any of Madge's baking. She *was* strong but looked like a puff of wind would blow her over. His dad would be at work and Megan was not up for company this week. 'Okay, why not? My treat though.'

'Certainly not, we'll go Netherlands,' she saw him looking at her with a puzzled expression, 'err... I mean Dutch.' *I can't get some of these sayings, they don't make sense at all.*

When they finished, they locked up and popped over to the cottage to let Stuart and Madge know they were leaving.

'Don't know what plans you two have got, but Duckie says, do you want to come in for some tea? She's made vegetable lasagne and there's plenty of it. I'll be eating it for days if you don't help out.' Stuart winked at them both.

It sounded much better than a burger, Murdoch thought, but as usual, didn't like accepting favours. 'We were going to…'

'That would be great, wouldn't it Murdoch, only if you're absolutely sure?' Merry interjected.

'*Absolutely* sure, come on in you two.'

Merry looked approvingly at the flagstone hallway filled with the smell of beeswax and baking. 'Just like home,' she sighed as she took her shoes off. About to ask her a bit more about home, Murdoch missed his chance as she literally skipped through to the kitchen, offering to help Madge before being shooed away.

Sitting around the worn, scratched table while Madge dished up, Stuart noticed Murdoch's finger tracing some gouges by the surface next to his plate. 'That'll be our Lily. Always sat here drawing as a little girl and she dug the pencils in so hard they went through to the table.'

'This looks like a flower in a pot, she's always drawing now, garden designs and stuff.'

Murdoch liked the idea of the table telling a story like that, he didn't even know if there were any photos of him as a child, let alone any physical evidence. Nothing he'd ever brought home from school had been displayed as far as he could remember and once his mother had left, his father wasn't interested. 'Merry, where is it you come from?'

'Oh, I've never really settled anywhere, I flit about you know? But I think I'd like to stay here awhile,' she added quickly.

'Do you have family here?' asked Madge, who was very curious about the newcomer.

'They're all over the place as well, but I can talk to them anytime I need to. Technology's wonderful, isn't it?' Merry beamed.

'Speaking of technology, how are you getting on with the phone, my boy?'

'Oh, great thanks, Stuart. I've already let Lily know about our new member of staff and I've just sent her a copy of the newspaper article.'

'What did you say about me?' Merry grinned, knowing full well that he'd taken a picture of her hair.

'Umm, just that we had a new person, a *lady*, she'll see you in the picture with the article I sent.'

'Of course she will, say "hi" to her from me.'

'We don't talk that much, it's not a regular thing,' he mumbled.

'When you do then. I'm sure you'll have a reason to message her again soon.'

After a delicious blackberry and apple crumble, they said they had to leave and were very grateful for the meal.

'Not at all, thank you both for the extra work you're doing.' Stuart said as he saw them out.

They walked together to the end of the road and Murdoch stopped. 'I'm going this way, how about you?'

'I'm over there,' she pointed vaguely, 'see you tomorrow Murdoch.'

'Do you have far to go?'

'Nah, I'll be home before you know it.' She strode away and when he'd gone a short distance, he glanced around to see how far she had gone along the straight pathway that followed the river. There was no sign of her. *Strange, she must have run.* Shrugging his shoulders, he carried on, unaware of the small butterfly hovering above.

* * *

Stuart and Madge arrived for Sunday lunch and were immediately offered a glass of sherry.

'Usual bullshit,' Stuart whispered as Robert went to pour them. Madge thought she'd much prefer a nice cup of tea but thanked him politely when they were brought over.

'Well, how are you two keeping then?' Their son asked, in a jovial fashion. 'You must be thinking about enjoying your retirement by now?'

'Hadn't given it that much thought, we both enjoy things as they are, don't we Duckie?'

'Definitely, I like to keep busy.'

Robert tutted with irritation at the use of the pet name. Corrine was keeping herself well out of the way in the kitchen, she never knew what to talk about when his parents were in attendance and was not looking forward to the lunch at all. Cooking wasn't her forte and they usually went out with friends. As a manager, Robert did have to work the occasional Sundays, but he managed to keep them to a minimum and she much preferred the carvery at the golf club or lunch at one of the nearby country hotels. Still, Robert had said this was important for their future, so she put on a smile and breezed through to the dining room with prawn cocktail starters, which were easy enough to do, especially when purchased at the deli and served up with thin slivers of brown bread and butter.

'Corrine, you look lovely as always, so kind of you to invite us over,' Madge said.

'Thank you,' she patted her hair. 'One likes to make an effort.'

The main course was roast chicken, Corrine didn't suppose they warranted anything better, but they seemed to enjoy it. Robert cleared his throat.

'Father, Mother, I want you to listen to what I have to say. Lily is doing a degree course, down in Cornwall, with the expectation that she will one day be running your centre. I cannot understand how you could shoulder her with such a burden at a time in her life when she is most vulnerable. Please let me finish,' he saw Stuart about to speak. 'I've said it before, the two of you aren't getting any younger, she is starting off in life and what would happen if she meets somebody and has a young family? That place will be nothing but a worry for her and a constant drain on her resources. It's not making enough money and it never will. There's too much competition around, surely, leaving her a nest egg to help set her up would be far better than saddling her with that dump to manage and what happens when the two of you... pass on?'

If they were beginning to be swayed, the word *dump*, undid everything their son had been trying to put across to them.

'Roots is not a dump, as you put it. It's been our life and Lily will be free to do whatever she wants with it when the time comes. Thank you for the lunch, I think we had best go now. Madge?' Stuart held out his hand and his wife, looking very shaky and upset, stood up.

'What do you mean, she can do what she wants? It won't be her decision.' Robert was getting very red in the face, he'd handled this badly, it wasn't going the way he had planned.

Stuart squeezed Madge's arm, warning her not to say anything. 'Maybe not, but *we* won't take her dream away from her.' There was no way he'd give Robert any inkling that the will had been changed.

'Oh dear,' said Corrine, looking flustered, 'Aren't you staying for dessert? It's crème brulee.' Another one bought from the deli and served in her own bowls. 'And I've put on the percolator for coffee?'

'Damn the coffee!' Robert threw his knife and fork down with disgust. 'I've tried to help and give advice and this is the thanks I get. Well, I hope you'll be satisfied when she's crying her eyes out because it has to be sold.' *But I'll make sure it gets sold before that ever happens.*

'Shall I switch the percolator off? It was lovely ground beans you know.'

'Sorry Corrine,' Madge said quietly, 'we'd better go before there's any more upset.'

Robert, thin-lipped, waited till they left and slammed the front door. 'They'll regret it, they must be getting feeble-minded. I'll have to keep a close eye on them.' *That would be handy, then I could get control.* 'Don't waste the crème brulee, bring them out and some of that coffee please. I'm sorry this lunch was a disaster. I'll open a bottle of wine.'

* * *

That night, Megan went to see Murdoch. She knew his father would be home, so wasn't worried about having to make an excuse not to have sex. She still didn't feel like it. They sat outside with crisps and a bottle of cola. 'I'm sorry I've been so poorly, I really don't know what the matter was, I'm so drained.'

'You're still a bit pale,' he said, putting his arm around her. 'I've been busy though, with some extra work, we'll make up for it later.'

She noticed the phone. 'Hey, that's new, I didn't think you could afford anything like that.'

'Ah, I was sort of given it.' He explained how Stuart hadn't wanted it and offered it to him.

'She's got a better one, that figures.' Megan said spitefully. 'Any more crisps?' As soon as Murdoch went to fetch them, she snatched up the phone and had a quick scroll through. There was an odd photo of someone's hair, which looked like a party wig, then she checked his contacts. *Lily!* Why was she there? Reading the text messages, she frowned. They seemed innocent enough, but she didn't like it. By the time he came back, the phone was back on the grass.

'Thanks. By the way, how's Lily getting on, with her course thing?'

'She seems happy. She asked me to let her know about things at work, so I've sent a couple of texts. That's... okay isn't it?'

'Yeah, sure. Why wouldn't it be?' she laughed. *As long as that's all it is.*

Chapter Ten

CHRISTMAS CACTUS – SCHLUMBERGERA

Can flower from late November to late January

It was almost the end of October and Lily was returning home for the first time since going to Cornwall. She'd been so busy, there had been no chance for a weekend visit but kept in touch with Murdoch who'd let her know what a success the pot painting had been.

They Q'd 4 an hour, Madge kept bringing squash and biscuits, & Flora helped with T & coffee for the adults. Merry lead them all in a sing-song & they sd it was the best fun ever. We were exhausted, but it was gr8. Loads of pots and bulbs sold. ☺ We were on TV!

She replied, *Wow, can't w8 4 all details. It's fab here, will tell u all soon. 2 much 2 txt.*

The pot painting had been a *huge* success. A press photographer came and took more photos and to Murdoch's mortification, the local TV news team arrived, shoving a microphone in his face and asking him about the idea. He had stuttered a bit, then found Merry at his side, explaining how it had been his and Lily, the owners' granddaughter's idea. Stuart was asked how he felt about it all. "He was delighted," he said, "to see young people getting involved with growing something and hoped the excitement would carry on until the spring when the bulbs would start to show themselves."

The parents had been swept along with enthusiasm, many of them also bought a selection of bulbs when they saw the pictures and ideas for grouping an attractive display. All in all, it had been a most successful weekend.

Merry had helped a gentleman a few days before they kicked off, who had arrived with boxes of plant pots and containers in all shapes and sizes. She studied him while helping to unload them all. 'This is very kind of you.'

'They're my wife's, she's the one who loves gardening but can't do it anymore and wanted the children to enjoy them. We read about your weekend in the paper.'

'She's not well, I'm so very sorry.'

'T-thank you.' *I didn't actually say she was ill, did I?* 'Young Lily, who served me last time, is she at university?'

'She's studying at the Eden project, who shall I say was asking?'

'She may not remember me, Mr Wavish, she helped me choose plants for my wife's window sill, that may jog her memory.'

'I'll make sure she gets the message, Mr Wavish. People go through bad times but they come out of the darkness and into the light where something is waiting for them.'

'A nice thought. Well, that's the last of the pots, goodbye and good luck with the weekend.'

'Thank you, I wish you well until we see you again.'

'I doubt if I'll be back this way.'

You'll be back

'We'll have to start thinking about Christmas now,' Stuart was in the tea hut with Murdoch and Merry. 'Getting present ideas ready for people perhaps? Mind you, your old place of work, Murdoch, Garden Zone, has pretty well cornered the market on that, we can't compete with them.'

'There's no need to compete, offer an alternative,' Merry suggested. 'An olde-worlde Christmas, that sort of thing. Proper hand-made wreaths and lots of dried flower heads for decorations, we can spray them gold and silver.'

'It's a bit late to dry stuff now,' Stuart said doubtfully.

'I've got a shed-full of the stuff,' chirped Merry. 'Hydrangeas, loads of seeds, poppy heads, teasels, lotus pods, cedar roses and fir cones, bags of them.'

'How are you going to get them here? you don't drive do you?' asked Murdoch.

'Nope, but you're taking your test next week, aren't you?'

'*Taking* it, yes, doesn't mean I'll pass.'

'Poof! Of course, you will. You can pick it all up the day after, you said you had a van, right?'

'Err, yes but...'

'That's settled then. I'll tell you where. Then we'll get spraying, we can do it all in the glasshouses, they're weather-proofed now. Hey, we could have a grotto in there, Stuart, you could be father Christmas.'

'Good grief, I don't think so, Mr Taylor would be a better candidate.'

'You could be a grotto fairy.' Murdoch, grinning, looked at Merry, who, to his surprise, appeared horrified.

'Oh no, that's not a good idea. Look at me, have you ever seen anything more un-fairy like?' To demonstrate her point, her gum appeared as a large bubble which then exploded onto her face. 'Oops.'

'You do have a point,' Murdoch said. 'Lily might do it when she's back, she's almost small enough to pass as one.'

'Perfect,' smiled Merry.

* * *

Lily was putting the last bits into her rucksack and tidying her room. It seemed forever since she'd been home, but it was only eight weeks. So much had happened, she couldn't wait to tell everybody.

'Hey Lily, are you nearly ready? I've had a text to say my lift is here.' Roo's voice came from below.

'Coming.' She had finally given in and gone out with him. He was actually great company, very funny and polite to everyone. He held the chair out for her, opened doors and was generally quieter and more caring than when he was in a crowd. The first time, he had given her a brotherly kiss on the cheek with a "let's do this again". Thinking that was the end of it, she was delighted when he surprised her with cinema tickets, a meal and didn't push for anything else. When he heard that she was going to book a coach home for half-term, finding out she lived near Salisbury, he said he was going on to Surrey and had a lift, would she like to travel up with him and be dropped off? Promising it was no trouble or inconvenience, he persuaded her.

Coming downstairs, she looked out of the door. 'Where's your lift?'

'Ah, it's a few streets away, you'll understand when you see. I hope?'

'What do you mean, is it *safe*?'

'Christ, Lily, there's nothing dodgy, I promise you. I'll explain in a minute.'

A little unsure, she followed him past all the newly built houses and into some quieter streets where older, large detached houses sat, bordered by beech trees, looking smug in their grandeur, soaking up the Autumn sunshine.

Halfway along sat a Rolls Royce and when the driver saw them, he jumped out and waited to open the doors. 'Morning, Mr Rupert sir, Miss, please give me your bags and make yourselves comfortable.'

'Roo, what the hell is this?'

'Thank you, John, this is my friend Lily, who we're dropping off near Salisbury.'

'Yes, sir. Let me know when you want to take a break and we'll stop. There're drinks and refreshments in the back.'

As Lily was putting her seat belt on and still slightly in shock at the opulence of her ride, a glass panel slid silently upward, cutting them off from John.

'Okay, I'd rather you didn't say anything to our housemates, if they do find out, it can't be helped, but I don't advertise it.' Rupert started.

'Advertise what? Are you... umm, a *Lord* or something?'

He laughed, 'No, I'm not, you don't have to bow to me, although that would be rather fun.'

'Don't push it.'

'Sorry. My parents are filthy rich, I use my mother's name because people would probably recognise my father's.' He told her what his dad was called.

'I don't know it, should I? is he important?'

'He thinks he is. He's a big newspaper tycoon, magazines, all that sort of thing.'

'Oh, right.'

'Is that it? Oh right? Most girls, when they find out, want to know what clubs I can get them into, or can I arrange for them to meet this or that celebrity.'

'That's not for me, I can understand why you keep it quiet, is that why you wouldn't let me pay for anything? It's very nice of you, but it's not fair.'

'I did it because I knew you weren't that sort of girl, I've got something else to tell you. I hope you aren't looking for a big romance, I like you and I want us to be friends and do things together, but I... have a partner, his name is Sam.'

She felt a Nano-second of disappointment, then nothing. 'Oh, I see. That's cool, are you using me to fend off attention? You do attract a lot.'

'No, I'm not worried about being upfront on *that* subject, I do genuinely like you, is that okay?'

'I guess so, but only if you let me pay sometimes.'

'Shut up, let's have a look at what goodies we've got.' There was a selection of cold drinks, crisps, pork pies, sandwiches and cakes amongst other things.

'No caviar?' Lily asked, grinning.

'Have a sausage roll and thank God there isn't, I hate the stuff.'

They dropped Lily at the bus station in Salisbury, at her insistence. She couldn't, just *couldn't* arrive home in a Rolls. Her mother would never stop going on about it. She was however persuaded, to let him pick her up on the way home, but only here at the bus depot again.

'I'll text you the time,' Roo said, giving her a hug. 'You have a good week.'

'You too.'

* * *

Peter Simmons gave a satisfied smile as he saw the message from his solicitor confirming completion of the purchase of the fields. Not long to wait now before he could start making the lives of the owners of Roots, a misery. He'd had a pathetic, bleating message from Robert Overidge, saying how stubborn his parents were and how he was 'still working on them', well, let him work. Now, he needed a legitimate reason to have heavy machinery, diggers and lorries going in and out of the place. With his architect already having been instructed, he had drawings for a modest leisure centre, with swimming pool, gym, squash courts and café. That would involve a *lot* of excavation. The plans would be popular, the current pool in the town was old and very basic. This one would have a children's pool, jacuzzies, and a sensibly sized spectator area. It was a no-brainer; the plans would be approved quickly and with little or no opposition. Not quite in time for Christmas, unfortunately, but with the Spring the garden centre would be looking forward to a lot of customers, customers who would be totally frustrated by the mess and delays on the lane, customers who would go to Garden Zone instead.

His planning consultant, Martin, had already had a meeting with the planning officer and it was very favourable. Also, having mentioned the possibility of development on the current garden centre, that was also now looked on favourably. He had absolutely no intention of building the leisure centre, of course, the preparation would take months and there would be all sorts of problems. When he had the okay for the other plans, his subsidiary company would have financial problems, he would step in and resubmit plans for more houses. Yes, wasn't it a shame about the pool, but he really didn't feel he could invest in such a large project. Pouring himself a whisky, he gave a silent toast to his email message.

* * *

By the time Lily got home and knowing she'd have to spend the evening with her parents when they got back, she checked in with her friends. Amy would be home tomorrow, from her course in psychology, but Laura had cried off, saying she had a lot of good invites over the week and would catch up at Christmas. Laura's pictures on Facebook were always with a crowd of friends, her arm around a different man each time. Regularly quoted as saying she "was loving every minute of her life studying for an English literature degree", Lily thought there was a sadness in her friend's eyes, belied by her smile. Laura wasn't happy unless she was the centre of attention and obviously had some competition with this new group of friends. Corrine arrived home first and Lily was quite touched by the shine of tears in her mother's eyes.

'Lily, you've grown up so much since I last saw you. I hardly recognised you.'

'I haven't changed, Mum, my hair might be an inch longer, that's all.'

'You look different to me, I hope you're remembering to use your skin products in that harsh outdoor air all the time.'

'Yes, Mum. We're not outside all the time you know, we're in the domes, and in class a lot as well.'

'You're near the sea, aren't you? You have to combat the salt.'

The salt? 'Yes Mum, I'm using all the stuff.'

'See that you do. Your father's picking up Chinese, a special treat, you can tell us all about it then. Not the gardening stuff dear, your social life, that's far more interesting. Boyfriends, for example, anybody on the scene yet?'

'There's a boy in the house and we're friends; does that count?'

'Now you're being silly again. I can see I shan't get anything of any interest from you at all.'

Lily knew her mother would die of excitement if she found out the full facts about the boy who was a friend.

Her father, when he arrived with the Chinese feast, at least asked about her course. 'What sort of things are you actually studying?'

'This year, I'll learn about plant and soil nutrition, a bit about landscaping and design and I'll have a work placement.'

'Work placement! Huh, we get those in the supermarket, never taken anyone on from it yet.' Robert shovelled in a forkful of sweet and sour pork.

Corrine poked delicately at her vegetable chow mein. 'It won't be that slave labour I keep hearing about on the news, will it? Picking fruit and such?'

'No Mum, it won't be anything like that. I think even Prince Charles approves of the Eden project.'

'Really?' her mother brightened considerably. 'It must be alright then, does he… ever pop down there?'

'If I hear he's coming, I'll let you know,' Lily grinned.

'Such a shame *both* the boys are spoken for, I expect they're interested in gardens and things.' She twittered on and Robert gave his daughter a conspiratorial wink.

* * *

Merry had Sunday off and as much as she didn't want or need it, she had to be seen to be fitting in, so spent her day collecting all sorts of seed heads and flowers and drying them with a wave that spread glitter all over the place. Soon she had a large collection as promised. These were tied together in bunches, the heap growing ever larger. They would not all fit in Murdoch's van. She'd have to pretend someone else had given her a lift with the first lot. Another wave and they shrunk to doll's house size, with which she filled a shoe box, that would do it, they'd all be restored to their full glory before anybody saw them.

Her thoughts went again to the man, Alexander Wavish. His poor wife would never know the joy to come. That was one thing her people were very strict about, absolutely no interference with the natural order of events. It was difficult, some were not able to resist the temptation, but it was always stopped and they were never given a second chance. Merry had no intention, however hard and unfeeling it seemed, to blow *her* chance. Certain things would happen in the time frame as they needed to, others, she *could* interfere with and she was looking forward to those.

In the meantime, Murdoch would be taking his driving test tomorrow. He would pass, with no help from her, and that would give him his own set of wings. Not literally, she chuckled, but he would feel as if he had them. She had made sure his van was a little more road-worthy than he believed it to be, there was no harm in doing something like that. Now she still had a few hours of late afternoon sun, so she joined the colourful butterflies in her cottage garden and enjoyed her own wings of mauve, pink and blue.

* * *

Lily arrived on Sunday, a little disappointed not to be meeting the newest member of staff, but really pleased to see her Grandparents and Murdoch, of course. Over a cuppa, she heard all the details of the pot painting and what a success it had been.

'Your Grandad was on the television and Murdoch and Merry as well. I've got it recorded,' said Grandma, proudly.

'Oh good, I'll have a look before I go home.'

'Oh, must you? I was stuttering like an idiot until Merry saved me.' Murdoch stirred his tea. He was looking at Lily. Eight weeks and she did seem a little more confident, more at ease with herself. Going away from home was good for her, he thought. 'I'm looking forward to hearing about what you do in Cornwall.'

As the centre wasn't very busy and Mr Taylor was around, she told them about the course and what she'd been studying so far.

'You're in some sort of houseshare I heard, what are the people you're living with like?' Grandad asked.

She made them laugh with her impression of Kate's northern accent and tales of Zoe's bossy organisation. She mentioned a boy called Rupert, who they called Roo, but skimmed over him quite quickly.

Interesting, thought Murdoch, wondering if Lily fancied him. *Rupert,* he could imagine what Megan and her friends would say about that.

After they'd finished, Lily went all over the centre, checking plants, and seeing what had changed. Very impressed with the vegetables, she saw several new crops coming through and some under polythene, ones that didn't like the cooler nights. Murdoch, noticing her interest told her what he'd planted, and explained about the glasshouses and Merry's idea for Christmas.

'Oh, that sounds fab, I can help with the spraying and stuff this week and start making up a few wreaths, she sounds like fun.'

'She's okay, a bit strange at times, but she can rattle off any name of a plant in Latin, and she knows all the conditions they like. I don't know how she learnt it all.'

'How old is she?'

'I don't actually know, she never really answers questions about herself. She dresses and looks young but seems sort of... old-fashioned in other ways, like I said, she's strange. You'll meet her tomorrow if you're here. I'm off for the day, taking my driving test.'

'Are you? Well, good luck, I'm hoping to start lessons soon, but it's a bit difficult at the moment. Maybe in the summer holidays?'

* * *

Amy came around in the evening and the two girls had a good catch up. She was also a bit worried about Laura. 'She doesn't really message much anymore or talk, only puts up lots of pictures.'

'Yeah, I thought that,' said Lily. 'She's moving on with new friends, I suppose, we'll keep in touch, let her know we're here if she needs us.'

'Yep. Listen and don't bite my head off, Garden Zone's got all their Christmas stuff, decorations and things out now. I'd really like to go and see it, will you come with me? You could be a spy if it makes you feel better.'

'We're doing stuff for Christmas as well, but it won't be out until November. Ours is going to be a more *natural* range. Okay, I'll go with you, just this once.'

'Oh great, how about tomorrow morning?'

Tomorrow? Murdoch was off and she could meet this 'Merry' in the afternoon, 'The morning's fine, shall we catch the bus?'

'Yep, we'll meet for the ten o'clock. An hour will be plenty of time to look around.'

They met as arranged, Lily felt very disloyal but liking Amy's idea of being a spy. Garden Zone was fairly busy, even though it was a Monday, it was half term and harassed parents were already trying to entertain children who were bored.

The Christmas section was enormous. All the tinsel, tree decorations and tableware were arranged in colour formation, so, if one wanted a silver Christmas, it was all there, with no searching to be done. Lily found it all very uniform and with no diversity. Wandering over to the floral decorations, she surreptitiously took some photos, she had no idea exactly how much stuff Merry had but couldn't see it coming anywhere near the volume offered here.

Amy joined her with a few red and silver bits she'd picked out for her tree. 'Sorry,' she muttered.

'Don't be silly, we're not selling that sort of thing anyway.' Lily's eye was caught by a tree-top fairy, wearing a long white dress and sporting flowing pink hair. It was rather sweet. 'Will you pay for that with yours and I'll give you the money in a minute? I just want to have a quick look at the indoor plants for gifts, section.'

She left Amy in the decorations and went over to the boxes of bulb present ideas and a large selection of Christmas cacti in different shades and also poinsettias. She noticed that there were quite a few buds on the cactus, but a gentle tap on the plant and some would drop off. It would be cold at night in this cavernous showroom, that wouldn't help them. The poinsettias were in a darker area and they needed bright light. There was a lady looking at them, Lily couldn't help herself. 'Excuse me,' she said. 'If you're choosing one of these, make sure you put it in the light when you get home and when you get to the till ask them to put it in a plastic bag, the cold can damage the foliage.'

'Do you work here?' The lady asked, looking at Lily's coat.

'I don't, but I do know a bit about plants.'

'Alright, pick one out for me please.'

Lily searched until she found one she'd be happy with. 'This one.'

The lady nodded. 'What about a cactus?'

'They're not in such a good condition. It's too cold in here at night, the buds are dropping. This is newer stock at the back I think, you may be safer with one of these, maybe...?' She crawled onto the shelving and reached across.

'Miss, can you get off there please?' An irate looking man was coming towards them. 'Is she with you madam?'

'No but she's been helping me.'

'Well she doesn't work here, allow *me* to assist you.' He glared at Lily and snatched the cactus from her hands, 'I'll take one from the front for you.'

Amy wandered over at this point, nobody noticing a strange glow coming from the little fairy in her basket. The woman took the cactus which promptly dropped every one of its buds onto the floor.

'Careful, don't shake it.' The man said curtly.

'Young man, I did not *shake* it. If this girl doesn't work here, she most certainly should. She knows a good plant when she sees it, you can keep your cactus.' She put the basket down and gestured to Lily. 'What do you do dear, if you don't work here?'

Lily took her arm and moved away from the man who was trying to kick the buds out of site under the racks. 'I work at Roots, the small centre at the other side of town, my grandparents own it.'

'Do you have poinsettias and cacti in stock?'

'We do, but not as big a selection.'

'Pick out one of each for me, and I'll collect them tomorrow. Your name is?'

'Lily Overidge.'

'My details, I'll see you tomorrow.' She fished a small card out of her bag and left.

'Who was that?' Asked Amy.

Lily looked at the card. 'Oh my God, it's the Countess who lives in that big Elizabethan Manor house, outside of town. She opens her gardens once a year for charity, they're fantastic I've heard.'

'Well, you impressed her anyway, come on, that man's looking daggers at you. Let's pay for these and get a milkshake in town.'

When Lily got to Roots later, she met Merry and liked her at first sight.

'I've heard so much about you Lily, it's good to meet you at last? Did you have an interesting morning?'

'Err, yes thank you. Has anyone heard from Murdoch?'

'About his test? Don't worry, he'll pass. I've got some of my stuff in the glasshouses, I umm, got a lift this morning. Come and see.'

'This is *some* of it?' Lily asked faintly. There must be three times what Garden Zone had on display. There was also a pile of spray cans in silver, gold, copper, snow effect and a few other colours. 'We'd better get on with it then.'

Her afternoon was spent sorting, trimming, spraying and when it was all dry, bunching and arranging the foliage for best effect. 'They look amazing, Merry. Thank you so much for all of these.'

'Nice to put them to good use,' she said. 'Didn't you say you had some plants to sort?'

'Did I?' *I'm sure I didn't tell her.* 'Yes, I'll do that now.' One cactus and poinsettia chosen, she took them into the cottage for safe keeping overnight, not really expecting to see the Countess again.

Murdoch had passed his test. His dad's friend, Joe, had taught him well if, a little unconventionally. There had been many demonstrations of, opposite locking and driving so smoothly a packet of chewing gum never moved on the dashboard. They had used a different vehicle almost every time, so Murdoch was no longer fazed by anything Joe turned up in. The examiner had said he was impressed and hadn't seen such confident handling from a youngster in a long time. Megan was thrilled and asked when he was going to get a *proper* car.

Mr Overidge was pleased as well. 'We can make use of you almost right away, well done my boy.'

'Let me tell you what happened to me yesterday,' Lily said and told the story, while Merry smiled quietly in the background. 'I'm just waiting to see if she turns up.'

The Countess did indeed turn up and was delighted with her plants. 'This is a nice little nursery, or whatever you call it, I've never been before. All that music and everything un-garden-like in the other place, it was *ghastly*. Tell me, will you be staying here?'

'I want to yes, but I'm doing a course first.'

'What course?' she fixed Lily with a beady eye.

Patiently, she explained and Stuart, who was beside her, told the Countess that it was their wish that Lily would one day run the place.

'You'll be back here at Easter again for the holidays?'

'I will, yes.'

'I'll have a proposition to put to you then. Easter, I'll be back.' She swept off with her plants to a waiting car.

'Like the Terminator,' muttered Murdoch, who'd caught the end of the conversation.

Lily spent the rest of the week helping to prepare the Christmas floral decorations and making one of the glasshouses more welcoming. Before she knew it, it was Sunday and time to meet Roo again in Salisbury.

'I'll see you all at Christmas,' she said. 'Don't forget to keep me up to date, Murdoch and, photos please.'

'I will.' After driving Merry to her cottage and picking up the rest of the dried foliage, he was feeling more confident, and after hearing Lily was getting a bus to Salisbury, wanted to offer her a lift. He was a bit ashamed of the van though, and he chickened out. Merry wasn't standing for that, she had a quiet word with Stuart.

'He really wants to offer Lily a lift, show off a bit you know, now he's passed his test, but he thinks she won't like going in the van.'

'Is that so? Let me sort that out.'

'Lily, Stuart wants me to pick up something in Salisbury for him, from a seed supplier? So, I could drop you off if you like?' Murdoch said nonchalantly.

'I was going to get the bus, but, if you're sure?'

'No trouble, whenever you're ready.'

Lily seemed quite happy in the van and chattered all the way. He dropped her at the bus station.

'Do you want me to wait, make sure you get your lift?'

'That's fine, I'm early. I'll get a cup of tea, thanks ever so much,' she stretched up and gave him a quick kiss on the cheek, then turned away in case he felt obliged to do the same.

He said a gruff goodbye, parked up and went back to watch, just to make sure she was okay. After about half an hour a *Rolls* drove into the pick-up area. He couldn't believe it when he saw her walk towards it, a tall guy got out, hugged her and she got in.

Who was he kidding, she moved in a different world. He came from the crap end of town, living in, one step up from a caravan and driving a beat up old van. Megan came from his world, she understood his circumstances. Lily was his employers' granddaughter, that's all she'd ever be.

Chapter Eleven

URTICA DIOICA – STINGING NETTLE

A plant most people avoid, rather than get hurt

Brian Lawton had started drinking again and not wanting Murdoch to know, was very secretive about it. Going to the pub at weekends had been accepted, but the nights were getting chilly and when he was working, as a lonely security guard, which as far as he was concerned, was a posh name for a night watchman, he had taken to having the odd nip of something in his coffee. This had now progressed to a small flask hidden in his jacket and on more than one occasion, he had fallen asleep. Thankfully, he had not yet been discovered and nothing had happened at the building site. A big development of posh flats, there was a lot of valuable equipment stored with daily deliveries of top of the range kitchen and bathroom fittings. The developer, a Mr Simmons, had arrived one night to check something and given him a brusque nod, Brian was obviously someone a man like that couldn't be bothered to pass the time of day with, or in this case, the time of night. Brian didn't care, he was earning a bit of money and that suited him.

He felt very guilty about the drink. His son always made sure there was a meal for him before he went to work and had asked him a few times to help on the allotment. Brian knew Murdoch was trying his best to keep him on the straight and narrow, but it was so hard. Night work was unsociable and he missed the easy camaraderie of the scrap yard. There was a chance he'd be able to go back there again soon, things had quietened down and the Old Bill had stopped sniffing around. He wouldn't need to drink so much then, he told himself. For the first time in his life, he was concerned about his son. The last few weeks, the boy had become less outgoing, giving short answers to any questions and generally seemed quick-tempered and surly. Maybe it was just a late teenage thing, what did he know about it?

* * *

Murdoch's behaviour had not gone unnoticed at Roots either. 'What's the matter with the lad?' Stuart asked Madge, 'He's not himself, that's for sure.'

'He's polite but distant,' Madge said sadly. 'Something's upset him, but he's not the sort to open up and you can't pry. We must just treat him as we always have and act as if nothing's wrong. If he talks to anyone, I would think it would be you.'

'I hope so, I don't like to see him troubled.' Stuart was concerned. He was fond of the boy and he'd been like this since coming back from Salisbury. Surely, he and Lily hadn't had a row? There was nothing in the letters they had from her to indicate that. She knew they liked to receive written news and she wrote every week, even if it was just a short note.

Merry did not seem quite her usual bright self either, but she had indicated that she was worried about him and "would try and find out what the matter was". She knew exactly what the matter was but was not quite sure how to bring the subject up. Worried that things would start to go wrong and that she may fail in what she had set out to do, she decided to confront him.

Murdoch was angry with himself for acting the way he did and angry with whoever it was in the Rolls, who had hugged Lily. Was it that, Rupert? it figured, with a name like that. What right did he have to feel put out anyway? She wasn't his girlfriend, Megan was, what was the matter with him? He was just feeling that life wasn't fair, well it *wasn't* and he had to accept it. Lily had been born into a nice middle-class family, good for her, he hadn't, so hard luck.

'Murdoch, fancy a coffee?'

Damn, it was Merry. 'Maybe later thanks, I'm a bit busy.'

'I've made it anyway, here you are.'

He sighed, stood up from his beloved section and stretched. 'Okay, ta.' He turned away, not inviting any conversation.

'Who's opened your cage?'

He turned back to her, an incredulous look on his face. 'Who's opened my *cage?*'

Oh dear, that wasn't it, what's the phrase? 'Umm, I mean, who's *rattled* your cage?' *that's it.*

Murdoch almost laughed, it was so ridiculous. 'I really don't know what you mean and is it actually, any of your business?'

'I don't like to see you upset, you can talk to me, I understand an awful lot of things you know. Look at those two butterflies over there.'

'Butterflies?' *What the hell is she going on about?*

'One is really colourful. The other one is pretty, but quite drab beside it, but they like each other, you can tell. See, they're flitting about together all over the place, their appearance isn't important.'

'And your point is....'

'My point is, it doesn't matter about differences between two creatures. If they are attracted to and, like each other, nothing else is of concern.' The plain coloured butterfly landed on her outstretched hand, while Murdoch looked on in amazement. 'See where the sun catches his wings, you can see colour there. Everybody has hidden depths which may not seem obvious to themselves, but other people see and appreciate them. This butterfly doesn't put himself down, he knows he's beautiful in *her* eyes.' She indicated the other jewel-like butterfly who was close and to Murdoch's eye, looked like something out of a colouring book.

How did she know the one on her hand was a *he* and why should he care anyway? He wavered slightly and then the prickly side came back. 'I really don't know what you're trying to get at Merry, and if you think you're helping, you're not. As I said, it's not your business, thanks for the coffee, but please, just leave me alone.'

Distraught and feeling stung, she walked away, she'd got it wrong, no, she hadn't. *I almost had him, it'll just take time.*

* * *

Megan was at work, looking over all the new samples that had come in. Mrs Overidge had asked her to sort them into small gift bags for selected customers. They were expensive products and she knew a lot of people who would pay for these, they were generously sized samples, not the sort of things that came in a magazine. She had built up quite a clientele of her own who were always ready to buy a little something. Any feelings of guilt she'd had about taking the money from Corrine's bag had long gone, that was an emergency and it wasn't as if her boss would be really hurt by the loss. If Megan was a bit short on cash, she didn't risk taking it from the till, but a few quid would disappear from the tip box and when it was shared out at the end of the day, she joined in the grumbles about the meanness of the clients.

She was getting a bit peeved with Murdoch, he was no fun at all, not like her usual crowd. He never wanted to hang out, having a few drinks and had even suggested they go for a walk one evening! A walk? In the shoes she'd been wearing? Driving out a few times, in that awful van, at least made a change, but he didn't drink at all when he drove, not that he drank much anyway. On the nights she didn't see him, saying they shouldn't live in each other's pockets, she would drift into town and find her old crowd, hanging around and having fun. Ryan and Davy took particular delight in winding her up about her drag of a boyfriend and when was she going to dump him? Trying to be loyal was difficult when even she was beginning to feel the same, he was so *moody* lately. If anyone had a right to be moody, it was her, after what she'd been through, all to make *his* life easier, she told herself, completely ignoring the fact she hadn't wanted a baby at all. She would give the girls a small perfume or skin cream sample and let them know what else she had and would come away with an order and a few quid richer.

* * *

Murdoch, on his own for the evening, was trying to shake off the bad mood he'd been in since dropping Lily off. If this Rupert was a boyfriend, so what? It was more the fact that he was obviously rich that galled him and he really hoped she wasn't keen on him just for that reason. Lily didn't strike him as that sort of girl, but you never really knew people, did you? He'd be very disappointed if that was the case. Rupert hadn't *kissed* her, they'd just hugged, as far as he saw at the time, but perhaps he didn't want to do that in public? Bored with what was on the TV, he was interrupted by a message notification on the phone. It was Lily.

Hi, not heard from u for a while. Is all ok? How's the Xmas stuff looking?

He ignored it for about half an hour, then sighing, picked it up. It wasn't her fault he felt the way he did but kept the message short and to the point.

Everything ok. V busy. There was no reply from her. He couldn't let her think he was at her beck and call every five minutes. Still bored, he ironed a couple of shirts, including some of his father's and took them to hang in the cupboard.

Brian's room was a mess. Murdoch had given up keeping that tidy, he did the rest of their home, small as it was, but tonight, it really annoyed him. Straightening the bedding, he then pulled some dirty clothes from the floor and noticed a butterfly in the room, trying to guide it outside, it flew under the bed. Kneeling down to shoo it out, his hand touched something and he leaned down further to see what it was. A shoe box? His dad didn't keep shoes tidy. Pulling it out, he had a quick look and saw it was photos and paperwork. None of his business, but a picture caught his eye, a baby, was that him? Murdoch was torn, he wanted to see them, but his dad had obviously kept this from him. Why? If they were of him, he had every right to see them, surely?

There were about a dozen photos in all, a couple of baby ones and then a few more, of a toddler and a couple of a young boy, by then he knew they were of him. His mother, he had forgotten what she looked like, the photo was of her and his father, it had been torn in half and then, stuck together again rather crudely, with tape. She looked very young, younger than his father, who had recently had a fiftieth birthday. There must be at least ten years difference between them. The background appeared to be a travellers' camp. Murdoch knew his father used to be part of that community before settling here, but his earliest memories were of the Park Home. If he had lived elsewhere, he didn't remember

There was a copy of his birth certificate, just the short one with his name and date of birth. He'd been registered in this county, so maybe they were living here then? There was no marriage certificate for his parents. Had they ever *been* married, he wondered? She had married since, but there were no divorce papers either. He looked again at the photo, he did look a bit like her around the eyes. They appeared to be brown like his, but the picture was too small to show much detail. No paperwork for his father at all, that wasn't a surprise. Finding one more of him and his mother he kept it to put in his wallet. The others he tucked back in the box, pushing it under the bed. The fact that the torn photo had been repaired made him feel a little better, his father must have cared, at some point. It made him curious and scrolling through information about birth certificates he realised with a full copy, he'd have the parents' details, where they lived at the time, that sort of thing. He didn't want to ask his father and he would need a copy one day. He applied online, mother's name? he wasn't quite sure. Lyn, he remembered people calling her that. Lyn Lawton? He'd try that, father's name no problem, so he would wait and see what it turned up.

* * *

Lily was quite taken aback by Murdoch's reply. It was so abrupt. Okay, he may be busy, but he could have done it later when he had more time. Was she being a nuisance? It wasn't as if she texted him every day and thought he'd not minded sending the odd message. To tell the truth, she felt very hurt but tried to be fair, maybe he was having a bit of an off day?

'Hey Lily, what's up, you don't look happy, didn't you like my lasagne?' Rupert grinned.

'It was wonderful, same as everything you cook, it's just stuff from home.'

'Personal stuff? If you need to talk, I'll listen, that's what friends are for, right?'

'It's daft, I told you about Murdoch, didn't I?'

'Yep, what about him?' The way Lily had mentioned him, so casually but praising him made Rupert think maybe there was something a bit more than a friendly acquaintance between them.

She told him about her message and showed him the last text. 'It seemed very offish, like, don't bother me again.'

'Maybe he *is* busy, you said he's never been like that before. Leave it a while, then message him about something important and see what comes back, you might be taking it a bit too personally you know.'

'Do you think?'

'I don't know, Lily, I don't know him. Did you... tell him about me?'

'Not *about* you, I mentioned you and all of us in the house, why?'

'Does he think I'm your boyfriend?'

'I never said that, why would I and so what, if you were?'

'He might not like it.'

'He's got a girlfriend, it's not that way between us.'

'A girlfriend, I see.'

'*I see*, what's that supposed to mean?'

'Nothing at all.'

* * *

The next morning, as Murdoch approached Roots, he noticed Stuart reading a notice on one of the gateways to the fields. Parking his van, he walked back. 'Anything interesting?' he asked.

'It's a planning notice. They want to build some sort of leisure centre here by the look of it. A pool, gym, and all the paraphernalia that goes with it.'

'Sounds good. The old pool is pretty crap now compared to some places and it'll bring people down this way as well, they might improve the road a bit.'

'That's true. We can look at the plans on the council website, you can look those up, can't you?'

'Yeah sure, it's quite easy. I can show you how to find things like that if you want me to?'

'I'm far too old to worry about that, I'll leave it to you young ones. Although, I've noticed Merry doesn't seem to want to use the computer, almost seems afraid of it.'

'I've never seen her with a phone either, odd for someone of her... age.' *Whatever her age is?*

As they walked back, Stuart faltered slightly and Murdoch put a hand out to steady him. 'Are you alright?'

'I think I overdid it a bit yesterday. Just short of breath and I felt a strain in my chest, must have been lifting those compost bags.'

Murdoch noticed how pale the man looked. 'You'd better get in and sit down for a bit. Have you got chest pain now, should I call an ambulance or I'll take you straight to the hospital?'

'I know what you're thinking, it's just a strain, don't worry yourself. See, I'm fine now.'

Murdoch wasn't convinced and decided to keep a closer eye on him. 'Okay, if you say so, but make sure you don't do any more lifting. *I'll* do that.'

'Don't go saying anything to my Madge, I won't have her worrying. And not a word to our Lily, either.'

Murdoch immediately had a flash of guilt over the text he'd sent last night. When he went to bed, he had regretted it but it was a bit late to apologise. Now he wasn't sure what to do, she had asked him specifically to keep an eye on her grandparents and let her know how they were. Stuart's colour had come back and he did seem alright now. Perhaps he *had* just overdone it. No need to worry her and in a way, he was relieved that he didn't have to message her at this time. He was ashamed about the way he'd been lately, it wasn't her fault he felt hard done by. He must shake himself out of it.

Merry had known what was going on but couldn't interfere in any way that might change the outcome. 'Ah, good timing, I've just made a cup of tea. It's a bit nippy this morning, so I thought we should all warm up before getting started.' She said as they came into the hut.

'Thank you, Merry, just what I need,' Stuart took it gratefully. He was not as calm as he outwardly appeared. He'd had a few twinges lately and, like Murdoch had worried about what it might signify. But he was alright now, he needed to take it a little easier maybe, he'd pop to the doctor for a check-up, just to make sure.

Murdoch had picked up the laptop. 'Here're the plans, Stuart do you want to take a look? Merry, they want to build a leisure centre on the fields, did you know?'

'Oh yes, I saw the sign.' *I'll be keeping a close eye on that.*

'It's quite involved,' said Stuart, studying it. 'Do you want to see, Merry?'

'No thanks,' she backed away. 'Screens like that make our... umm, *my* eyes go funny. It's a shame, but there you go. I have to live without it.'

'Is that why you don't have a phone?' Murdoch asked.

'I can manage in an emergency, goodness, you wonder how people ever *existed* before they were invented.' She laughed, and there was the sound of a faint tinkling echo. 'Now then, what are you doing about Christmas trees? You ought to have them for the beginning of December.'

'Not something we've ever done,' Stuart scratched his head. 'But I suppose there's no reason why we shouldn't?'

Murdoch's mind immediately shot back several years, to when his father had mentioned that Harry needed him for a couple of nights' work as well as the day job in the yard. Brian had been drink-free for a few days and a lorry load of Nordic Spruces had mysteriously arrived and been sold by the side of the road next to the scrap yard. A wad of notes appeared and they actually had a chicken and other goodies to eat on Christmas day. There were not many bonuses after that. 'With other Christmas stuff we're doing, it seems silly not to, shall I source some suppliers?'

'If you would, Murdoch, I'd be grateful, we better get on with it then, I'll tell Duckie, she'll be excited.' Stuart felt much better and said he'd see them shortly, pleased to see Murdoch had perked up a bit.

'How many trees do you think, Merry? We need to advertise them really.'

'Could we do some of those flutterers? With all the information I could deliver them to the area.'

'*Flutterers?* Do you mean flyers?'

'Oh yes, of course, silly me, I do say some daft things. That… machine there, it prints doesn't it?'

'Yes.' Smiled Murdoch. 'It prints. I still don't know how many to order?'

'What about a hundred, with scope for more if necessary?'

'We'll never sell a *hundred.*'

'Course we will, especially with the fly papers. You do that and print out as many as you can, I'll start delivering tonight.'

Murdoch looked dubious. 'Let me get a date so I know when the trees will be here first, then I'll put that on. We'd better run it past the bosses first.'

Stuart and Madge also thought a hundred Christmas trees very ambitious, but Merry's enthusiasm persuaded them. 'There are about fifteen thousand people in this town and around the outskirts, we'll never be able to cover them all, or print out that many adverts.' Madge said sadly.

'Give me what you can and leave it to me.' Merry smiled secretively. 'I've got friends who can copy and deliver some.'

One hundred trees were ordered, which had to be paid for, but Merry assured them, they'd make a tidy profit. Murdoch designed and printed one hundred and fifty flyers before the ink cartridge ran out. Merry assured him that was more than enough and tucked them away in the little bag she always brought with her. A bag that they only just fitted into but was capable of holding a cake tin on occasions. It must be some sort of stretchy material, thought Murdoch.

When Merry was back at the cottage, she immediately spread out the flyers, another word she had to remember, and waved a glittery swirl over them until they multiplied into thousands. As the glitter settled, another swirl shrunk each one to the size of a pinhead. She stuck her head out of the door and whistled. Within minutes, a crowd of her usual butterflies, looking more like striking night moths with the setting of the sun, were given a pile each and instructions on where to go. Merry was pleased. As soon as one of those was pushed through a letterbox or one of those feline doors, it would expand to its proper size and nearly everybody in town would see them.

A week later, a large lorry trundled down the road and delivered the trees. They piled some up by the gates, with the others inside the centre where they had cleared a space. At least at this time of the year, there weren't so many plants to worry about.

'People surely won't want to buy them this early, the needles will all drop off before Christmas day.' Stuart shook a tree he had taken out of its netting to prove a point but they all stuck firm.

'These are *special* trees,' Merry waggled her eyebrows. 'They won't drop until after New Year.' She'd already made sure of that as they were being unloaded. By midday, they'd sold one dozen and the people who came had looked in the grotto area, bought some dried arrangements and said they would bring their children to see Santa at the weekend.

Murdoch, after much thought, took a picture of the trees and sent it to Lily with a short message.

This is why I've been busy.

Chapter Twelve

GALANTHUS NIVALIS – SNOWDROP

A welcome sight that Spring will soon
be on its way.

Lily had packed her bag for the Christmas visit home and was looking forward to it. Her father had asked if she would like him to drive down, but Roo had already offered her a lift again. They were teased mercilessly about their friendship, as most people knew where Roo's preferences lay and they thought it strange that the two of them seemed to be such close companions. The truth was, they had forged a deep friendship, one Lily would never have expected, but they got on so well and could talk to each other about anything. He told her how difficult his life had been when he was younger, confused about his sexuality and worried about how his parents would take the news.

They were sat talking, over coffee. 'I can understand how people feel suicidal,' he said. 'It was actually my mother who suspected and brought up the subject, it was such a weight off my mind. My father, I think, was a bit disappointed, but he's used to it in the circles that he moves in. In the end, I had it quite easy compared to some.'

'I'm so glad for you, is this Sam... the one?'

'We've only been together for seven months, we'll see how it goes. I'd like to think so. Now we've just got to get *you* sorted out.'

'I'm too busy to think about that, I really enjoy what we do here and *we* have so much fun together, I don't need anything else at the moment.'

'I've made it one of my modules, as part of the course to fix you up with someone.'

'Don't waste your time. Change the subject, what will you do for Christmas?'

'Lunch with the family, my younger sister makes it special for all of us, she's fourteen, but still acts like a child where presents are concerned.'

'It's a bit stilted at my house, everything has to be just so, but I go to my grandparents for tea and stay for boxing day. It's much more relaxing, my mother won't have chocolate or sweets around, but Grandma and I can almost finish a tin off while we watch TV.'

'Well I don't know where you put it all, you're like a reed and you tuck into my cooking alright.'

'Are you saying I'm greedy?'

'I don't have to say it, you are!'

When Zoe came into the living area she tutted to see them both laughing and hitting each other with cushions. 'You two are such children, I hope you're going to tidy up when you've *finished*."

'Yes ma'am,' Roo saluted and they both collapsed into giggles again, to Zoe's disgust.

'I'm glad to be going home to some civilised company for a few weeks,' she huffed and left them laughing even harder.

* * *

The salon was exceptionally busy on the run-up to the holiday. Most of the appointments were being squeezed in the last week before they shut at lunchtime on Christmas Eve. Megan was the one who was jiggling the appointment book and trying to placate angry customers who couldn't understand why they were unable to have a last-minute facial. 'I'm *so* sorry Madam,' she said to one irate lady who had come in person to argue about it. 'These appointments get booked weeks in advance, we always try to remind people. When was it you were last here?'

'It was July before I went on my summer vacation with my husband, Hugh,' the woman snapped.

'July? I see, that's the problem. Our *regular* customers would have been more prepared, we've had notices up since September.' Megan quite enjoyed seeing the woman's face get redder by the minute. If anybody would benefit from a relaxing facial, this old fart would.

'Well, I think it's disgraceful, do you have a cancellation list?'

'We do, but that's got quite a few names on it already, but I'll certainly add you. Would you be able to come in at short notice?'

The woman looked at Megan as if she had sprouted a second head. 'Short notice? I'm a very busy woman, young lady, I can't just drop everything and rush here at *your* convenience.'

Megan was about to give a rude retort when she saw Mrs Overidge. 'We'll do our very best, if you'd like to leave contact details, Mrs...?'

'Thank you, Megan,' Corrine said, a few minutes later. 'This is a very difficult time of year, I'm afraid you'll get a lot of that. Now, I wanted to let you know that you'll all get your Christmas bonus as usual. I'm not able to put it up this year as I mislaid some money a few months back and it's left the business a little short.'

Megan flushed. 'I'm sorry to hear that Mrs Overidge but thank you anyway.' *Didn't think someone like her would miss it that much.*

Megan was determined to get Murdoch out on New Year's Eve for drinks with her friends. It had been a long time since the bar-b-que and there would be people there he hadn't even met, so clashing with Ryan could probably be avoided. He couldn't use the excuse he was driving because they planned a pub crawl, so he could damn well drink for a change and have a bit of fun. She'd also invited him for Christmas lunch, after persuading her mother to squeeze him in. He said thanks but didn't want to leave his father on his own for Christmas. She wasn't happy about that at all. What would happen if they set up together, would she be expected to entertain that drunken old soak at regular intervals? Murdoch said his father had cut down a lot, but she didn't believe it for one minute. Also, she was expecting something a bit special this year. They'd been going out for quite a while now and she reckoned it was time he produced a ring of some sort, something, just to show a commitment. Oh yes, she'd act all surprised and flustered, but if it wasn't forthcoming, she wouldn't be happy about that either, even if they didn't end up together, she'd get a ring out of it.

* * *

On the pretext of going to the post office, Stuart was at the health centre instead. 'I'm sure I'm wasting your time doctor, but to tell you the truth, although I laughed it off, it did scare me a bit, at my age you know?'

'You were very wise to come in, Mr Overidge. From what you tell me and the brief examination I can do here, I would like to send you for some tests, an ECG and a stress test.'

'I know what an ECG is, but a stress test? I'm not stressed about anything.'

'Not that sort of stress, you'll be on a treadmill or static bike and be monitored. I'll refer you and you'll get a letter quite soon.'

'I don't want my wife to worry if there's no need. Can I come and check here for my appointment?'

'I do understand, but isn't it better she knows, rather than be confronted with a possible situation she might find upsetting or that scares her?'

'I will tell her if the tests show anything, just... not yet.'

He walked through the town afterwards, then past some of the smaller houses newly built on the site of an old factory. Pleased to see some of the centre's plant pots in windows and on doorsteps, he knew it wouldn't be long before the bulbs started to show growth. He remembered Lily's face when she was little, checking every day to see when seeds started to break through their soil covering and stretch up to the light. It was like magic, she used to say.

Lily. He couldn't afford for his health to go downhill, she needed to concentrate on her course for the next two years. Well, not quite two years now, but he wouldn't let her worry about him or have any ideas about giving up and coming back to help. She was too young and needed to live a bit before taking on such a responsibility.

Young Murdoch would need to step up and do a bit more in the day to day running of the place. They'd have to increase his salary of course, but they could afford that, Murdoch was responsible for bringing more custom in along with Merry, who was also full of ideas.

There was something that puzzled Stuart. Merry had given him some bank details for her wages and assured him that she was receiving them. But, the business account didn't tally with the amount going out, almost as if it never left their bank, although on the statement it did. He couldn't understand it. They must be taking more at the till than was being registered, but how? Maybe Murdoch could work it out, he'd talk to Madge about making him some sort of manager. The lad needed something, a purpose, this might do it and it would be a weight off his mind.

* * *

Robert Overidge was on the shop floor and the supermarket was very busy. Screaming children, couples arguing and the noise of till drawers opening and closing. It was music to his ears. A spotty-faced youth on work experience tapped him on the arm. 'Woman down there on till sixteen says can she speak to you?'

Till sixteen? Wasn't that Szarlota? 'Thank you, get some more Christmas stock out, they're going mad in the seasonal aisles.' He hurried off.

Szarlota was on the verge of tears. Robert immediately called a supervisor to take over the till and helped the poor woman away from the hubbub of noise. 'Come to my office and tell me what the matter is.' He guided her through the aisles, thinking how soft and warm her arm felt and tried not to think about how the rest of her would feel. She thanked him and snuffled into in a hanky as he sat her down and shut the door firmly. 'Now then, what's wrong, anything I can help with?'

'I am very sorry, but I not feel very well.'

Robert took a step back, he didn't care for illness around him and she did look like she had a bit of a temperature. 'You had better go home then.'

'I not *ill,* I mean I very tired, I was coughing in night, so sleep difficult.' She coughed as if to demonstrate and her chest wobbled alarmingly in the low-cut top beneath the uniform sweatshirt which was partly unzipped. If it had been any other member of staff, he'd have called them to task, but couldn't bring himself to mention it where she was concerned.

He had to grip his desk to steady himself and his nerves, it was a fine chest at the best of times and when it was heaving like that... 'Have some water, you should be in... bed,' he said faintly, 'with some hot lemon and... and cough medicine.' If Corrine coughed or laughed, nothing moved at all. All hard planes and sharp angles, that one. Nothing wrong with being trim of course, but a woman should *give* a little, not feel like a piece of hardboard.

'I need to earn money, for family in Poland.' Cough. Wobble.

'You are obviously not well enough to be on the shop floor; a few days won't affect your wages I assure you. I think I ought to run you home right now. You're a valuable member of staff Szarlota and you must look after your body... err, yourself.

Robert forgot his aversion to sickness as soon as Szarlota was in the car. She gave him directions and they arrived at the blocks of rather run-down flats in an area he tended to avoid.

'Zank you so much, you very kind. I will try be back in few days.'

'I will see you to your door.' He said gallantly, hoping the car would be safe where he'd parked it.

'No, is alright. My flat very small, not what you used to I'm sure.'

'Don't be silly, I would feel better knowing you're inside and warm.'

The flat *was* small but very clean, neat and tidy. There was evidence of children, but she'd said they were both at school. A photo showed what he guessed was the two of them, a boy of about twelve and a girl, maybe nine or ten? Nice, tidy looking kids. It was cold in the flat.

'You need some heat Szarlota, where's your boiler?'

'In kitchen, I put in on when we home, can't...' cough, 'afford it all time.'

Robert quashed the feelings of guilt, thinking how warm *his* house would be when he went home after work. 'I need you back at work, so I will help you a little with your bill this month. Christmas is an expensive time, here.' He pulled out a couple of twenty-pound notes and put them on the table.

'I will not take that, I am not to be bought.'

'Szarlota! What are you implying, I am trying to help you, what did you think I meant?'

'I so sorry, I mean, you no need to pay me. I like you very much. I get lonely sometimes... with no man.'

'Y-you do? No man? You're a very attractive woman, *I* think.'

'You like me?' Her cough seemed to have eased and her chest was right in his eye-line. 'I have cough liniment, is that right word? It needs to be rubbed in, to chest, you help me?'

Oh God. 'Anything I can do to help, of course, but I can't stay long. The store, you understand.'

'I understand, will not take long.'

He left forty minutes later in a haze of contentment which was harshly blown away when he saw his car, his pride and joy BMW tourer, sprayed with 'posh wanker' across the windscreen. Another half an hour, with the help of some boys who'd probably done it anyway, and why weren't they at school? scrubbing it off for a tenner between them and he was back at work.

* * *

The grotto, which had been going well, even with a miserable Mr Taylor as Santa, was going to run every day when the schools broke up for the holidays. That had also been advertised on more flyers when they saw the success they had been with the trees. Another hundred had been ordered and every night, when their stocks of dried, sprayed flowers and seed heads seemed to be getting lower, Merry said she'd re-arrange them and come the morning, there appeared to be plenty again. The Overidge's had never seen so much money come in at this time of the year and Madge was overcome, wanting to invite everybody over for a party at Christmas. 'Even Robert and Corrine can come,' she said, 'Christmas is a time for family and friends.'

'Our Lily's home tomorrow, she'll have parties to go to I expect. Check a date with her first.' Stuart advised.

Merry was thrilled to be invited and said any day would be fine with her. 'Arrangements are always vague with me, I can see everybody I want to at some time.'

Murdoch wasn't too sure about it, he'd feel quite out of place. The only people he'd be at ease with were his co-workers, if it was just them perhaps, but not Lily's parents, they'd look right down their noses at him, he was certain of it. They'd said, bring somebody. Megan? Yeah right, he could just imagine it, laughing at all of them and getting drunk. no chance. She wasn't turning out to be the sort of girl he'd thought she was, but Christmas wasn't a time to cause upset and he had already bought her a present. He'd saved for weeks to get a handbag she'd pointed at, on one of the days she dragged him around the shops. Pretending not to take any notice which annoyed her, he'd clocked it. He thought it a ridiculous amount for a *bag*, but he wanted to get her something she would like.

He'd had a call from the Register Office about his application and the fact that the name he'd given for his mother didn't match the records. He explained how she'd left when he was young, there was no paperwork for her, there was no other family and Lyn, was the only name he remembered, because he had all the other details correct, they agreed to send it. "No, sorry, they couldn't tell him anything over the phone." He was curious as to what it would show.

'Murdoch? You were miles away my son, did you hear me?'

'What? Sorry, Stuart, I missed that.'

'I said, Madge and I have something to tell you, will you pop up to the cottage before you go home?'

'Yeah sure,' he answered, wondering what it was.

He found out after a cup of tea and three of the mince pies that Madge had baked. He listened in disbelief, as they explained how they wanted to promote him to under-manager, with a pay rise. Stuart, particularly, was finding a lot of the work too much for him now and Mr Taylor wasn't a help in the heavy work department. He'd earned it, they said, but they'd like to tell Lily before it was general knowledge. As she was going to be in charge of the place one day, they felt she should hear it from them.

Although he'd always known Lily wanted to run it, hearing it officially brought it home. It may be several years away, but looking at the Overidge's, it could be sooner rather than later. They weren't young anymore and then, she would be his boss. *That little slip of a thing telling me what to do*. It was unfair to think that way and he knew it, she had never treated him on anything but a level playing field and many times had asked his advice or been swept away by his ideas. But actually, being in charge, was a bit different. 'I don't know what to say.'

'You don't have to say anything now, sleep on it.' Stuart slapped him on the back. 'We don't want to lose you to a better-paid job, you're far too valuable to us.'

'Thank you.' He'd never felt of value to anyone.

Merry was walking up from the grotto area and saw Murdoch on his way out. 'All locked up and ready for tomorrow,' she smiled. 'You look thoughtful.'

'Do I? maybe. Come on, I'll give you a lift, I don't want you walking along by the river in the dark.'

'That's kind of you, but I'll meet my friends there, I won't be alone.'

'We never see your friends?'

'They're very shy. Oh, look! The little clump of snowdrops by that street light, they've come into flower. Do you know, some people won't have them in the house? They think they're unlucky. It's best to leave them outside because as soon as it's a little warmer, the bees come out of hibernation and there's lovely nectar for them.'

'Don't see many snowdrops before Christmas.' Murdoch was amused by her chattering.

'It's been mild. They're the teardrops of the snow, did you know that?'

'What snow?'

'Don't spoil it. The snow cries as it melts and Spring comes, this little plant is telling us that it won't be a bad winter.'

'Honestly Merry, you do come out with some fantastic nonsense. Are you sure you don't want a lift, it's very dark.'

'Look over there, see those lights, that's their... umm, torches, they're waiting for me. See you tomorrow.'

He watched her skip off into the darkness and then the lights went crazy and he heard childish laughter. She must be okay.

* * *

As the Rolls pulled into Salisbury bus station, Roo pressed a small gift-wrapped package into Lily's hands. 'A present for you.'

'Roo, we all did a secret Santa, we agreed.'

'Yes, but I couldn't risk putting this in. It's a personal gift, I really wanted to get it for you. Please, Lily, don't make a thing of it, take it as it's meant, from a friend.'

'Oh Roo, you shouldn't have, but thanks.'

'You don't know what it is yet and *don't* open it until Christmas Eve night.'

'Not Christmas day?'

'I think the night before is special, magical, don't you?'

'I guess. You have a good time with your family and Sam.'

'I shall text you New Year's Eve and I want to hear you're out with some handsome hunk. Take a photo and make me jealous, come here.' Giving her a hug and a kiss, he waited until she was on her bus.

Lily was excited, she always loved Christmas and was looking forward to seeing the grotto at Roots. She was torn, should she give presents to Murdoch and Merry? She didn't want to look like the big, *I am*, handing out a token and she really couldn't give something personal. She'd have a look around town, maybe a gardening diary or something like that? Also, when should she give it? If it was early, they would rush out to get her something and that wasn't what she wanted. But, if she left it too late, they'd be embarrassed if they hadn't given her anything. It made her cross, why was present giving so difficult at times? Looking at the one from Roo, she wondered what it was.

Chapter Thirteen

ROSMARINUS

A gift of Rosemary signifies love and
remembrance

Alexander sat with his head in his hands, trying not to cry. Rosemary was going downhill fast and he just prayed that she'd get her wish and see Christmas. They had both known this time would come, but it did not make it any easier. Adamant that she didn't want to go into a hospice unless the pain really became unbearable, she wanted to look at her garden for as long as possible, there were a few snowdrops out and she was so pleased to see those. The white flowers, bowed down, to protect the pollen that would be appreciated if it became mild enough for the bees to awaken, ruffled slightly in the wind.

Her friend Elizabeth, the Countess, had brought her a beautiful poinsettia and told her the story of how she had acquired it. 'I was very impressed with the girl, she seemed to know her stuff. I told her I'd be back to see her at Easter, I want her input for my summer opening.'

'I won't be there this time,' Rosemary said sadly.

Elizabeth, about to retort, bit her tongue. The reason they were such good friends was that they had always spoken their minds and never indulged in insincere flattery, or nonsense. 'Maybe not, but you'll always be there in my mind, your suggestions have been invaluable over the years. I will miss you, very much.'

Nothing else needed saying. They sat in companionable silence until Alexander brought in coffee and biscuits. Black, as Elizabeth liked it and very weak for Rosemary, who would probably only have a few sips and not bother with a biscuit.

'I was telling Rosemary the story of this poinsettia and she said it was the girl who probably served you.' Elizabeth filled in the details.

'Lily, I wonder what she was doing up at Garden Zone? A reconnaissance mission I expect,' he chuckled. 'Always good to see what the opposition is up to.'

* * *

Corrine wondered what on earth was the matter with Robert. He had come home, two nights ago with a bunch of awful supermarket flowers and a box of chocolates, as if it were Valentine's day? 'You know I don't eat chocolate,' she had said. 'And you'd better stick those in a vase, I've got wet nail varnish. I let Megan do them today and they're not very good, so I had to take it all off.'

'Well, Lily will like the chocolates, sorry I forgot.'

'Forgot? I haven't eaten chocolate for years, but it's the thought I suppose. Pour me a glass of wine, would you?'

He rushed to do her bidding. The thrill of the afternoon mixed with his guilt was giving him indigestion and he gulped his wine down before refilling his glass and taking both in. 'Here you are dear, so, not so good at the salon then?' She looked at him in surprise, he never asked about the salon and he panicked. 'I-I mean, you mentioned one of the staff? Is she not working out?'

'She's willing enough, a bit rough around the edges but she'll do for the more mundane jobs. I suppose *you're* pressed for time at work at the moment?'

He flushed slightly, remembering how Szarlota's chest felt when it was pressed against him. 'I'm going to take a shower before dinner.' *A cold one.* 'Do you want to go out tonight? Lily's home tomorrow, so we'll get Chinese again, she liked that.'

'Yes alright.' She studied her, *pink perfection* nails, yes, much better.

* * *

Lily was home with a week to go before Christmas, the grotto was open daily and she was delighted when she saw it. Careful not to be over-friendly towards Murdoch, who she thought tended to avoid her, she felt very at ease with Merry. Grandad had said earlier, that he'd like her to pop up to the cottage when she had a minute as there was something he wanted to talk about.

'I think that's a wonderful idea.' She said when he and Grandma told her about their offer to Murdoch. 'I worry about you both doing so much and he's very capable and has settled here really well.'

'That's what we thought.' Grandad said, 'And there's something else we'd like to discuss with you.'

She listened, getting more upset by the minute. 'You've changed your will? I don't want to think about your will, you've got years yet, both of you and how's Dad going to react?'

'There'll be enough for him, with our policies. He would sell this place, Lily, before we were even cold. I hate to say it, but it's true.' Stuart also looked upset. 'It's a safeguard for you *and* the garden centre. We know you'll do what's right, and in the end, *if* it has to be sold, it'll be *your* decision, not your Father's. We'd appreciate it if you kept this quiet for the time.'

'I'm not going to say anything, Dad will go mad, but I hope it's not going to happen for a long time yet.'

'We're not *planning* on it happening any time soon,' Madge said, with a smile. 'Now, I want to do a little party here over the Christmas period. Let me know as soon as possible when you're free.'

'I'm here for Boxing Day anyway, what sort of party?'

'Mainly for the staff, a little thank you for everything they've done this year. We'll ask your parents, but I doubt if they'll come. Did you want to bring anybody?'

'Not really, it'll be little old me on my own.' Lily kind of wished Roo could be there, he got on with anybody and was very entertaining. Would Murdoch bring his girlfriend? Probably and why should she care? She wanted them to get back to the friendship they had before this... awkwardness there now seemed to be between them. It would be good to resolve it before she left again and she'd like to tell him about her course and what she was doing, knowing he would be interested.

She also heard about the leisure centre. 'The pool in town is really naff, it sounds great. When's it happening?'

'I doubt if many people will object, so as soon as they get the okay, I guess.' Stuart stoked the wood burning stove. 'Weather won't be too good for a while, but that doesn't stop builders. A lot of work to be done there. They'll be busier than we are in January and February, that's for sure.'

'It's quiet at the moment, I'll take a cup of coffee down to Mr Taylor, even with that little oil stove he's got, the grotto isn't the warmest place.' Lily put the kettle on. 'Maybe what we should have done is to use the staff tea room, it would be a bit cosier for him.'

'We can plan it better for next year, that's a good idea, Lily. Murdoch and Merry did a fine job lining the place with crepe paper and making it look like a little house, not a greenhouse, but the wooden hut would be better. Next time eh?' Stuart felt a slight twinge in his chest and was getting breathless again. 'I'll join you shortly, just got a bit of paperwork to sort.' He made it to the small dining room which was empty and sat down. He wasn't right, he knew it deep down, he'd have to pop to the surgery to see if his appointment had come through.

Lily gave the grateful Mr Taylor a hot coffee and listened while he moaned about greedy children these days wanting all sorts of technical nonsense and looking disappointed with the small gift they received from him. She doubted if he ever managed a, *ho ho ho*.

Murdoch almost bumped into her as she came out of the grotto. 'Sorry,' he mumbled.

'You and Merry did a really great job here, I wish I could have helped.'

'Thanks.' He decided he couldn't exactly ignore her, but it wasn't a good idea to be *too* friendly, not when she'd be his boss one day if he was still here of course. 'How's Eden?'

'Oh, it's such an amazing place. I've been doing plant nutrition and soil science. Next term its plant use in landscape, which I'm keen on anyway and we're doing basic nursery work as well.' She chattered on and he listened, interested in spite of his misgivings. Then she changed the subject. 'Grandma and Grandad told me what they want you to do, I think it's fantastic, there's no better person for the job.' She went slightly pink. 'Grandad's very fond of you, you know. I think he wishes his son, my dad, had been a bit keener on the garden side, but he just wasn't interested. He doesn't like me doing any of this, he can be a real pain.' She was surprised how Murdoch's face clouded over.

'At least he cares about your future. *Some* people's dads couldn't give a toss. You don't appreciate how lucky you are, Lily, to have parents who care about you.'

'What do you mean, yours don't?'

'My mother left me when I was eight, with a drunken father, satisfied now?'

'Murdoch, I-I'm so sorry, I didn't mean...' She felt awful.

He gave her a cold look and walked away leaving her almost in tears. *Christ, what's the matter with me? I shouldn't have snapped at her like that.* He noticed her miserable face for the rest of the day as they tried not to let their path's cross and he felt like the biggest jerk in the world.

Merry also noticed and felt upset. Why did those two rub each other up the wrong way? She flitted between them, making conversation and trying to cheer them both up. It was Christmas, for goodness sake, a magical time for everybody.

Lily drew a little card towards the end of the day with a note, "*Sorry I upset you, I didn't mean to be nosy or anything.*" The picture was of two plant pots, with cross faces, turned away from each other, was it too childish she wondered? She slipped it into his coat pocket and then later, changing her mind, went to retrieve it, but the coat had gone and Merry told her he'd left early to deliver some stuff for Stuart.

* * *

Brian was tucking into the cottage pie his son had made. 'This is good, aren't you having any?'

'Maybe later. I'm not hungry.'

'What's up with you? You've got a face like a smacked arse. Girl trouble?'

'Nothing, don't worry about it. Just... stuff.'

'You seeing that Megan this evening then?'

Murdoch shrugged his shoulders. 'I'm going out for a walk, have a good night.'

He climbed through the hedge at the back of the site as he didn't want to walk past Megan's home. It wasn't that he didn't want to see her, he wouldn't be good company and preferred to be on his own. It was cold and dark so he shoved his hands in his pockets to warm them and felt a piece of card, pulling it out, he moved under a streetlight to see it properly. He stared at the drawing in total bemusement and turned it over to see Lily's message. Great, now he felt even worse, although he had to smile at her little cartoon. He would have to apologise, it was uncalled for, the way he'd spoken to her. Perhaps he should get her a token Christmas present? Just a fun thing, but something she'd like. It was late night shopping, he'd go and have a look.

Megan, not having had a satisfactory reply to her enquiry as to whether or not Murdoch wanted to meet up, had also taken herself into town. Buying one item and slipping two or three into her bag, soon had all her siblings taken care of. She purchased some socks for Murdoch and managed to bag a hooded sweatshirt without being seen. It was a bit bulky, but she made sure her previous purchases were all on the top and also made a point of chatting in a friendly manner to the harassed woman on the till saying what a nightmare this late-night rush was.

Very pleased with herself she texted Ryan to see who was about and getting a message that they were at the Drunken Duck, she started to make her way there when saw Murdoch through the crowd. He hadn't seen *her* and he was looking in a jeweller's window. *Oh my God, he's doing it, he's buying a ring.* Not close enough to see what he was actually looking at, she watched him go in and saw the assistant pull a tray from the window. Keeping a low profile, she saw him leave and then scooted over to have a look. There was quite an assortment of things, but there *were* rings in the vicinity that she'd seen the tray taken from. Not hugely expensive, but respectable enough. Something to look forward to and worth getting bladdered for tonight, with the crowd.

At home, Murdoch opened the small velvet pouch. He hadn't intended to buy anything like this but glancing in the window as he walked past, saw the selection of charms. They weren't very expensive, not like the gold selection, but a particular one had caught his eye. A little silver watering can. It was perfect for her. He'd write a funny message with it, so it couldn't be taken the wrong way. She was bound to have some sort of chain or bracelet to put it on, he thought, he wouldn't buy that as well, it would look as if he'd spent too much. It would get their friendship back on track but he would never be over familiar with her, it couldn't be like that anymore.

He took a letter from its hiding place behind the breadbin, not wanting to open it while his father was around, he guessed it was his birth certificate. They had a mailbox outside, which Brian never checked so Murdoch always sorted the post when he came home.

There was his name and date of birth, born... at home, that surprised him, here, in the very place he was sitting now. Father's name and occupation, scrap metal dealer, mother Caroline, that explained the Lyn, with a surname of Carruthers. So, his parents weren't married and they had both signed the certificate. It didn't help him a great deal but at least he knew his mother's name and maybe, could find out something about her? If they were living here, some of the older park residents may talk to him. The Watkins perhaps? They'd always been kind to him in the past and they may know some more. He wouldn't bother them now, maybe after Christmas?

* * *

It was Christmas Eve and the centre was closing early, the last tree had been sold and finally, the decorated foliage was down to a few lonely stalks. Stuart had nipped out in the morning and brought gingerbread treats from the market for everybody. He'd also checked his medical appointment which was in early January.

For the last few days, Murdoch and Lily had an unspoken agreement. Talking only about work, they were polite but not over-friendly. Now, as they were getting ready to close up, Lily had a tray full of cups and plates to take up to the cottage and was trying to balance it and open the door, when he came in.

'Let me carry the tray.'

'It's okay, I can manage.'

'Let me carry the *tray.*' She handed it to him silently and he sighed. 'I hope you have a good Christmas Lily, and… thanks for my card. It's surprising what you can find in a coat pocket.' With a ghost of a smile, he carried the tray up to the cottage and they didn't speak again until everybody was leaving.

Mr and Mrs Overidge gave all the staff an envelope. 'It's not much,' Stuart said, 'A little something for Christmas and we'll see you all on Boxing Day evening for a buffet supper.' Even Flora Harvey had been chirpy all morning and had bragged to her neighbours about her party invitation.

Merry threw her arms around Murdoch and Lily as they walked out. 'Happy Christmas, both of you. I love this night, it so magical. See you in two days.'

'Bye Merry, are you with people tomorrow, you're not on your own?' Lily asked, suddenly realising Merry had never mentioned family or who she spent time with.

'I'm never on my own, what are you doing now?'

'Umm, meeting up with my friend Amy for a bite of lunch and last-minute bits, what about you Murdoch?'

'Some food shopping for tomorrow, I'm cooking for me and... my dad.' He didn't look at Lily.

The drunken father? She hoped he would have a good day.

They parted ways and, because she'd forgotten her gloves, Lily automatically put her hands in the pockets of her coat. Feeling something, she pulled out a little velvet pouch, tied with tinsel.

It's surprising what you can find in a coat pocket.

Opening it carefully, nestled in the palm of her hand was the sweetest silver watering can, almost dolls' house-sized or for a fairy garden she thought in delight. It had a loop at the top and she knew she had a chain that would fit it. It was perfect and now she didn't mind the fact that she'd bought a nice set of garden gloves for him and the same for Merry, although hers were in pink. They were left at Grandma's, for Boxing Day.

She didn't show the charm to Amy, but they had a burger together and did a bit of shopping.

'Have you heard from Laura?' Lily asked.

'Yes, she's home, very busy she says. *But*, she will grace us with her presence on New Year's Eve and we're hitting the town, no excuses. I've sent the word out to as many of the old crowd as possible. We're meeting in the Five Bells at nine o'clock. So, eat first.'

That evening, Lily threaded the watering can onto the chain and put it around her neck, she loved it. Then she reached for Roo's present. It was a pair of silver drop lily flower earrings. She put them in her ears, took a selfie and sent it to Roo with a thank you message.

Back came, *Ur welcome kiddo. Out on the lash + Sam. Love the charm as well xx*

They did go together very nicely she thought, perfect for the holiday season.

* * *

Rosemary did see Christmas, although she slept through most of it. To Alexander, it was just another day. She'd wanted a few decorations, so he tried to make her room look festive, but it meant nothing to him. He would be facing life without her and that was not a matter of months anymore, even weeks, now, it would be days. At least she wasn't in too much pain. It was an awful time. Just waiting. What really brought it home was when she wanted to discuss her funeral. They weren't regular churchgoers, so she decided on a celebrant, who had already visited and spoken with her about what was to be said in the eulogy. She wanted a woodland burial, she was quite emphatic about that, to give back to the earth. He accepted that, he didn't particularly like cemeteries and they'd always enjoyed forest and woodland walks.

He sat with her, unable to concentrate on anything, certain he would face the New Year alone.

* * *

Christmas Day for Lily was quiet with a lunch out which she didn't enjoy. Having expected to eat at home, her parents surprised her with a five-course hotel special and entertainment. She had some nice presents but spent most of the time wondering if Murdoch was okay, how bad his father actually was and wishing she was at the cottage with her Grandparents. She was dropped off there in the evening, her parents declining the invite for the buffet the next day but popping in and having a drink so as to appear sociable. They couldn't get away quickly enough. Lily could relax at last and stretched her toes out to the fire. One of the special trees stood in the corner, which she'd helped Grandma to decorate ten days ago. On the top sat her pink-haired fairy, quietly glowing and glittering in the reflection of the firelight.

Murdoch and his father ate at four o'clock, Brian only having woken up at two, after a late night out, drinking. The small turkey crown, being kept warm for so long, was not at its best and it was eaten in relative silence along with the re-heated veg, potatoes and gravy. There were no Christmas decorations. Murdoch had brought in some fir branches and a bit of holly, only to hear, 'What's this shite taking up room on the table?' It was dumped outside.

Brian gave a loud burp and leaned back. 'Very nice Son, very nice. Did us proud as usual. Sorry I slept in a bit, I was celebrating. Thanks for the shirt. I didn't wrap it, but there's twenty quid by the kettle for you.'

'Thanks, Dad. Celebrating what?'

'Being taken back on at the yard. More sociable and a damn sight warmer in the portacabin than the shed I got for my night work.'

'That's good then. I'm pleased for you.'

'They didn't appreciate me, those ponces. Hey, you work down by where that new leisure centre's going, don't you?'

'Yes, why?'

'The owner, smarmy piece of work, I overheard him the other night. He comes in sometimes to check things, I'm invisible to him of course. I was doing me rounds and I heard him talking on the phone.' Brian picked his teeth while Murdoch waited for whatever jewel of information his father thought he had. 'He was saying, the go-ahead for the leisure centre will be given first week of January, and they're to start digging and making as much mess and inconvenience as possible. What's that all about then?'

'I don't know,' Murdoch was puzzled. Mess, and inconvenience to who? The garden centre was the only thing that would suffer. He might mention it quietly to Stuart. 'Thanks Dad, it may be nothing but always good to get a heads up. Would you like some pudding?'

He slipped over to Megan's in the evening and watched as she tore the paper off the large parcel he gave her. She'd looked surprised when she saw him arrive with it and when she saw the bag, her face fell. She opened it, taking out the paper as if looking for something else.

'It was the one you liked wasn't it?'

He must be saving it for New Year's Eve, yes that's when he'll ask me. 'Absolutely the right one, I-I was just surprised you remembered. Thank you. Here's yours.'

Socks and a very nice sweatshirt that looked expensive. 'Thanks Megan, it's great.'

She had a house full, so he left fairly soon but not before she'd extracted a promise from him about New Year's Eve.

* * *

Mr Taylor, looking jollier than Lily had ever seen him, arrived first on Boxing Day. Flora was next with Mr Harvey, a quiet, sad-looking man, who glanced around, muttering to himself. Thankfully, Merry arrived, with a tray full of ginger cake bites and marshmallow Father Christmases.

'Happy Christmas everybody.' She looked radiant, with completely pink coloured hair matching the tree fairy and a glittery dress which shed its sparkle all over the carpet.

Murdoch turned up with a bottle of wine and some soft drinks which he took to the kitchen. He'd glanced quickly at Lily, noted the charm around her neck and was quietly pleased.

Lily hadn't worn the earrings, she thought it a bit much for this occasion, and she sought him out once people were moving about and chatting. 'Thank you for this Murdoch, it's absolutely lovely. There's a gift for you under the tree and one for Merry,' she added quickly.

He was pleased with the gloves and Merry was delighted with hers, saying how they matched her hair. Food and drink disappeared and then Murdoch said, sorry, he had to go because he was meeting somebody.

Megan, thought Lily. She obviously hadn't wanted to come with him. She was glad he liked the gloves.

* * *

New Year's Eve and Amy came to collect Lily for the night out. 'You look lovely and what beautiful earrings.'

'From a friend, and so was the charm,' Lily said, not realising she'd made it sound as if they'd come from the same person.

The Five Bells was heaving but they spotted a couple of ex-school friends and Laura, holding court with stories of her exciting life. An hour or two and three pubs later, Lily was feeling a bit the worse for wear. Another very noisy crowd pushed their way in.

Murdoch saw Lily right away and knew she'd had too much to drink. Her eyes were very bright and she was giggling loudly. She was obviously with a crowd of friends, so he hoped they were looking out for each other. She looked very nice, in a fairly tight, short dress and she was wearing the charm and some earrings that looked like a flower, from what he could see. She spotted him just as he was looking.

'Murdoooooch!' She shrieked. 'Happy nooooo year. Oh and Megan, yoooo too.'

Megan, who was fairly drunk gave a wave. 'That Lily looks alright, scrubs up okay.' She couldn't wait for midnight. She'd hinted to the sneering Ryan and Davy about what was going to happen and made them promise not to cause any trouble.

Ryan had clocked Lily. She was a bit of alright, he thought. More upmarket than his usual type but she seemed to be up for a laugh. 'Who's that girl who knows you both?' he asked Megan.

'Oh *her*? That's Lily, works with Murdoch, her folks own the place or something.' Bored, she draped herself over Murdoch who, fed up by this time and having been forced to have a few drinks, was not in the best of moods.

Merry, who'd had one of her, *feelings* that something was going to happen, also squeezed her way into the bar. She spotted the pair of them right away, surrounded by a bad aura, quite prevalent. *Oh dear.*

It was getting close to midnight and Ryan was making his way towards Lily. Megan was in a high state of anticipation. Murdoch just wanted out of there and Merry was on tenterhooks.

The landlord rang a bell. 'Okay everybody, here they come.' He wacked up the volume on the TV and everyone started the countdown.

BONG!

Huge cheers greeted the first strike, Megan waited breathlessly.

'Happy New Year,' Murdoch kissed her.

Nothing. She waited, smiling at him, still nothing.

'What's the matter?'

'I-I thought...'

'Thought what?' at that point, he heard a scream and turned to see Lily struggling in Ryan's arms. Leaving Megan fuming, he was there in seconds just in time to hear Lily saying, 'I said no! leave me alone.' He hooked an arm around Ryan's neck and pulled him back. 'She said no, you dumbass.'

'Oi, gerroff, mind your own business, shithead.'

'Are you alright Lily?' Murdoch asked, not letting go of Ryan.

'Yeah, thanks. He's drunk, that's all.'

Megan came up as Amy found her way over to Lily.

'Murdoch, what are you doing, stay out of it.' She glared at Lily.

'Friend of yours, is he?' Amy's glare shot between Megan and Ryan. 'You'd better get him out of here.'

'She's right, get on out of it Ryan.' Snapped Murdoch.

'Look after your own bird,' Ryan said, furiously. He hadn't realised how strong Murdoch was, the arm was like an iron bar around his neck. 'Where's her bleeding ring that she's expecting?'

'Ring?' Murdoch stared at her. 'What ring?'

'I saw you, at the jeweller's, buying something. I thought you were going to propose.' Megan wailed.

'*What?* I'm eighteen, I don't want to get *engaged*. The jewellers was nothing to do with you.'

'Who then?' demanded a red-faced Megan.

'Ooh, was it *him* gave you that stuff?' asked Amy innocently.

'Hah, been caught out have you, you prick? Let go of me, I wouldn't touch her if you've had yer paws all over her.' Smirked Ryan

'What *stuff*?' Megan demanded, 'what's been going on?'

'*Nothing's* going on, we bought each other little Christmas presents, that's all?'

'Jewellery! That's not a *little* present. You know what, Murdoch? stuff your *little* present and the poxy bag you bought me.' She emptied the contents of her bag into a carrier she grabbed from one of the girls in her crowd and threw the bag at him, catching him square in the eye.

'Hey.' He yelled, letting go of Ryan, who promptly got a quick punch in, sending him to the floor, before scarpering. 'Megan, wait.'

'He bought you all that?' Amy was asking.

'No, just the charm, the earrings were…' A slap across her face from Megan stopped what she was going to say.

'Keep him, you slag!'

Merry had seen enough. A quick wave and a swirl of glitter had everybody in the pub moving to create a barrier between the two groups, although she was careful to make sure Murdoch was on Lily's side.

'You lot, out now before I throw you out.' Shouted the barman to Megan's group.

Looking daggers at Murdoch and Lily, she flounced out.

Merry was holding a bag of ice to Murdoch's eye and Lily was crying in Amy's arms. Laura seemed to be enjoying the situation and was taking pictures on her phone.

'Murdoch, I'm so sorry, do you want me to speak to M-Megan?'

'No, stay out of it, Lily. He didn't hurt you, did he?'

'He bruised your arm,' Amy pointed out. 'What a dickhead.'

'I'm alright, really. You can explain to her, can't you?'

'I don't know if I can be bothered. Merry, I'd like to take a couple of days off. Would you explain?'

'I can explain,' Lily began.

190

'Forget it,' he snapped. 'You've got to get back to Cornwall in a few days anyway, that's more important for *you*. If you're not hurt and your friends here can look after you, I'm going home.' He walked away.

'I'll make sure he gets back alright,' said Merry. 'Don't worry Lily, it'll be fine.' *I've got some serious thinking to do here.*

* * *

Rosemary slipped away in the last hours of New Year's Eve. It was peaceful and as if she'd just fallen asleep and hadn't woken up again. Alexander sat with her all night, waiting until the morning before doing anything. He had to let her go now.

Chapter Fourteen

ANEMONE

Also known as Windflower

Lily left for Cornwall without seeing Murdoch again. Merry tried to reassure her that everything would work out for the best, and that Megan probably wasn't meant to be. 'It wasn't your fault Lily, he stepped in to help and well, it all blew up from there. He just needs to sort his head out.'

Roo had messaged her three times during New Year's Eve and rang later the next day because he was worried about her. She was very upset and said she'd rather talk when she saw him. He knew better than to press it and told her a few funny stories from his time at home and at least left her feeling a bit better.

Merry was in a quandary because after watching the evening events, she knew exactly what Murdoch needed, and that was Lily. Technically she wasn't here for the girl, would that be seen as interference if she was to help her a little as well? There were many rules to adhere to, all of which the fairies broke occasionally from time to time. However, those instances never went unnoticed and there was usually a reckoning.

She needed some advice and her usual mentor, Fae Dorothy Grim, was away. Her best friend Homity Dearfrog would help, but she was already under scrutiny for a minor infringement, so perhaps not. Merry scratched her head trying to think. She was dealing with a boy, so perhaps she ought to ask one of the male fairies? Faroe Frightday and Giford Fayheart were free at the moment, or they had been when she started this latest mission. Her mind was made up. This was a delicate situation and as far as she was concerned there was only one outcome for the, *happy ever after*. She felt a little shiver at the thought of Giford. He was a strange choice as a Godfather, deeming the people he was supposed to help as beneath him and often treated them with contempt and derision. Maybe he *had* to do it as some sort of reparation for another misdemeanor? She called him a friend but it was really by association from her friendship with Faroe. Giford was a rather magnificent specimen in male fairy circles, Merry wished he would take a little more *personal* interest in her.

Murdoch purposefully waited until he knew Lily had gone, before he went back to work. Megan had stayed away and when he did text her so see if she wanted to talk, she blanked him. He wouldn't go chasing her, in some ways, although he felt bad about it, he was relieved. He knew deep down, that they didn't have much in common and her idea of a fun night out was a nightmare for him. He was better off without her, in fact, he felt at times, he was better off without anybody.

He knew if Ryan had hurt Lily or really frightened her, he could have done the prat some serious damage and that rather unnerved him. Was it because he knew her so well, would he have felt like that if it was any girl? He liked to think he would step in and help anybody but Lily did rather bring out the protective streak, she was small and it made her appear helpless, which she wasn't, of course. By the time he saw her again, things would have settled and she was with Rupert anyway, wasn't she?

* * *

Planning had been approved for the leisure centre and Peter Simmons got the ball rolling. Within hours, a large excavating machine had arrived on site and three tipper lorries were waiting to be loaded.

Murdoch was watching from the gateway with Stuart and was about to say what his father had told him, when Stuart said something that made him stop.

'I took your advice and went to the doctor, he's sending me for some tests in a couple of days. I'm only telling you at the moment, so you know what's what. I won't have Duckie worrying if there's no need.'

'Oh okay, well, I'm glad you're being checked out.' He didn't want to cause him any stress, so kept quiet about his misgivings. Feeling the need to share them with somebody, Merry sprang to mind and finding her on her own a little later, was the perfect opportunity.

'Mess and inconvenience,' Merry repeated. 'Are you quite sure those were the words?'

'According to my father, yes, and he did appear to be sober at the time.' Murdoch said wryly.

'I've had a bad feeling about what's going on there, and my feelings are never wrong. You and I need to keep a close eye on what's happening. *I* think they're going to make life difficult for this garden centre and we can't allow that.'

'We can't?' Murdoch grinned for the first time that year.

'No. We need to document everything, photos, you can do that on your phone thing, and have it all ready if needed.'

'Needed by whom?'

'All sorts of people,' she said vaguely. 'Law people and press maybe. Just make sure it's done, what have you got to lose? Don't tell the Overidge's, we mustn't worry them. They'll see it happening of course, but we must reassure them and tell them it won't last forever.' *Which it won't, I'll take care of that.* 'Now then,' she continued. 'What about you, are you alright and what happened with your girlfriend? Don't go all quiet and broody on me Murdoch, I'm not nosy, I'm concerned.'

'I don't go quiet and broody!'

'You do and you know it.'

He glared at her, then sighed. 'She's not my girlfriend anymore and before you say anything, I'm not actually that upset. We weren't really suited. Was Lily alright?'

'She was very subdued and seemed upset about what *she* thought she'd caused. I told her it wasn't her fault, but she ought to hear that from you.'

'Yeah, I know.' He kicked the ground moodily and went quiet.

'You're doing it,' warned Merry.

'*Okay*, I'll talk to her, just... not yet.'

* * *

Roo listened to Lily's story and told her not to be so silly. 'It wasn't your fault at all, his girlfriend sounds like a right mare, he's better off without her. He didn't *have* to help you, he *wanted* to. The fact that he took a knock, which doesn't even sound serious, is by the by. We men are prepared to accept that sort of thing,' he said with a smirk. When he heard her snort, he knew he was getting through to her. 'If another guy came onto my Sam, I'd go berserk.'

'What if a girl was doing the, coming on?' she smiled.

195

'He'd be scared shitless,' laughed Roo. 'Give it a few days and message him. Tell him you really appreciate what he did and hope things have settled down, then leave it to him.'

'I'm glad I've got you to talk to, my friend Laura thought it was funny, she wasn't much help.'

'He sounds an okay sort of guy, seriously, you can also say sorry that it caused him a problem, but *don't* apologise for anything else.'

'I won't, thanks. It's a shame because things were just settling down again after I upset him before.'

'Before, what else have you done?'

'It was what I said.' Explaining to Roo about the, *dad*, conversation and writing the card made it all seem rather silly now. People said things all the time, they didn't mean to cause upset.

'It's obviously a sensitive subject. He must have had a difficult upbringing if it was just him and his father from when he was eight. He obviously had to work and couldn't go to university or anything like that, even if he'd wanted to.'

'I didn't look at it like that, you're probably right.'

'I usually am,' he smirked again.

* * *

When Murdoch drove to work the next morning, the lane was blocked by a lorry, backed into a gateway and being loaded with soil. 'Can you back in a little bit further?' he asked politely, 'So I can get past?'

'Sorry mate, the field's a mud bath, I'll never get out again.' The machine that was loading the tipper, disgorged another ton or so of earth, half of it missing the spot and going all over the road.

There's the mess and inconvenience, thought Murdoch. He backed up and parked further away, walking down the lane to work.

'This'll be going on for quite a while I'm afraid,' the driver said cheerfully, not looking sorry about it at all. Murdoch nodded and when he was past, took a couple of photos without being too obvious about it.

January was always a quiet time in Roots, but the next few days saw no customers at all. Mr Taylor and Flora both complained about having to walk through clods of earth to get there at all and eventually Stuart told them both not to bother for a few days, they weren't busy and there was limited work that could be done at this time of the year.

Murdoch was worried about the bulb competition. In a matter of weeks, the children who had picked early flowering bulbs would be bringing their pots in to be photographed for final judging.

'I'm sure the main clearing, or whatever it is they're doing, will be finished by then,' said Stuart, but he sounded worried.

'I'm not so sure,' Murdoch argued. 'They don't seem to have done that much. One lorry load with an equal amount of earth on the lane and now another one blocking the way.'

After three days, Merry decided it was time to step in. The first lorry that arrived, as it backed into the gateway, found it's gears slipping and it shot backwards, its rear wheels sinking two feet into a mud hole. The front end was still sticking out into the lane, but there was certainly room for cars to pass. They heard the shouting and revving of the engine in the tea hut.

'What the hell's going on out there?' Murdoch went to investigate and came back looking very happy.

'Lorry's stuck and it's not going anywhere for a while. It threw up so much mud all the men look like they've been dipped in it and I don't think it'll be easy to get a big enough vehicle to pull it out. The lane's too narrow. What a shame.' He grinned at Merry.

* * *

It was the day of Rosemary's funeral. Alexander sat in the front with Elizabeth with some of Rosemary's friends from her book club and gardening circle, filling the row behind. She had no family to speak of, an elderly sister who wasn't well enough to make the trip and a nephew who was an undesirable as far as Alexander was concerned. *He* was just hoping for something from the will as Alex and Rosemary had no child of their own, or at least not one they knew the whereabouts of.

Percival, had offered his condolences and volunteered his services in any way he could help. Alexander was not impressed. 'I'm a barrister and still in charge of all my faculties. I think I know what has to be done. Rosemary did leave you a small bequest which you'll be contacted about.' *Percival*, what sort of a name was that? Alexander had always thought and now, didn't wish to encourage any more conversation.

Percival was also sitting in the front row, looking suitably distressed and probably, Alexander thought, trying to guess the value of his bequest. It was what Rosemary wanted, her sister didn't need it and this young man was the closest thing she had to a child of her own, she'd said. The fact that he hadn't visited his Aunt once during her illness rankled, but he would make sure her wishes were fulfilled.

He and Rosemary had come to a decision, ten years after Caroline had disappeared. A trust fund had been set up to include the house and monies after both of them had passed. If Caroline was found it would be hers and any children that she'd had would be included. If children came to light, with no Caroline on the scene, they would benefit. Percival would also receive something and if after another ten years nobody was found, he would get a bit more and the rest would be split between certain charities. Looking at Percival's sly face, Alexander prayed again his daughter was out there somewhere and would one day, appear on the doorstep.

Back at the house with a spread arranged by Elizabeth, Alexander gave her a small parcel. 'It was Rosemary's precious garden journal, with all her notes and some pressed flowers. She wanted you to have it.'

'Oh, thank you Alex, I know how she treasured it, as will I. I know you'll be alright, but if you ever need someone to talk to…'

'Thank you. I suppose I had better talk to other people and Percival, unfortunately.'

'It's not really for me to say, but the way he's eyeing those paintings on your wall, I would say he's the avaricious type.'

'You're not wrong Elizabeth.' With a sigh, he began to circulate.

* * *

Peter Simmons' wife was rather concerned when she saw his face turn puce whilst listening to a phone call.

'What do mean stuck, how did that happen? Get it out of there.' Silence. 'No *room!* Sort it out, that's what you're paid for. I want that driver sacked. Gears slipped, a feeble excuse.'

He slammed his phone onto the table. 'Imbeciles! I shall have to go out for a while.'

'Oh, must you?' she was quite relieved, finding life with him rather wearing at times and it meant she could sit and watch *Loose Women* in peace with a nice cuppa and a couple of biscuits.

Peter was fuming. It had gone to plan for three days, with nothing able to move through the lane, which he planned to widen later, now that he owned those other fields. The trouble was, he didn't want to risk being seen there, but he supposed it would only be Robert Overidge who would recognise him and it was highly unlikely he'd be around.

Robert was at that moment driving to Szarlota's flat. They had agreed a routine and he would make sure he had a meeting to attend or some suppliers to see when she was on a day off. The children were back at school and it was the first time he'd been able to see her for a while. He had to ring and check first, in case one of them was ill and he'd done that, delighted that the coast was clear. It was just a bit of fun, nothing serious, he told himself and he also made sure to park some distance away this time and walk.

She greeted him, wearing a wrap in a nice warm flat. He had slipped her a little more cash, saying she and the children mustn't get cold. The wrap was removed to reveal stockings and suspenders with a thong and nothing else. He thought he'd died and gone to heaven.

'I'm supposed to be seeing some fruit suppliers,' he panted as she dragged him into the bedroom. Melons came to mind as he buried himself between her two magnificent orbs.

His *fruit* meeting lasted an hour.

Peter stomped towards the stricken lorry, staring in horror at the mud-caked men, trying to shovel gravel and chippings in around the wheels.

'We won't get this out today guv.' One of them said. 'And there's rain forecast as well, that'll make things worse.'

'I don't want to hear that, get it done asap. At least the time of year means the road isn't too busy anyway but I still want as much inconvenience as possible.'

'We could have a lorry, dump sixteen tons of gravel in the road, we need it here, it's perfectly feasible and we can't shovel that fast.'

'You might have redeemed yourself, I'll order it now. Is that green van further up one of the garden workers?'

'A young lad guv, we ain't had no complaints as such, yet.'

'Well, make sure you do.' He made a quick call and being told the gravel couldn't be delivered until the next morning, decided to go and check on his other project, the flats, many of which had already been sold off-plan and a lot of profit was going to be made there.

* * *

Stuart had to climb over gravel and catch a bus for his appointment. He had chest pain by the time he got there. They took one look at him and dispatched him straight to the medical assessment unit. After tests consisting of the ECG he had been expecting and blood samples which had to be checked, the consultant came to talk to him. 'Mr Overidge, it appears you may have had a small heart attack. We need to book you for an angiogram, we'll do that as soon as possible and, in these circumstances, we usually like to keep people in, but you do seem well recovered and you're quite fit from what I hear.'

'It's my outdoor work, doctor. I was a bit worried but I've given up the pipe now, not that I smoked a lot.'

'Well that's good. It's a small step but it's a start. Now, do you have somebody to look after you at home?'

'Ah, Yes, I'll have to own up to all of this now, won't I?'

'You certainly will, Mr Overidge. Somebody else will talk to you about diet and exercise and we'll see what the angiogram shows. How are you going to get home?'

'I'll phone the lad who works for me, he'll come.'

'Okay, tell him about two hours, then you'll be ready.'

Stuart rang Murdoch and explained. 'Please tell Madge something suitable and I'll tell her the truth when I get back.'

Madge took the news of Stuart's possible condition, surprisingly well and berated him for not telling her sooner. She had stern words with Murdoch as well. 'Obviously you knew something, but I guess he told you to keep quiet, so I respect the fact that you did, but now that I know, you keep an eye on him and tell me if *anything* happens, understand?'

'Yes Madge, I did think you ought to know and he said he would tell you.'

'Humph, well he's had to now, hasn't he? One thing, Lily is *not* to be told, neither of us wants her worrying and we'll make sure, when and if she does find out, that she won't know *you* knew anything about it, alright?'

'I'd appreciate that, there's been a few difficulties between us, I don't want to add to them.'

* * *

The pile of gravel had been on the road for two days before Merry saw fit to interfere again. *I'm not having this, they can't get away with it.* The weather had forecasted gale force winds and they were blowing up well by lunch time.

The workmen had retreated to their portacabin for a cuppa and to get out of the wind. The lorry was still stuck in the mud and they made token gestures of gravel shoveling, telling Murdoch, when they saw him in the mornings, that they were building a ramp. He would just nod and then take more photos.

Merry was a short distance away watching them. It took a bit of concentration, but the wind blew itself up into a mini whirlwind, whizzing over the pile of gravel and then onwards to the cabin.

The men inside, were sat at the table, eating sandwiches and drinking their tea. 'Blimey, that wind's a bit fierce.' Said one, as some gravel stones rattled on the outside. Within a minute it sounded like they were being attacked. The cabin shook and was bombarded with gravel on all sides. It began to tilt. 'What the hell?' shouted another as they found themselves upside down, with the entire contents of their room on what had been, the ceiling.

Fighting their way to the door, yanked it open to find gravel pouring in. Climbing out, they saw the lorry, now on its side, the gravel heap strewn across the field, with the majority of it piled up against their wrecked building.

'Must have been one of those mini storm things, Simmons will never believe it, he'll go ape.' The foreman said gloomily. 'Bloody jinxed on this job, we are.'

Again, the commotion was heard in the cottage, where Murdoch was having his lunch well out of the wind. He came out to find Merry staring at a scene of devastation.

'A small tornado,' she said, calmly. 'They're all okay, I saw them running around. That'll keep them busy for a while.'

'I can't believe it,' said Murdoch. 'Do you think we should do anything?'

She thought for a moment. 'Nah. There's enough of them, and what can we do? Nobody's hurt, come on, let's go tell Stuart and Madge the story. I saw it all.' *Didn't I just?*

When Merry was by the river on her way home, Faroe jumped out in front of her.

'Hey Merry, that was pretty spectacular, is that sort of thing allowed?'

'I think so,' she answered, innocently.

'Far too over the top if you ask me, you should let them sort out their own problems.' Giford, *Giford,* was leaning against a silver birch tree, his white-blond hair camouflaged by the bark. His arms were folded and he was glowering at her.

I didn't ask you, she was tempted to say. 'Perhaps a bit, but they're *nice* people Giford, something you don't seem able to accept. I wanted to ask both of you for some advice, actually.'

'Ask away.' Faroe smiled. 'Come on Giford, walk with us and be gracious enough to impart some of your wisdom.'

Giford stretched up, gracefully, like a cat and stepped onto the path. 'If I must. What *have* you done to your hair, Merry?'

Since Christmas, she had changed it again and it was now a vibrant orange with purple tips.

'It's called *fun,* Giford, something you should try sometime.' Ignoring his condescending look, she filled them in with all the latest including, how she felt Lily was the one for Murdoch and how could she help things along?'

Giford looked at her in disbelief. 'That wasn't part of your mission, was it? You're interfering too much. Can't he even sort out his own love life? Pathetic!'

'If you're supposed to be helping him, I don't see what's wrong with it?' Faroe grinned. 'Come on, let's go back to your cottage and work out a plan.'

Giford, having nothing better to do, sighed and followed them. 'Your little stunt obviously explains why all the wood anemones closed up their petals, they knew a storm was coming.'

'It was very *localised,* it didn't affect the woodland at all and you know it.' Merry retorted and smiled at him.

* * *

Everybody in the house share was trying to warm up after a cold day. The biodomes were a godsend, but the journey home was on a bus with broken down heating and *somebody* had switched the heating timer off here as well. As Zoe was supposedly the one in charge of that department they all denied any knowledge of it. Roo just made a chilli and they gradually thawed out. He spoke to Lily later.

'Listen, I have an invitation for you. Do you *particularly* need to go home for the week in February?'

'I guess not, it *is* only a week and not much happens at Roots at that time of the year. Why?'

'My parents have a ski lodge for that week. They've said I can bring a few friends, have you ever been skiing?'

'Never, but Roo, I can't afford...'

'They're treating me, it's an early birthday present. Sam will come and he's looking forward to meeting you. He's never skied before either, so you'll have that in common. My sister will be there, anyone you'd like to bring?' he asked casually.

'N-no. I think I'd love it but what about all the stuff? And are you asking anybody else from here?'

'It's awkward, I can't ask them all and Zoe would be a nightmare measuring out the Gluhwine, you're my *friend,* so it's okay. Most of the equipment will be there, you just need a snow suit really. We'll go up to Plymouth on Saturday and do some shopping and,' he stopped her before she could argue. 'If you're short, *moneywise* that is, *I* will treat you.'

'It's not fair Roo,'

'I don't care, I *want* to. No arguments.'

Chapter Fifteen

RIBES UVA-CRISPA – GOOSEBERRY

Plant between late autumn and early spring

Peter Simmons was in grave danger of bursting a blood vessel while talking to Martin and the architect. 'A tornado! Can you actually *believe* that? They had the bloody local television news filming the damned truck laying on its side and the upside down portacabin. I've now got the council building inspector down there, looking into what we're doing. Apparently,' he glared at Martin, 'they didn't realise there was going to be quite so much excavation and heavy plant going up and down the lane.'

'Well, to be fair, neither did I,' Martin said defensively. 'You just asked me to check out the feelings that planning would have towards a leisure centre and that was no problem.'

Peter ignored him. 'I've got to meet him later. They're talking about us having to widen the road before any more work is carried out so that we don't block it, that was the whole point of the exercise! I don't need all this extra expense.'

Jeremy, the architect, chipped in. 'You would have had to widen the road anyway before the leisure centre opened and for the garden centre development, at least you own the surrounding area now.'

Peter didn't say that he had no intention of building a leisure centre, not enough profit in that, but yes, if he built more houses, the lane was a bit of an issue. It spoilt his plans for isolating Roots however, he'd now have to think of something else.

* * *

A few days later, Murdoch and Stuart were talking about the work having come to a halt. It seemed plans were now in place to widen the road and it would take a while for the surveying to be done and for highways to be involved. The timing was perfect, as children began to bring their pots of bulbs to be admired and photographed, with a prize being given each month for the different types. The local paper reported the ongoing story and also praised the centre for encouraging the children to take an interest in the growth of plants.

It was an ideal opportunity for Murdoch to send Lily some pictures. A few of the pots and the story, with a quick message.

Hi. Hope all good ur end. Bulb comp going well as u can c. V quiet here apart from that. C u end Feb?

It was a while before he got an answer, but during the day she was probably busy, he told himself.

I'm so pleased. I'm away 4 a week so won't b back till end March. Plz keep me updated.

Away? She hadn't mentioned that, but then, why should she? They hadn't exactly had a cosy chat before she left. When her name came up in conversation he asked Madge if she knew that Lily was away till Easter.

'Oh yes,' Madge replied. 'She said she's off to Austria for a week, with a friend and his family, skiing, would you believe? Hope she doesn't break her leg.'

Skiing? With a *friend*? Rupert, it must be. Murdoch felt angry. Her Grandfather was in poor health and she was off *skiing* with her boyfriend. *She doesn't know,* a little voice said in his head, but he ignored it. Yet another example of the different world she lived in and *another* reason not to get too friendly.

Merry saw how closed up he had become again and tried to put into practice the advice she been given by Faroe and, begrudgingly, by Giford. 'What are you so niggled about?'

'Nothing,' he muttered as he checked his plants under the polythene tunnels he'd fashioned to protect them.

'Well, in that case, we can go out for that burger we promised ourselves and I don't want to hear any excuses from you.'

'I...' a burger *did* sound good, even if he had to listen to her prattling on. 'Okay, a burger and that's *it.*'

'Chips as well I meant.' She looked crestfallen.

'Yeah, chips as well.' He had to smile. She took things very literally at times.

Later, when they sat with their burger, chips and a drink, she tried to get him to open up a bit. 'You let Lily know about the bulb thing in the paper then?'

'Yeah.'

She tried again. 'After you did that, you went all *Murdoch,* like you do and I heard you asking Madge about what she was doing in February.'

'So, what if I did? She said she was going away for a week, that's all. I just wondered.'

'Ah, I see. And what *is* she doing?'

'Going skiing with her *boyfriend* and his family.' He stabbed a chip into his sauce as if he was trying to kill it.

'Boyfriend? Are you sure?'

'Pretty sure. I saw him pick her up last year when I dropped her at Salisbury.' He described the car and the little remarks that added up.

'Add up to five you mean. If it's the one she's mentioned to me, he could be just a very good friend. Roo, or something?'

'Rupert. Even his name sounds like money. Why's she going with his family?'

'I don't understand what you mean. Money and Rupert don't sound anything alike? As to your other point, maybe they asked if he'd like to bring a friend?'

'Well, isn't this cosy and I thought it was just that, *Lily*, you were sniffing around?' Megan stood looking daggers at him with some of her crowd in attendance, Ryan keeping well back, Murdoch noticed.

'Not that it matters now, but I wasn't sniffing after *anyone*.' Murdoch stared at her, noticing how spitefully she looked at Merry. What had he ever seen in her? 'Merry's just a… friend.'

'Interesting choice of friend,' Megan sneered. 'Choose her because her hair looks like one of your plants, did you?'

'Do you think so?' Merry was delighted. 'I was trying to get the effect of Candy Pop and Lady Purple. Those are Petunias.' She added, at Megan's blank look.

'I don't give a shit what it is. Were you coming onto him before New Year?'

'I don't comprehend your meaning?'

'Are you for real? Well, it's quite obvious what was going on,' She leaned over the table and put her face close to Murdoch's. 'I'm well shot of you and just so you know, I aborted your baby.'

He went white, there was a buzzing in his head and voices sounded far away. Merry took one look at him and put out a hand to stupefy him for a few seconds, while a dozen or so rats came streaming from the kitchen, running across the floor.

Pandemonium reigned. People screamed, including Megan and there was a stampede for the door. In seconds the place was empty except for the two of them and the staff, looking puzzled, wondering what had happened as there was no indication of what had caused the panic. Merry pressed a glass of water to Murdoch's lips.

'I-I… did you hear what she said, Merry? She did *that* without telling me?'

'She's gone now and she said it to hurt you. If it *did* happen, there's nothing you can do, but the way she looked at that guy you throttled at New Year, just before she said it, makes me think *he* may have had something to do with it.'

'How can you think that?'

'One of my feelings and they're usually right, as I told you. Now, let's get you home.'

* * *

Corrine dished up one of the Supermarket's frozen specials for tea while Robert poured a glass of wine and eyed his plate. 'Take one of those potatoes off, would you? My trousers are getting a bit snug, I need to cut down a bit.'

'Seeing as how they haven't actually done up around your *waist* for some time, but lower down under your stomach, how is it you've only just noticed?'

'I… it's New Year and all that, isn't it? I keep seeing the magazine covers in our racks, new body, new you, all that sort of thing.'

'Well, I won't discourage you of course, you could cut down on the cheese and biscuits as well.'

'I suppose so,' he said, glumly. That might be a step too far, he liked his cheese, but Szarlota was quite… inventive and he wanted her to be impressed with his physique.

'Oh, I forgot to tell you. I posted Lily's passport as she asked me to and, could you transfer some money for her?'

'Passport?'

'She going to Austria for a week, staying in one of those ski lodges, I wish I'd had a chance to take her shopping. There are so many fashionable après ski clothes about.'

'Skiing!' Robert spluttered. 'How can she afford that?'

'She's not paying. She's been *invited* and the friend's parents are treating him and a group for his nineteenth birthday apparently. But she needs spending money, I don't want her looking like a pauper in front of his parents.'

'*His*, what boy is this and should she just be going off with people we know nothing about?'

'She explained it to me on the phone. Apparently, his family are *very* well off and he's asked her because they're such good friends. He's called Rupert, what do you think of that?'

'Not a lot. So, are they... you know?'

'Are they what, having *sex* do you mean? It's perfectly normal you know, even for someone of your age. Why have you gone all red?'

'It's warm in here.' He loosened his tie. 'Alright, I'll transfer some money for her, anything that takes her interest away from this garden nonsense can't be bad. Rupert, you say? I could get used to it I suppose.'

'She'll look so sweet in those sunshade things they wear.'

'She'll probably be face down in the snow most of the time, she's never been on skis before.'

'Some of the Royals' go skiing, don't they? That would be nice if she mingled with them.'

Sometimes, Robert thought, his wife was away with the fairies.

* * *

Stuart had angina, which was confirmed after the angiogram. Madge had insisted on accompanying him and they listened while the consultant explained that there were signs of coronary heart disease which was affecting his arteries. It may be that he would need stents inserted in the not too distant future, the procedure for that that would be similar, but a little more involved from what he'd just experienced. In the meantime, a change in diet would be beneficial along with some exercises, which he gathered, had already been explained. Stuart was given some medication, an odd-looking spray with instructions to use if he felt a pain and reassurance that he would be monitored closely and a further decision would be made when necessary.

They went for a cup of tea in town before going back to Roots. 'I'm wondering,' Stuart began, 'Whether we should have a re-think. You know we could transfer ownership of the property to Lily and still live there.' He squeezed Madge's hand. 'We have to face up to it you know but it would solve a lot of problems. There's room for her as well if she *wanted* to live with us. Legally, speaking, it might be better if it was her address.'

'We're going to have to tell her about your condition.'

'Yes, I know. We'll do it all at Easter. I don't want to cause trouble between her and her father, but Robert's not going to like it at all.'

'Lily won't want bad feeling either,' said Madge. 'It's a delicate situation.'

* * *

Lily and Roo finished early on the Friday before half term. She was staying at his house for the night because the flight time meant they had to be at the airport by six in the morning.

'This is where you live?' She could hardly speak as they pulled into the mock Georgian, mini-mansion.

'Too much?'

'God, it's fantastic.'

'It's just a house Lily, don't be fazed by it. People are more important than their belongings. Sam felt the same when he saw it for the first time.'

She found it hard *not* to be fazed, when they were greeted by a housekeeper, but felt more at ease when the woman hugged Rupert and gave him a kiss. 'Your parents are in the lounge, welcome to you Miss Lily, Mr Rupert will show you to your room after you've met them.'

A young girl came rushing down the stairs. 'Rupert! And you must be Lily, hi, I'm Bella.'

Lily knew Roo's sister was called Arabella and if that had been *her* name, she'd want to shorten it as well. 'Hi, Bella, nice to meet you.'

'My friend Becky's coming with us and she's never skied before, so she'll be learning with you.'

'All my family ski,' Rupert said, almost apologetically, 'but we get together for part of the day and the evenings of course.'

His parents were very down to earth and welcoming, to Lily's relief. Sam arrived soon after them and gave her a huge grin.

'So, you're the one keeping Rupert out of trouble, good for you. I don't know what I'm doing on the snow either, so we can make fools of ourselves together.'

She saw the looks that passed between him and Roo and envied their closeness and feelings for each other.

* * *

Murdoch found it hard to believe that Megan could have kept such a thing from him. Was Merry right about Ryan? If she was, then Megan had cheated on him anyway, but what if it *had* been his? He had a right to know and to be part of the decision. No way was he ready to be a father, but if he'd had to, he would, although, he could have been bringing up someone else's child without knowing it. In a way, he was glad the choice had not been given to him but was still angry. He'd been treated like a fool, that wouldn't happen again.

At work, he thanked Merry for her help that night, he'd been in a bit of a daze and couldn't really remember going home. Yes, he was fine, he told her and just wanted to get on with his work. He was watchful of Stuart, always making sure the man didn't overdo it and never hesitated to run any errands that were needed. His job became his life, with no time to feel sorry for himself or miss companionship of any kind.

Merry was sad for him but knew he needed time to sort out his feelings, she was just there, to lend a hand, make idle conversation or suggestions and didn't push in any way. Lily was away, so it was a perfect time for the wound to heal.

* * *

The holiday was wonderful. Sam, Lily and Becky got on well with the ski lessons, Becky made friends with some of the younger people in the class, giving Lily and Sam time to get to know each other. During the evenings, they had fun with meals and nights out in the snow-covered town. Bella and Becky were typical fourteen-year-olds, giggling and chatting with phones always in their hands.

Lily took lots of pictures, she'd never seen scenery like it, the week sped by and it was time to head home.

'Roo, I can't thank you enough or ever pay you back, this has been such an experience, it was something I'd never thought I'd do.'

'You being here was payment enough and I told you, my parents were happy for me to bring friends. My Dad's trying to accept me and Sam, but it made it easier in the daytime and when we were out, us being in a threesome.'

'I was afraid I was in the way.' Lily said, having felt like a gooseberry at times.

'I promise you, you weren't and Sam likes you as well, which is great. I love you to bits Lily and if I was straight, I'd be right in there.'

'I... guess that's a compliment, would you really?'

'You can't see it, can you? How fanciable you are.'

'Umm, thanks.' *Am I?*

As they had to travel back to Cornwall on Sunday, Lily stayed another night at Roo's house. His mother said it had been delightful to meet her and was glad her son had such a good friend while he was studying. She hoped Lily would visit them again.

* * *

The building site had been quiet for a few weeks. Planning had been granted to widen the road and the wrecked portacabin and the sideways lorry had both been removed with nothing to replace them. Peter Simmons was not going to spend money on the road without the purchase of Roots, so a story went out about the firm who were building the leisure centre being in financial difficulties, with the possibility of other investors coming up with the money. That would all take time and give him a chance to think of another way to get the garden centre in his grasp.

* * *

The obsequious little man from the council, as Elizabeth viewed him, had been with her for at least an hour. Praising her efforts to raise money for charity, with the opening of her gardens, he had called initially to discuss some dates. He was trying to persuade her to join a Summer special involving several gardens in the area. 'If you could see your way to opening every weekend over the Summer holiday, Countess... I'm sorry, *Lady* Foxmore, it would be a real event and much appreciated.'

'Every weekend? That's a lot of extra work for the staff here, I may have to give that some thought.'

'Yes, yes of course, I quite understand.'

'I don't think you do. For every person who comes to enjoy and appreciate what is here, there is another who leaves litter, picks flowers, when strictly asked *not* to and even some who come with a trowel and try digging them up. That's why I need a lot of people to keep an eye out.'

'Perhaps we could get the girl guides and scouts involved? The older ones I mean, who could act as marshals. Perhaps, you might think about opening up your house?'

'Certainly not! I don't want a lot of strangers nosing around. This is a private house, not, *through the keyhole*, they would be even worse than in the gardens.' Elizabeth sighed. It would look very churlish to refuse and perhaps if they had a refreshment marquee, it would help to pay the extra wages of staff asked to work more hours. 'Let me give it some thought and get back to you, Mr... Jessop, wasn't it?'

'Yes, wonderful, your ladyship, err... Lady Foxmore. Is it possible, your son, t-the Earl, might attend one weekend?'

'I can ask him,' Elizabeth was quite amused. Her son, James, did indeed hold the title now. It was quite an insignificant Earldom and the best part of it was the beautiful Elizabethan Manor house that had been in the Foxmore family for generations. James was a parliamentary secretary and loved London. He did visit, on odd occasions and regarded the house as an unnecessary expense. His wife, Lady Clara, despised it, calling it old and draughty, she visited it on even fewer occasions.

Mr Jessop went away, a happy man and glad that his wife had made him watch *Downton Abbey*, so he knew the correct form of address for a Countess.

* * *

Murdoch was meeting a chef and a buyer from one of the most prestigious restaurants in the area. Having already provided them with samples of his more unusual vegetables, they had come to see his set up. 'I decided to concentrate on these uncommon varieties, the types you can't get so easily. It would be a selling point on your menu.'

'You can provide a selection, seasonally, all through the year?' asked the chef.

'I can, here's a list I drew up for you, month by month. Yours is a small but very select clientele, so the amount you would need weekly would be more than manageable for us. I've priced the selections for you as well and that includes the cost of fresh, daily delivery.' Murdoch handed them a folder with all the information, which they began to study. He stepped back to let them talk. Stuart had given him full control of distribution and he wanted to prove himself.

The buyer scanned the prices and with a nod from the chef, he smiled. 'No room for negotiation?'

Murdoch smiled back. 'The prices are competitive, I think you'll find.'

'Fair enough, okay, you've got yourself a deal. Don't let us down.'

'I won't, thanks very much.' He watched them leave with a great feeling of worth and satisfaction.

Merry came over and high-fived him. 'Well done you, Lily *will* be impressed, she told me she knew you'd get this off the ground when it was talked about. She's home tomorrow, for Easter.' She added casually.

'Yeah, I know.'

* * *

It was mid-morning on Lily's first day back at Roots before she actually had an opportunity to speak to Murdoch. He came into the tea hut while she was boiling the kettle and almost turned around to leave, but she saw him. 'Hi there, tea or coffee?'

'Coffee, please. Um, you okay?'

'Fine, Grandad told me about the restaurant, that's great news. What are you growing for them at the moment?'

This was safe territory and he relaxed. 'Spinach and fennel, artichokes and asparagus. I brought a lot on under cloches and I used the greenhouse. I told them I was cultivating unusual varieties, it's all good bullshit for their menu.'

'That's the sort of thing that impresses my mum,' she passed his coffee and their fingers brushed for a second. 'Murdoch, about New Year...'

'Don't go there, please. It wasn't your fault, so let's just leave it, okay?'

'Okay, but, I did appreciate your help, I need you to know that. We are still friends, aren't we?'

There was a silence, then he tweaked her hair. 'Yeah. We're friends.' Taking his coffee, he went outside and let out a breath he felt he'd been holding for weeks.

There was a letter for her up at the cottage.

'It's been waiting for you for a couple of days,' Grandma said. 'Expensive looking notepaper.'

'And hand-written as well,' Lily said as she opened it. It was from the Countess, Elizabeth, Lady Foxmore. She asked if Lily would be kind enough to give her a ring and come for lunch one day next week. If there was anybody else from the centre who had an eye for design and was as helpful as she had been, they would be welcome.

'Why don't you ask Murdoch, then he could drive you?' Madge said with a twinkle in her eye. She would like to see the two of them getting on a little better. 'You can tell him what the Countess has said, he *does* have an eye for design, he did it in his course, just hasn't had much opportunity to use it.'

Merry was on a day off, she never wanted them, but it would look most odd if she didn't take them. She would spend those days flitting through the woods, hoping to see Faroe and of course, Giford. Today, she couldn't believe her luck when she came across him, on his own, crouched in a tree stump, studying a clump of fungi. 'Giford, be careful, there's not mushroom for you there,' she said and fell about laughing.

He looked at her blankly. 'That is amusing, I suppose. Have you nothing you can interfere with, instead of bothering me?'

'I am on one of the nuisance days' off. I shall visit the centre shortly in another form. Where's Faroe?'

'He's been given a job. Another human fool who can't see where they're going wrong.'

'When are *you* going to have an assignment?'

He crawled out of the stump and stood up, towering head and shoulders over her. 'They are waiting for a situation that will suit my temperament,' he said, in a supercilious voice.

Merry burst out laughing again. 'Then we'll all have to wait until the gooseberry bushes start singing.'

Giving her a disgusted look, he disappeared in a flurry of glitter.

When she had recovered, she set off in butterfly form.

'I can't see what help I'd be and I'm very busy here.' Murdoch said when Lily made her suggestion.

'You've got a day off Tuesday, haven't you, could you spare a couple of hours then?'

Intrigued by the invitation, but not wanting to show it, he shrugged. 'If I do some allotment work first, I could be done by eleven.'

'That's great, where shall we meet? Shall I come to you?'

'No! I mean, don't go out of your way. Can I pick you up at the end of the high street? Then we're on the right road.' The butterfly, swooping around his head, nodded with approval, shaking glitter over his hair and shoulders.

'I'll phone her then and say it's two of us, you've got...' she put her hand up and brushed glitter away.

'I don't know where all this stuff keeps coming from,' he said. 'Must be in the greenhouses from Christmas.'

'You've got some in your eye, some green bits.'

'Have I?' he rubbed them, 'Nothing there.'

'Oh no, it's actual colour, showing up in the sunlight, I never noticed before.' *I thought they were just brown.*

'I better get on,' he said.

If the butterfly's face could have been seen, it would have shown a beaming smile.

Chapter Sixteen

DACTYLORHIZA VIRIDIS – FROG ORCHID.

Easily overlooked in its habitat of short grassland

Brian was delighted to be back at the scrapyard. Although some days were hard work, he had the company that he enjoyed and there were always a few cans around in the makeshift office. All sorts of people used to drop in, friends of Harry, who would know of a deal to be done somewhere. It may involve the scrapping of a car, with no questions asked, or interesting items that would change hands for some ready cash. Since the jewellery discovery, it had quietened down but was now beginning to get back to normal. Harry revelled in it, he was the big fish in a very small pond, some might even say a goldfish bowl, but it suited him. Some days he would flash the cash, others he'd be skint, but he always had the scrap which was more or less, legitimate. Brian was careful never to take anything home again, but once or twice, on the pretext of helping his son on the allotments, he had buried oilskin-wrapped packages. He was careful to make sure they were on old Watkins plot and not Murdoch's.

Murdoch had been hoping for some time to talk to the Watkins, but Jean had been in hospital, with her husband visiting most days. She was home again now and having left it for a while, he took some flowers and his usual box of produce and knocked on the door.

'Come in lad, nice to see you, how're you keeping?' Ken beamed as he took the box.

'I'm very well thank you, how are you, Mrs Watkins?'

'I'm on the mend, Murdoch dear, come and tell me all your news.'

Over several cups of tea, he brought them up to date and told them the story of the mini tornado.

'I saw that on the news,' said Jean. 'You were lucky it missed the garden centre.'

'Yes, it was quite amazing, just the one field.' Murdoch had thought about it many times and couldn't make any sense of it. 'I wanted to ask you both about something if I may? I don't want to ask my father, he always gets in a mood if my mother is mentioned.'

'What is it you want to know?' Jean asked softly.

'I got a copy of my full birth certificate and it says I was born here, in this Park, were you here then?'

'We were and I actually helped you into the world, you were a strong lad, even then.' Jean smiled. 'You were squalling when the ambulance arrived and your mother wanted to send them away and said she was fine. They checked her over and a midwife came. That was that really. Nurse and health visitor popped in for a bit, but your mother didn't want to have anyone interfere, as she put it. I know you had all the injections and all the check-ups you should have had.'

'It's hard to remember, do you know anything about her, did she ever talk about any family?'

Ken answered. 'Brian told me she'd joined the group when she left home, wasn't happy, it seems. They settled here when they knew she was pregnant. I can't tell you much else.'

'I know she dyed her hair blonde,' Jean continued. 'When it was growing out, it was dark, like yours and she had brown eyes. You look like her, I think, from what I can remember.'

'She was called Caroline Carruthers, that's what it said on the certificate.' Murdoch was pleased with the small bits of information, but it didn't really help him in finding out if he had any family. 'It said she was born in this county, but I don't know her exact date of birth and I couldn't find anyone of that name on any searches for a ten-year period around when she would have been born.'

'Well, she called herself Lyn, that's all I know. Sorry Murdoch, we can't be of any more help.'

'That's okay, thanks for what you did tell me.'

* * *

On Tuesday, as the green van pulled up, Lily got in with a portfolio. At Murdoch's questioning look, she explained. 'I brought these to show the Countess the sort of things I've drawn up before and stuff I've done at Eden. Apart from my parents' garden, I've never actually planned a layout for anybody.'

'Me neither, only in my head. Her grounds must be enormous, I don't know what she's got in mind. I looked them up and they're very well established. It was you that impressed her, so I guess she thinks your input is worth hearing.'

'I've never seen her gardens, she only opens them once a year and I've always been on holiday, so I'm quite excited.'

Her enthusiasm was rubbing off on him and he also noticed she wore the little watering can charm, which made him feel ridiculously pleased. She didn't appear to be wearing any other jewellery, so nothing *Rupert* had given her. Don't be daft, he told himself, if she's with him, that's it and she's not for the likes of me anyway. We're friends, work friends, that's all. He turned up the volume on the rather basic and tinny sounding radio so the conversation dwindled for a while.

'I think it's this way,' she said after a while and pointed to the next sign.

Turning off, he remembered the map he'd looked up and knew it would about two miles. A sign for Foxmore Manor appeared and they turned into a driveway, bordered by rhododendrons and camellias, which were large and obviously had been there for many years. As they rounded the bend, a beautiful house, with black and white timbers and leaded windows stood in front of them.

'It's out of a storybook isn't it?' Lily gasped. 'I thought Roo's house was breath-taking but this is wonderful.'

'Roo's house?'

She didn't notice the edge to his voice. 'Yes, in London. I stayed there the night before we flew.'

He didn't really hear what else she said, his hands were turning white from gripping the wheel so firmly. *She stayed at his house? In his room?* It was none of his business, he told himself, *again,* but this Rupert character better not mess her about.

She was still chatting. 'His family were all really nice and it was good to get to know Sam.'

'Err, yeah, sure.' He'd stopped by the front door without realising it. *Who's Sam?*

Elizabeth had seen them arrive and was waiting on the steps. 'Lily, thank you for coming and you must be, Murdoch?'

'Yes, Lady Foxmore.'

'Oh heavens, call me Elizabeth, please. We have an hour before lunch, so I suggest I show you around, you can get the feel of the place and I'll explain what I want.'

She led the way through the gardens, pointing out how old the oaks were and showing off the watercourse that ran through the wooded area, falling into small pools at different levels. 'That was new two years ago, so I want another feature. Something interesting and different, over here, I thought.' She led them to space which was shrouded by trees, giving a lot of shade and not much other growth. 'There's a challenge for you both. Come and have lunch now and then I'll leave you to walk around again and see if you can suggest how to transform it.'

Lunch was a selection of salad, with slices of cold game pie and the tiniest, buttery new potatoes. Dessert was a warming, rhubarb crumble with lemon cream. Elizabeth moved the conversation away from gardening, grilling them both about their lives and ambitions. She was very interested in Lily's stories about Eden and decided she *must* make a point of visiting it. The young man, Murdoch, was not at ease talking about himself, she could see that, so didn't pry any further, after he'd said it was just him and his Father. She thought he was very good looking and reminded her of someone, but she couldn't quite think who. Once they got back onto the subject of gardening, he came out of his shell and contributed as much, if not more, to the conversation, than Lily. 'Why don't you two go and look on your own? I'm not expecting you to come up with something today, you'll probably have to give it some thought.'

'Yes, Lad... Elizabeth, that was a lovely lunch, thank you.' Murdoch was keen to get outside. He *did* have an idea, one he felt sure Lily would agree with. He was surprised during lunch when she was talking about her housemates and mentioned Rupert, as her new best friend. A bit more than that, surely?

As soon as they were outside Lily turned to him, an excited look on her face. 'I've got the perfect suggestion for it.'

'So have I.'

'A stumpery!' they both said in unison, stared at each other in astonishment and Lily started to laugh while Murdoch managed a smile. 'Okay, that's settled then,' he said, 'Let's go and do some sketches and make notes.'

They spent nearly another hour, drawing, pacing the area for measurement and discussing the various designs that could be done. When they got back to the house, afternoon tea was produced.

'This is very kind, we weren't expecting all this.' Lily said, eyeing the massive scones and a large tub of cream.

'It's nice to have to some sensible company, did you think of anything at all?'

Lily saw that Murdoch was happy for her to explain and she did so, showing some of the sketch ideas and a list of mosses and ferns they had in mind.

'I visited the Highgrove gardens last year and the one there is magical,' Elizabeth was thrilled. 'You will need to speak to my gardener, I'm sure he took some tree stumps up at the end of last year, they're probably hidden away somewhere.'

'We could go to the reclamation centre, they may have old railway sleepers, things like that we can use. Is there a budget for this?' Murdoch was having more ideas and was eager to get it started.

'As long as it's sensible, I shall leave it up to you. When you've chosen what you want, ring me and I can pay over the phone I expect. Do you have all the plants you need at your centre?'

'Not all of them,' Lily admitted. 'It's quite specialised, but we can source them from suppliers.'

'Excellent, it will be a work in progress for the visitors this summer and of course, I shall credit you both and Roots.'

'Thank you, that won't do us any harm at all. Murdoch will be doing nearly all the work, I shall be back at Eden until mid-July, but I have a week at the end of May as well.'

Murdoch glanced at her. *Not off with the boyfriend again then?*

As they were driving away, Lily was chattering about the stumpery and how much she wished she was around more and would like to help with it.

'Shall we stop at the reclamation centre now and see what they've got?' Murdoch asked.

'Oh, could we, if you've got time, please.'

It wasn't far out of the way and would still be open so he headed in that direction. He didn't want to dampen her spirits and was also keen to see what was available.

There *were* some old railway sleepers along with several logs and tree stumps of different sizes. Lily was like a child at Christmas, discovering bits and pieces and every few minutes, he'd hear, *come and look at this*. One such summons did unearth something rather wonderful, it was an enormous piece of driftwood, gnarled, curled and bleached white.

'That won't be cheap,' Murdoch said. 'Artists and sculptors like that sort of thing.'

The price was astronomical for, *a bit of wood,* as she called it, but after phoning the Manor and getting the okay, Elizabeth said she would be down in the land rover with her gardener in the morning. When told it was for Lady Foxmore, the staff put it all to one side and said there was no problem, she could pay tomorrow.

Walking back to the van, Lily tucked her arm into Murdoch's. 'This has been such a good day, I'm so glad you came as well, it wouldn't have been half as good on my own.'

He wasn't quite sure what to do. Having her arm there, felt... nice and natural. Did girls do that sort of thing with a male friend? Just because he'd had no experience of it, he didn't want to react in the wrong way so he relaxed as best he could and tried not think how warm her skin was, or how her hair just brushed his jaw and smelt of lemons. 'It was a good day, and it's a shame you're not here to see the whole project through, but we can keep in touch about it,' he said nonchalantly. 'You've still got a week, haven't you?'

'Oh yes, if she's getting all that stuff tomorrow, we'll sort out another day to have them placed, if that's okay with you?'

'Yeah, sure.'

* * *

Peter Simmons took his wife out on one of the rare occasions that he wanted a companion for a meal, it was her birthday, after all, it was the least he could do. It had worked out quite well as he wanted to try a restaurant he'd heard was exceptional. So, here they were, sitting in the Sanglier et truffe, with menus in hand.

'Oh dear,' she said. 'It's all in French, I'm not sure what to ask for.'

The head waiter, who had been hovering nearby, was at her side in an instant. 'Allow me to assist you, Madame. Our special tonight is Navarin of Lamb, with *petit* roast potatoes and the freshest of vegetables delivered this morning.'

Peter tutted irritably, he usually ordered for his wife. 'Fancy name for lamb stew, isn't it?'

'It is much more than *stew*, Monsieur.' The waiter sounded most insulted.

'It sounds lovely, I'll have that thank you.' Natalie said firmly. It was so nice to be treated with a bit of respect and not as part of the furniture. A birthday card *had* been forthcoming that morning, but not one that appeared to have had a lot of thought given to it. Peter had also given her, a few quid, as he put it, to buy something smart and there was this meal tonight.

'I'll have steak and chips, or frites or whatever you call them.' Peter glared at the menu. He was damned if he'd have *Pierre*, explain it to him.

'Entrecote steak avec pommes de terre ébréchées. Merci, *Monsieur*. Madame.' He smiled at her as he scooped the menus up. The man was a *cochon,* he thought.

'He's only being nice to you for an extra tip.' Peter remarked and looked around to see if there was anyone he knew. Natalie looked down at the table and moved her cutlery slightly, for want of something to do and so as Peter wouldn't see the sudden shine of tears. She'd taken care, she thought, to look nice tonight but as usual, there was no compliment forthcoming.

The meal was delicious, the lamb melted in her mouth and the vegetables were an absolute delight. Tiny spears of asparagus in butter with some pan-fried artichoke hearts. Natalie had once served the tinned hearts and Peter had turned his nose up at them. She watched him sawing at his steak and when he swallowed, his eyes bulged slightly and his throat swelled. Her mind went to one of the nature programmes she always enjoyed. A frog, trying to attract a mate with its vocal sacs swelling. She had to hold her napkin over her mouth to hide the smile.

When it was time to pay to pay the bill, it was presented on a silver dish. 'I hope everything was to your satisfaction?' The waiter looked at Natalie.

'Humph, it would have to be for what I'm paying.' Peter fumbled for his wallet.

'It was very nice, and the vegetables were amazing.' Natalie smiled back.

'They are specialised and from a new local supplier, *Roots* nursery, do you know of it?'

'I think I have heard....' The silver dish clattered to the floor and Peter's face was as red as his napkin. 'Are you alright dear?'

'Yes,' he snapped. 'Is that correct? That garden centre is doing your vegetables?'

'Our légumes spécialisés are from there, yes Monsieur. People have been most complimentary.'

'Have they indeed?' *Right, I'll soon put paid to that, they won't be supplying you for much longer.* He'd have to get onto that first thing in the morning. Martin wouldn't go back there, not after the wasps, he'd have to do it himself. He could take Natalie, she could chat away to whoever was there while he sussed the place out properly. What would it take, weed killer? Or some other sort of chemical, they wouldn't be special then, would they?

'You're smiling, you must have enjoyed it?' *or perhaps you've got wind?* Natalie thought wickedly.

'It was alright I suppose. A lot of money for fancy named food. We best get home, I'm taking you out in the morning and we should have a bit of birthday bedtime.'

Oh no, I'll give him a large brandy and hopefully, he'll fall asleep.

* * *

Robert was nodding off in front of the television. It had been a busy day at work and he'd also fitted in a visit to Szarlota. Her children had been at an activities day, so it was a bonus as he'd expected a quiet Easter holiday as far as *his* activities were concerned. She had, as usual, worn him out, the woman was insatiable.

'Robert! What are you grinning about? This is serious, for my business, so make it yours.'

'Eh, what, sorry, you were saying?'

'I was *saying*, that my accounts haven't been balancing for months. I know I'm not an accountant, but I've gone over and over it. There're small amounts of money missing most weeks that I can't find anywhere and my stock samples don't add up either. This has never happened before in all the time I've been a manager and I may lose the franchise.' She was almost in tears.

Robert immediately felt very guilty. 'Let me have a look at it, Corrine, you go and pour us a glass of wine, it can't be that bad.'

Four hours later, he had to admit that it *was* that bad. 'The only thing I can put it down to is, that somebody's pilfering. It hasn't been noticed because the till deficit has appeared recently. You said the tips had been lower a while back, didn't you?'

'All the girls were complaining, so I had a locked box for them, which I open at the end of the week and share out. That was about the same time as the till started to not balance. I think you're right Robert. How awful though, one of my girls must be doing it, and taking the stock. I always let them have samples, but these are large numbers of lipsticks and skin care samples that have disappeared.'

'Who's the newest person there?'

'Megan, but I can't accuse her. She's always so helpful and just because she's the last in, it doesn't follow that she's a thief. Maybe one of the others is struggling for money.'

'I'll get our security chappie to fit up a small camera that looks at the till drawer. You'll soon have proof of who it is.'

'Is that allowed?'

'It doesn't matter if it catches a thief? And you're not spying on their work or private time. Once they're confronted, they won't be crying *unfair* anyway.'

'Oh Robert, you can be so wonderful sometimes.'

He felt very uncomfortable.

* * *

Merry was pleased to see that Murdoch and Lily had obviously got on well on their day out. The two heads were together, bent over the laptop, making notes, discussing ferns and mosses and other shade-loving plants. They were also planning which day next week they could return to the manor. Smiling, she made coffee and then stepped outside to see two people. One, she recognised from the golf club and the building site, a person that needed to be watched.

The woman he was with, seemed genuinely interested in the plants, while he wandered around as if looking for something specific. She followed him without being noticed, down towards the vegetable area. The section that Murdoch had cultivated was fenced off from the public walkways, but he was paying it particular attention.

Peter studied the vegetables without much interest, he wanted to know how he could get to them. No lock on the gate, so that was easy enough, but even though it was quiet, he couldn't risk being seen. He still wasn't sure of the best way to go about ruining the produce, poisoning the soil could take a while and if the restaurant were depending on daily deliveries, something more instantaneous might be beneficial. Along the side of the plot was a hedge and grass verge backing out onto the lane. He could feed something through from outside, bleach, through a hosepipe maybe, or even diesel from his vehicle, yes that was it. He could drive down in the night and do that himself. He turned to see an orange haired woman right behind him.

'Can I help you?' she said, looking most *un*helpful.

'No,' he said crossly. 'I'm just here with my wife, over there, she's the one who's buying.'

'Interested in vegetables, are you?' Merry was picturing him with a turnip as a head and it was very tempting, but that was a step too far, much as it would have been satisfying.

'Not really, no. Excuse me, I'll join my wife.'

Natalie had already picked out a rose bush and because Merry had followed him up the path, he hurried his wife out and paid for it, gritting his teeth.

'A nice choice,' said the elderly lady behind the till. 'It has a lovely scent.'

'This is much nicer for plants than that big new place, a very old-fashioned cottage garden appeal about it. Don't you think so, Peter?'

'If you say so, I wouldn't know. Hurry up, I need to get diesel on the way home.'

Natalie smiled apologetically at Mrs Overidge, who looked at her sympathetically as she passed over the change.

Peter was aware of the strange orange-haired woman who was, as he saw it, glaring at him. She quite unnerved him, but he didn't know why. He listened to Natalie all the way home, saying what a nice place that was and a shame they didn't have more time to look around. Filling the car up to the brim with diesel, he knew he had some old hosepipe at home and he began to feel better.

* * *

Megan was not very happy. She noticed Murdoch, most days, going to work and studiously ignored him. Her plan had been to let him stew for a while and then allow him to crawl back to her. That hadn't happened and when she saw him with that *ridiculous* creature in the burger bar, she'd flipped. Thinking back, they hadn't appeared all lovey-dovey, so perhaps she *was* just a friend. It was too late to do anything, now she'd blurted out about the abortion. Ryan had also been very suspicious and she wished he hadn't heard it. He was sure something had happened between them and kept pestering her about it.

Work also was a problem. Mrs Overidge had taken to locking the samples away and had introduced a new tin for the tips, which was also locked and shared out at the end of the week. A bit of till dipping had to be done, but it was risky. She'd got used to the bit of extra money every week and was missing it. Looking around for something else had been a waste of time, salon work in the town was limited and she was far too lazy to set up a mobile business and she couldn't drive anyway, another thing Murdoch could have helped her with.

She noticed Brian Lawton weaving his way home, drunk again! 'Evening Mr Lawton.'

'Eh? It's Megan ain't it? Not seen you around for a while.'

'No. Murdoch and I split. Is he with anyone else now?'

'Split? That's a shame, no, I don't think so. A girl like you could have anyone though I reckon, he didn't know when he was onto a good thing.'

'Obviously not. Oh well.' She was seething. Having messed up by confronting him, she'd lost him. Well, she'd show him what he was missing, tomorrow, she'd take a wedge from the till and buy an outfit that would knock him out. She would have to try and make it seem that someone else had done it.

* * *

Merry had flitted off in butterfly form to follow Peter. She watched him fill his car up with smelly diesel and when he got home, he put a length of hosepipe in the car boot. She overheard him telling the woman that he had to go out around midnight to check on one of his sites, he didn't trust the security guard, he said. Back at the centre before she was missed, she pottered about, still pleased to see the other two acting in a friendly fashion.

That night, she was waiting. Peter Simmons pulled up quietly by the hedge and turned his engine and lights off. Using a small torch, he threaded the hosepipe through the hedge, and then took another small piece of tubing, which he fed into where he had put the diesel. Merry watched, fascinated, as he sucked and quickly put the end into the hosepipe. She could smell the diesel going through the hose.

He never took any notice of the brightly coloured moth as if flew past him, over the hedge. As the diesel came out of the other end, it turned to water and so did what was in his tank. Finishing up, he retrieved the hose and tried to start his car. The engine turned over... and over... and over. Half an hour later he called his breakdown service.

Merry watched, with great amusement as they checked everything and then discovered his fuel tank was full of water.

'That's not possible, you idiot! I filled up this afternoon and I *drove here*. Explain that.'

'I can't sir, I'm just an idiot. You need the tank drained, shall I call a breakdown lorry or do you want to leave the vehicle here?'

Another hour and a breakdown lorry arrived, hauled his car up, and an irate Peter climbed in before it drove off.

'There, little veggies, you've had a nice drink tonight.' Merry smiled.

Chapter Seventeen

PROPAGATION

The breeding of a plant from the parent stock.

Elizabeth was delighted to see Lily and Murdoch again and walked down to the stumpery area with them. All the wood had been delivered and her gardener, Sid, was waiting with a small forklift to place the heavier tree roots where directed.

'I'll be doing the planting over the next few weeks, but Lily and I have selected and ordered everything we need. By the summer it will be something to look at, even if it's not fully established.' Murdoch showed her their final plans.

'It's perfect and I like the little pathways you've included and the seats. I'm sure it will be quite a talking point.' Elizabeth beamed. 'I was telling my friend Alex all about it and he's looking forward to seeing it. He's met you, Lily.'

'He has? I don't know an Alex…'

'Wavish, Alexander Wavish. He said you were most kind when he was choosing plants for his wife. She was very sick and sadly, she passed away, quite recently.'

'Oh yes, I remember. I'm so very sorry, he was such a nice man.'

'He is *still* a very nice man,' Elizabeth smiled. 'And he was interested in your idea and the fact that you both came up with it. When you've finished here, come up to the house. Mrs Conday has made some pasties, which I'm sure you can help us out with.'

By the time they had everything in place and were happy with it, they were both starving and made short work of the delicious pasties.

'I expect you've had those down in Cornwall, haven't you?' Elizabeth asked Lily.

'Yes, quite a few times, they were lovely on a cold day. I'm looking forward to proper Cornish ice cream when the weather gets warmer.'

'Hopefully, that will be soon. That's very sweet, your little charm necklace, most appropriate.'

'Oh, err yes, Murdoch actually gave me that for Christmas.'

'What a nice thought.' Elizabeth noticed with interest, that Lily looked quite shy and Murdoch slightly embarrassed by the reference to it. *So that's how it is then?*

* * *

Peter had taken to his bed for the last two days, thinking he was going mad or having some sort of breakdown. Natalie had listened to his story in total disbelief.

'But I saw you fill the tank on the way home, it must have a leak and the rain got in, or something.'

By that time, he was too exhausted to even argue with her. He was very overworked, that was the problem, a day or two's rest and he'd be back to normal. He couldn't understand why everything seemed to be going wrong at the moment.

Natalie wasn't worried, she watched what she wanted on the television and suggested he take a sleeping tablet to help him rest. She ordered a takeaway pizza, something he would never eat, unplugged the phone and switched off his mobile, so there were no disturbances.

* * *

Megan had slipped eighty-four pounds from the till over the last three days. On her day off she went shopping, splurging it all on a couple of dresses and a new pair of shoes.

That evening, Robert sat Corrine down in front of the laptop and whizzed through to the places he had marked on the camera's timeline. 'There you are, as plain as day. You can see quite clearly what she's doing.'

'That sneaky little bitch. How dare she think she can steal from me. I was always so nice to her as well.'

Robert rather doubted that but was in agreement with her sentiments. 'I'll put these sequences together and you can confront her. I think you should inform the police, it's not like she only did it the once.'

'I suppose so, but it seems harsh,'

'Harsh my arse, she's a thief! Do you want her to get another job somewhere and do it to somebody else?'

'Well, no. Let me challenge her first. Umm, do you think you could be there as well?'

'Of course.' He puffed up with self-importance. 'I'll be with you before you close tomorrow, I've had to deal with things like this before. Don't forget to put all these ten-pound notes that I've marked, in the till.'

* * *

Lily said goodbye to Elizabeth and told her she couldn't wait until the end of May to see how it was all coming along. Murdoch had an open invitation to come and go as he wished to do whatever work was needed.

'I'm so envious that you'll be doing this now and I have to go back.'

'Yeah, but your course is important, isn't it?' Murdoch gave her a quick look as he drove. 'And you'll want to see your... friends.'

'Of course, but my heart's here and always will be. Roots, is my future.' She glanced at him, but his eyes were back on the road. 'Grandma and Grandad want to speak to me tonight, something very important they want to discuss before I go again.'

Where does Rupert fit in with all this, I wonder. 'Better get you back then. Err, will you be staying there late? Are you okay to get home?'

'Oh, I hadn't thought. I might stay. T-thanks, though, for the offer.'

'No worries.' *I'm just looking out for you, that's all.*

* * *

Megan was sweeping out the salon floor and planning how to let Murdoch see her in her new clothes. Mrs Overidge had been in a strange mood all day, very skittish and now she was looking out of the window every couple of minutes.

'Girls, you can go now, Megan, would you mind staying on a short while longer, I will need you in a moment.'

'Yes, Mrs Overidge.' *Hope this isn't going to take too long.*

'Oh good, here's my husband.'

Robert came in, looking very solemn and officious. 'Corrine, are we ready?' He set up the laptop beside the till and made sure the footage was ready.

'Megan, would you mind having a look at this?' Corrine's voice was a squeak, she didn't like confrontation and was glad of her husband's presence.

Look at what? Their sex video perhaps? She sniggered to herself as she walked over. The snigger was replaced with a feeling of dread as she saw film of the till. A few transactions with some of the other girls, followed by herself, putting in a twenty-pound note, offering change and then putting it in the tip box, in sight of the customer but not quite closing the drawer. A moment later, sliding the drawer open, her hand palming the same twenty-pound note and closing the drawer.

'There're more instances of it, what do you have to say for yourself, Miss?' Robert challenged.

'It's nothing, I was just rearranging and tidying the money that's all. It's not what it looks like.' Megan was flustered, she felt hot and knew her face was getting red. 'How could you accuse me of theft.' She burst into tears.

Corrine began to wobble but Robert stepped in firmly. 'It's perfectly clear if you're innocent, you won't mind showing us your purse, will you?'

'My purse?' she thought quickly, there was only the ten-pound note taken today, she didn't have a lot to show. 'I'll go and get it, then you'll see and I want an apology.'

'I'll come with you,' Robert marched her to the staff room where she retrieved her bag. Back at the counter, he asked her to tip all the contents out on the desk.

'You can't make me do that!'

'Shall I call the police and show them the evidence so far?'

'Oh, alright then, if it satisfies you.' Everything was dumped out in a flourish.

'One moment,' said Robert as he opened the till. 'Mrs Overidge stocked the till with specially marked ten-pound notes this morning, some will have gone as change of course and others would have come in, but she made sure the marked ones were always at the top. They have a little square with a cross inside in the top right-hand corner. Would you have any of those ten-pound notes, I wonder? I will give you the chance to admit it by telling you I have seen today's footage.' He was really enjoying himself, hating staff who took advantage like this little baggage had. 'Please open your purse and take any notes out.'

Megan felt sick. With a shaking hand, she removed two fives and three tens from her purse, for a moment her heart lifted, there was no mark to be seen. Then, Robert turned them over and there, on one, in the corner was the mark he had described.

'I don't think you have any excuses, do you? This was all filmed as well, by the way. Anything in the till area has been, for the last week. You got greedy, otherwise, you might have got away with it. I'm sure my wife will not require notice from you, you may leave immediately. This evidence will be passed to the police and we *will* be making a statement. Keys, please?'

Without a word, Megan stuffed everything back in her bag, except the keys and the offending banknote. Corrine wouldn't look at her, there was no support there. She'd blown it big time and would find it hard to get another job, even if she was in a position to and not banged up. Head bowed, and too proud to cry in front of them, she shuffled out of the door.

'Oh Robert, that was horrible, you were magnificent.' Corrine threw herself into his arms.

'There, there, it's all over, I suggest we get the locks changed immediately, just in case. I'll call someone now and then I'll take you out for supper.' He was feeling quite aroused by his helpless wife fawning over him and thinking he was the cat's whiskers. It was a long time since he'd felt so... manly, in her presence. 'I say, Corrine, I could call the locksmith a little later, why don't you show me one of your massage beds and offer me some, *extras?*' Winking, he patted her bottom, not as round and cushiony as Szarlota's, but familiar and one he was well acquainted with.

She giggled. 'What a naughty suggestion, come on then.' Locking and bolting the door, she switched off the reception lights.

* * *

Lily was speechless. 'You can't do something like that, this place *belongs* to you.'

'Yes, and when we're both gone it will belong to *you.* This will be less stressful at a difficult time. We've talked it over and it's the only solution. It would make sense if you actually made this your address, you half live here anyway and we'll be your tenants.' Grandad tried to reassure her.

Grandma took her hand. 'We'd worry all the time about how you would manage, my darling. This is the best way for everybody. It won't change anything, theoretically, you'll be responsible for the bills, but we'll sort that out between us, it won't affect our lives in any way. We don't want to leave you a poisoned chalice, what good would that be to anybody?'

'We both plan to live for quite a while yet,' Grandad said gruffly. He was now very aware of his condition and intended to keep himself in the best health possible. 'Tomorrow, we'll go to the solicitor's office and get everything signed, I want to get this done before you go away again.'

'What about Dad? I can't keep this a secret.'

'You don't have to tell him right away. You'll be gone for about six weeks. We'll tell him it was *our* decision and that'll give him time to calm down a bit.' At least, Stuart hoped that would be the case. 'We seem to have skipped a generation,' he said sadly. 'We like to think you're a cutting from *our* stock that we've propagated into a strong plant.' He smiled, knowing that she'd appreciate that explanation.

Lily was glad she'd already let her parents know she was staying over in the cottage that night as she didn't think she could face them.

In the morning, Stuart asked Merry if she would be alright with Mr Taylor for an hour as he wanted to borrow Murdoch.

'No problem, we'll be fine, take as long as you need.'

Stuart then went to Murdoch. 'Madge and I have to go to the solicitors with Lily and Duckie's not keen on me driving so, how would you feel about driving my car this morning for us? I know it's a bit different to your van.'

'When I was learning I drove almost everything except a tractor, I think I could cope.'

'Excellent, we'll leave in about twenty minutes then?'

Lily opened the door of the car. 'Oh, Murdoch, hello. Grandad, you're not driving?'

'I'm getting on a bit now love and my eyesight's not what it used to be. I wouldn't want to cause an accident when there's no need for me to drive. Murdoch here, makes a good chauffeur, don't you think?'

'He's a very good driver,' Lily smiled at him and wondered why he suddenly looked so grim-faced. His moods seemed to change with the wind.

Chauffeur, well, she'd know, swanning about in that Rolls. 'Where is it you want to go Stuart?'

'The main high street, if you don't mind waiting for about half an hour, I thought we could all have some breakfast together?' Stuart suggested.

'Well, I have had something, I can wander around for a bit?'

'Rubbish, a growing lad like yourself can manage a fry up, I'm sure. I've err, had my breakfast too, but I'll have something.' Fry ups were definitely off the menu for him now, but he didn't want Lily to suspect anything. He and Madge had also decided not to mention his condition this time around, she had enough to think about with this.

Murdoch met them afterwards, mildly curious about what they'd been doing and said he'd just have a coffee.

Stuart tutted. 'Don't be silly, it's my treat, have the works, you too Lily. Madge says you're too thin, like a dandelion seed, the wind would blow you away given half a chance.'

They went up to the buffet counter together. 'It does look rather nice,' she said. 'Can I talk to you, a bit later, in private?'

'If you want.' Realising he sounded a bit abrupt, he softened. 'Here, have a couple of hash browns.' He scooped them onto her plate along with sausages and bacon. 'Stuart's right, you need fattening up.' He grinned.

'I do *not*, thank you, but I'll have some of those mushrooms please.'

Stuart had beans on toast and Madge had the same, with a few rashers of bacon. 'We don't eat as much as we used to, but I still enjoy my baking.'

'So do we.' Lily and Murdoch spoke as one, laughed and enjoyed their meal.

* * *

Merry was watering some of the young bedding plants when she saw a man she recognised from the golf centre. Lily's father.

He stared at the orange-haired apparition in front of him. 'I'm Mr Overidge's son, is he about? There's no-one at the cottage.'

They've gone out for the morning, I'm sorry, can I help?'

'No, you can't. What about my daughter?'

'She went as well; shall I tell them you called?'

'Blast,' he muttered. 'I'll come back later, I'm free today.' He stared at her again. 'Have we met?'

She stuck her hand out. 'Merry, Merry Faith Good, pleased to make your acquaintance.'

He looked dubiously at the earth-covered hand. 'Quite so. Tell them I called, I'll be back later.' *I'm sure I've seen her somewhere before.*

Merry chuckled as he walked away. If she still had the blue hair, he might have remembered, it was great fun changing it all the time.

Robert looked around the centre as he left. It was tidy and well-organised, it looked... prosperous. How very annoying, he'd wanted to have another go at his parents about selling. Time was pressing and the developers wouldn't wait forever. He wondered what had happened about the leisure centre that was supposed to have been built across the lane. Having seen that ridiculous news story about the tornado, he thought what a shame it hadn't flattened the garden centre as well. He only wanted the best for his parents, he told himself, it was in their interests and those of the family. They could move into one of those nice little assisted living apartments in town, much better for them and he wouldn't have to worry as they got older, in fact, he'd brought some brochures to show them. If Lily didn't have Roots at the back of her mind all the time, she might decide to go in a different direction and get this gardening craze out of her head completely.

Later, a cloud of colourful butterflies surrounded Merry as she worked. 'Don't lecture me, a little sprinkle of special dust will help these struggling seedlings. Where's the harm in that?' The said seedlings, which were much smaller than they should have been, shot up at least a centimetre and took on a much healthier and sturdy appearance. 'There, that's better and nothing too outrageous. They'll be proper little plants by the time the bedding rush starts. People are already coming to buy baskets and pick up leaflets for ideas. We'll start planting up our own baskets and tubs soon.'

'Who are you talking to Merry?'

She turned to see Murdoch's amused look. 'To the butterflies, one can have a very sensible conversation at times.'

'Well, they don't answer back, do they?'

'Not so as you'd notice. The Overidge's son was here looking for them. He's coming back later. I didn't like the look in his eye.'

'What sort of look?'

'Oh. You know.' She gave a vague wave. 'Anyway, they need to be warned.'

Again, he looked amused. 'I'll go and warn them then.'

'What does he want?' Madge demanded. 'He can't have got wind of what we were doing, surely?'

'No, but he's up to something, that's for sure. Lily, it might be better if you weren't around. Murdoch, you've got to deliver restaurant vegetables, haven't you? Fancy having an assistant for the day, you don't need to hurry back?' Stuart was delighted to have an opportunity to push them together again.

Murdoch wondered what they were so worried about and if it was what Lily had wanted to talk to him about. 'Yeah, sure. If it's alright, I've got my own stuff to deliver and sell which I was going to do later, but if you want her out of the way, I could do that. I'll make the time up.'

'You'll do no such thing. Keeping Lily out of the way for the moment is a good afternoon's work as far as we're concerned. Go on, the pair of you.'

'When you've done the restaurant, could we drive somewhere and just talk for a bit, I need to tell somebody or I'll burst.' Lily looked agitated as she asked.

Oh God, she's getting engaged. 'Are you sure I'm the person you want to talk to? Perhaps... Merry?'

'No, you'll understand better and you already know a bit about how things are fixed.'

She *is* getting engaged, he thought and wondered why his chest felt like it was filled with lead. He said nothing more until they got to the restaurant. 'The vegetables aren't needed first thing, as long as they have them by late morning, they're happy. They don't serve before one o'clock anyway.' He introduced Lily to the chef, she would be in charge one day, it made sense.

After they had left and were on route to the next stop, it was still on his mind. He definitely couldn't stay when that happened, she was constantly in his thoughts and what could he offer her, even if she was interested? Rupert, or some other boyfriend would always be on the scene. 'I really don't think I'm the person you need to talk to.'

'Please Murdoch. I can't talk to my parents yet, although Dad may have found out.'

Found out, wouldn't they be pleased? Christ, maybe she was pregnant? Megan hadn't talked to him, but Lily felt she could? 'I'll drive somewhere quiet.'

* * *

Robert came back, saw his parents and said he wanted to speak to them both. 'Look, I'll come straight to the point. I insist that you think seriously about selling this place. I'll do it all for you, you needn't worry about anything. I've brought you these to look at, a nice place for you as you get older. I'm not prepared to let Lily waste her life, thinking that she can run this place. It won't be up to her.'

Stuart struggled to keep calm, now was *not* the time to get stressed. 'I appreciate your concern Robert and don't worry, you'll be looked after when we're both gone. But the garden centre no longer belongs to us.'

'W-what! You've sold it, without consulting me?' He saw all his dreams turning to manure.

'Not sold it, no, we've given it away, to Lily. She is the owner now and there's a covenant which says it can't be sold for any other purpose than a garden centre for a minimum of twenty years after our death.'

Robert felt for a second that his *own* death was imminent. His face was the colour of a purple-dome Aster and his voice came out as a squeak. '*Lily!* Are you quite mad? You must be, how dare you do something like that behind my back. Well, it's not going to happen I tell you. You... you'll be hearing from my solicitor!' He stormed out in a rage and roared up the lane, tyres screeching.

'I need to sit down,' gasped Stuart. 'Don't panic, I'll be alright, it just upset me, that's all.'

Madge dabbed her eyes, 'Me too.'

* * *

'You *own* the garden centre, what you mean, actually *now?*' Murdoch was shocked but pleased she was neither pregnant or engaged.

'Yes legally, but nothing's going to change.' She explained the reasoning behind it. 'They don't want me to have to sell it.'

'I can see the logic, so why are you upset?'

'I'm not upset, *exactly,* but it's going to cause a lot of bad feeling and it'll upset Grandad and Grandma if Dad starts on at them.'

That gave Murdoch a bad feeling, it wouldn't be good for Stuart. Desperately wanting to tell her, he couldn't betray a confidence. If things did turn serious, he would reconsider.

'I'm sure they thought it through and have done the right thing. Will this change anything for you, course wise, I mean?'

'No, I'll finish it. The business side will be more relevant now and I couldn't run the place yet, even though I like to think I could and I-I'd really like your help as well.'

'You would?' *Oh Hell.*

'I can't imagine you not being there now.' *I don't want to do it without you.*

'Let's see what happens, shall we? I'm sure Stuart and Madge will be holding the reins for a while yet.' He spoke the words carefully, any doubts he had were kept hidden.

Chapter Eighteen

ENTANGLEMENT – MUEHLENBECKIA FLORULENTA

Commonly known as tangled lignum

Peter Simmons switched his phone on to see fifty-three missed calls and umpteen messages. The last five calls were that afternoon, from Robert Overidge with messages insisting Peter ring him immediately. To his annoyance, his wife Natalie, had gone out, leaving him to sort out something to eat and make his own coffee. When he began to feel human again, his mind cleared. There had just been a series of unfortunate events, things did not go smoothly all the time, he knew that from past experience, so why had he got so worked up about it? That was passed now, time to move on and he was going to sort that garden site out once and for all. He wondered what Overidge might have to say.

He soon found out, the man was apoplectic on the phone. Some story about his addled-brained parents signing it over to their granddaughter, his *own* daughter, going behind his back! When he found out the girl was only eighteen, Peter almost laughed. He'd make her an offer that she could only dream about. What young girl would turn down a money offer that he had in mind?

She'd have her very own money tree plant, he chuckled. He was on the phone with Martin immediately.

'I've got a job for you. What?... Yes, I know I haven't been available, never mind that now. I want you to find out everything you can about Overidge's daughter, Lily, I believe her name is. She's at that garden centre. It'll be worth your while, trust me.'

* * *

Lily knew she'd have to go home and face her parents and was dreading it.

'Well, I wondered when you'd show your face,' her father went on the attack immediately. 'So, what's the big plan then?'

'Nothing's going to change,' her heart was hammering but this is what her grandparents wanted. 'It's been done this way to make things easier and so that I don't have to sort it all out later. I can see you're upset, but you knew they always wanted me to have it, so what's the problem?'

'The problem?' he spluttered. 'The *problem* is, that you're saddled with a money-eating, failing site which *I* was negotiating a fine price for. A price that would do all of us well.'

'You were negotiating? It wasn't yours to do *anything* with. How could you?'

Corrine was standing in the background, wringing her hands and looking upset. 'I don't understand either. Does this mean we won't have our cruise?'

'Damn the cruise! That was just a small part of it. Well Lily, now that you're a big property owner, you can fund your own lifestyle and start by paying rent! I won't be made a mug of.'

Lily was pale and near tears. 'I'll move to the cottage, you won't have to support me anymore. I'm sorry Dad, that you feel like this, but I didn't ask for it. It's what they want and I shan't let them down, Roots is getting more and more custom, it *will* be a success.'

Packing her things and listening to her parents arguing downstairs, she texted Murdoch asking if he could do her a huge favour and pick her up with her belongings. *How am I going to manage the rest of my time at Eden without their help?* There was a serious chance she may have to give up the course. Silently, bags and boxes were carried down to the front door.

Her father, stony-faced, turned and went out into the garden. Her mother, looking puffy-eyed, gave her a hug. 'I don't really understand it all, but Lily, will you be alright? I mean in that tiny cottage?'

Mum, the cottage is lovely, that's not a problem, I don't like this horrible atmosphere with Dad.'

'But does it mean that you're going to spend your life messing around with plant pots and things?'

If Lily hadn't laughed, she would have cried. 'It's more involved than that, don't worry about me. Murdoch's here, that's his van. There's some stuff I'll come back for if that's okay?'

'I won't let your father throw anything out, trust me. He'll calm down, I'm sure it's all something of nothing.'

'Well I wouldn't say that, Mum, but thanks.'

Murdoch came up the pathway. 'Everything all right?' he asked, seeing her white face and red-rimmed eyes.

'Pretty horrible, I'm moving out. You obviously found the house okay?'

'Stuart explained where you lived. I'll give you a hand. *Jesus,* what have you got in here?' he lifted a box.

'A few books and all my drawing stuff.'

'A few books? If you say so.'

Lily didn't say she'd had to slide it down the stairs, one step at a time but watched as he hoisted it up and carried it, fairly effortlessly, to the van. She followed with a bag and noticed that he'd swept out the inside of his van and removed all his tools, laying a blanket down to protect her things. 'I really appreciate this, its very kind of you.'

'Don't be daft, it's nothing, let's get the rest of it.'

* * *

Brian Lawton was in trouble. Having removed one of the buried packages, he'd taken it where he'd been told and been given an envelope full of money. This, he was supposed to give to Harry in the morning. Stopping off at the pub for a few, he realised he was short of cash and meeting up with a group of acquaintances who were buying rounds, didn't help. He dipped into the envelope showing it off, to impress. They wouldn't miss a few notes, he told himself and if they did, he'd say it was an emergency and pay it back.

Several hours later, when he staggered home, the envelope had gone. Blearily, he remembered being jostled at the door when he was leaving, by a group of youngsters. Some thieving little turd had taken it. He started to sober up very quickly. Of course, he could be half honest and say he'd been mugged, but there wasn't a mark on him. What could he do? Murdoch was asleep and he'd be no help. The van! That was insured, wasn't it? People around the site always had the odd petrol can stashed away, if the van was torched, there would be insurance money. Brian could come clean then and promise to pay it back. His son wouldn't want to see his father beaten half to death which could happen, there had been a *lot* of money in that envelope. He went searching.

Murdoch heard crashing about and sighed. Dad was slipping back into his old ways and he didn't know what to do about it. Then, he realised his father had gone out again, what was he doing?

It was no good, he had to get up, so he dressed and lit the gas hob to boil water for coffee, which took ages on the small stove so, while waiting, he stepped outside to try and see his dad in the darkness.

Brian was in luck. Behind one of the houses was a plastic milk carton and it lay next to the petrol lawnmower. Sniffing, he affirmed the contents and then realised he had no matches so went back home, missing Murdoch who had gone in another direction but was now also on his way back.

Brian, who was still rather drunk swayed unsteadily on the steps. Pushing open the door, he lurched and tripped, the carton flew out of his hand, hitting the edge of the cooker which caused it to split and the petrol shot out, over the kettle and hob.

Murdoch was close when he saw the light as the door opened. *Thank God he's back again.* Then, a split second which forever ingrained itself in his memory. There was a tremendous roar, his father was silhouetted in a blinding light, followed by a terrified scream and flames shooting out of the door. Murdoch saw a figure, his father, falling down the steps in a ball of fire.

* * *

At six o'clock in the morning, the phone woke Lily. There was a message from Murdoch.

At hospital. Don't have anybody.

Dressing quickly, she tapped on her grandparent's door.

'Lily, what's the matter?' Madge was already awake, listening to the radio.

Murdoch's at the hospital, I don't know any details. I've got to go.'

'I'll drive you,' Grandad was getting out of bed.

'No, it's okay, there's a bus at the end of the lane, they run from six. I'll phone you when I know what's happened.'

'I hope he's not been in an accident. Anything we can do to help, we will. You tell him, Lily.' Grandma insisted.

On the bus, another message came.

Shdn't have txt u, was upset. Plz ignore.
2 L8 on my way

After some confusion at the desk, when no Murdoch Lawton was on the system, they said they had a Brian Lawton, was he a relative?

'Yes,' said Lily, afraid they may turn her away. 'Where is he please?' Upon being told he was in the burns unit, she rushed up two levels and spoke to a ward clerk, explaining that she'd had a call from Murdoch. Asked to wait, she sat nervously, not knowing what to expect.

He came through, a shadow of the Murdoch she knew. 'I'm sorry, you shouldn't be here, I messaged you in a panic.'

She jumped up, not noticing his hands were bandaged. 'I'm here now, what happened?'

'M-my dad, there was... a fire, it was awful, I-I couldn't...' He fell to his knees and she held him, horrified by what she'd heard. Stroking his hair, it wasn't until he put his hand over hers, that she realised what she was doing and saw his hands. 'Are *you* alright?'

'Some superficial burns where I tried to smother the flames. Thank God I had that blanket in the van, I'd dumped it on the grass and forget to put it away, it probably saved his life. Our home is gone, everything's gone. I've... got nothing.'

'Oh Murdoch, you've got all of us, you're not alone.'

'I'd put my jacket on so at least I've got my phone, wallet and van keys. I don't know what to do Lily, what am I supposed to do?'

'Well the first thing you're going to do is check your father and then, I'm taking you downstairs for coffee and something to eat.'

'I can't, he needs me.'

'Is he conscious and talking to you?'

'Well... no, but...'

'When he *does* need you, you'll be no good to him in this state. You need some sleep as well. I'll stay and if they call, I'll wake you. I'm also going to get you some fresh clothes, and I don't want to hear a word of argument.'

About to protest, he sagged and gave up. 'Are you this bossy with Rupert?'

'Why on earth would I be bossy with him?'

'Don't you tell your boyfriend what to do?'

'He's not my boyfriend.'

'He isn't?'

'No, what made you think that? He's a very good friend, that's all.'

'Just... a friend?'

'Mr Lawton, your father is awake.' A nurse interrupted them. 'He's very weak and finds it hard to speak, but he's asking for you.'

'I'm coming. Lily, will you wait for me?'

'I'm not going anywhere. I'll let my grandparents know what's happening.' She sank down onto the chair. What a terrible thing to have happened, she couldn't imagine how she'd feel if she lost her home and all her belongings. At the end of the day though, that's all they were, belongings. Mostly replaceable, people weren't. She was due back at Eden in two days and knew she couldn't leave Murdoch like this. She messaged Rupert, with a quick explanation and said she'd be at least a week late and would tell him everything later. A phone call to the cottage and Grandma said she'd sort out some clothes right away and get Merry to bring them over. He would come and stay with them, there was a small room he could have and they'd sort things out from there.

Madge soon had a bag of essentials, as she saw it. T-shirts, a couple of jumpers and some trousers that Stuart still had from his younger days. She stuck in a belt in case it was needed but Stuart had been trimmer back then. Some socks, a washbag with soap and a razor and a comb.

'Do you think that's alright Merry? I'd like to give him some money, but he's such a proud young man I don't want him to take it the wrong way.'

'I think that'll do him very nicely and if we can persuade him to come back here, there's time to sort it out.'

'I hope they had insurance,' Stuart muttered. 'He lived over in the Park homes you know. From the little he ever said, I think it was one of the older, very basic ones, not these plush things you see in the adverts.'

'If he does need money, we'll have to make it some sort of loan, he'll never accept it otherwise.' Madge was fretting. 'That poor lad, I just want to give him a hug.'

Hopefully, Lily was doing that, thought Merry. She'd known something was going to happen but again, couldn't interfere. She *could* make sure the clothes fitted him properly at least and a little shake of glitter in the bag sorted that out.

Madge had also packed some sandwiches, cakes, pork pies and flapjacks and provided some bottles of juice. 'Find out if there's anything we can do to help, Merry.'

'I will and I'll tell him I'm seeing to his patch and all the vegetable deliveries, he's not to worry about a thing.' *They'll never have seen veg like it.*

Murdoch sat by his father's side. The doctor explained that Mr Lawton was a very lucky man. Because of his son's prompt actions, the flames had been doused quickly, but there would still be scarring. There was no smoke inhalation which was positive and apart from a small area on one side of his face, the scarring would not be visible. He left them to talk.

'It was my fault, Murdoch I'm right sorry.' Brian groaned.

'Dad, don't talk, you're in pain.'

'Things I need... to say. Was there much damage?'

There was no point in lying, he'd know sooner or later. 'Everything's gone, we'll have to start again.'

'Everything?' Brian felt a glimmer of hope amongst the guilt.

'Yes, all I've got are the clothes on my back and the van of course. Nothing could be saved.'

'Oh yes, the van.' He closed his eyes. 'Don't go, I'm not sleeping.'

'We'll sort it out, *I'll* sort it out, you just concentrate on getting better.' Murdoch couldn't blame his Father, that wouldn't get them anywhere. Time for recriminations may come later.

'I'm going to be in here for a while yet, the doctor says. Listen, you need to go and see Harry. Tell him what happened and make sure you say *everything* was burnt, including the money.'

'What money?'

'He'll know, just tell him. Wait, there's something else. I'm a liability to you, I know that. Don't argue with me.' Brian tried to sit up and fell back, gasping in pain. 'Give me a minute.'

Murdoch wasn't *going* to argue, he made sure the oxygen mask was back in place and told his father to take his time, feeling desperately sorry for him.

Brian tried to grab his son's hand which was not easy, considering the thickness of dressings he had on his skin and pulled the mask off again. 'I've got no family, I was a traveller, you know that. That's where I belong, I've always been tangled up with them and when I'm better, I'm going back. I don't know how yet, but I will. Your mother, she came from around these parts. Ran away from home when she was about your age and changed her name I think. I met her a few years later and then we had you.'

'From around here?'

'That's what she told me. She lived up country for a while and when we settled here, she said no one would know her because she'd changed her hair and used a different name. She did love you, Son, in her way, but she was never really happy, not with me anyway.'

'Thanks... for telling me.'

'She taught you to speak well, and you haven't lost that, which is good. You make your own way now, without me to worry about.' He closed his eyes again and this time, he did sleep.

Lily was pleased to see Merry arrive with a bag and small picnic basket. 'You got here quickly.'

'Did I? That's good. There're some clothes for Murdoch and food for you both. You're to bring him back to the cottage when he's ready and that's an order tell him.'

'What's an order?' Murdoch stood there, his question directed at Merry, but his eyes on Lily. *Just a friend.*

'I'll let Lily explain, I need to get back and you're not to worry about a thing, it's all in hand.' She gave him a quick hug, leaving glitter all over his singed shirt. 'There's a shower room downstairs, you may want to use it, see you later.' She disappeared as quickly as she had arrived.

'How is he?' Lily asked, thinking Murdoch looked a little better.

'Not as bad as it could have been, but it'll take a while before he's up and about. He's in the best place here, that's for sure. What have you got there and what, was an order?'

'In a minute, eat this sandwich, I'll get a coffee from the machine, then do as she says and shower. I'm sure there's something in here that'll fit you. I'll wait outside in the garden area and then we'll eat some more and talk.'

'Yes. I want to... talk.'

* * *

Robert Overidge was sitting in his solicitor's office, already in a bad temper, having had to take the morning off work. Now, he was being told, there was nothing illegal in what his parents had done, Lily was an adult and unless it could be proved she had coerced them, or their minds were failing, there was really nothing he could do.

Were their minds failing, if so, how could he prove it? Deep down, he knew they were both as sharp as the knife in his toolbox, but he felt betrayed. The fact that *he* had been trying to sell their livelihood, passed him by. He left in a huff and phoned Peter Simmons again.

'Actually, Robert old chap, I don't think we can do any deal after all. It was a nice thought but I think it's time we went our separate ways.' Peter sounded very superior and not in the least regretful.

Robert was beyond furious. Everything he had planned; all the schemes and dreams, were gone. Szarlota was becoming a little demanding and expecting favours at work. She'd had the temerity to mention how, he mustn't upset his wife, and now he lived in fear that she might expose him in some way. No fool like an old fool was the saying. He wasn't *old,* but old enough to know better. Now he'd upset Lily as well and she would hate him. No, she wasn't capable of hating anybody, but there was bad blood between them now. Maybe if he let the dust settle, they could have a civil conversation and come to some sort of understanding.

* * *

'You look better, and the clothes fit okay.' Lily smiled as Murdoch came out into the garden.

'God, I feel better and I'm starving.'

'Here.' She passed over a plateful of food and a bottle of juice. 'Why did you think Rupert was my boyfriend?' She waited patiently while he ate and avoided her eyes.

'I saw him pick you up when I dropped you at Salisbury and you went skiing with him, what would anyone think?'

'Did that bother you?'

'It's your business who you go out with.'

'I love Rupert, but not like that. He's a very special person to me but he's more likely to ask you out, than me.'

'Ask *me.* You mean, he's...'

'Gay, yes. He's with Sam, that's a male Sam, by the way.'

'But he's got a Rolls Royce.'

'So? His parents are rich. That's not why he's my friend. You'd like him if you met him and I've talked to him about you as well.'

'What possible interest could I be to someone like that? And what have you said?'

'Someone like that? There you go, getting all anti when you don't even know him. You've been funny with me for months, was it because of him?' Lily was beginning to feel a bit squishy and warm inside. He was looking at her so... intently.

'*Funny* with you?'

'You'd be really nice sometimes and then you'd go all quiet or almost ignore me. What did I do wrong?'

'You didn't do anything wrong. I thought you were with someone else that's all.'

'And... you didn't want me to be?' She moved closer.

'No. I was with someone else then, but, I kept looking at you and thinking what it might be like.'

'I've thought that for ages. Ever since I broke my heel in fact.'

He was also moving closer, so close their faces were only inches apart and then suddenly he pulled away. 'I'll tell you something my Dad said to me. My mother, she left when I was eight, I told you that once? She was from around here apparently, she'd run away and went up North with travellers before she met my Dad. She changed her name though. I always wondered about her. Lily?' he said softly.

'Yes?'

'I'm sitting here in borrowed clothes, a few quid in my wallet, a crappy van and nowhere to live. I would like us to give things a go, but not like this. I've got nothing.'

'It doesn't matter.'

'It matters to me! I need to get on my feet before I do anything else and that's going to take time, I don't even know where I'm going to sleep tonight.'

'Well, that bit's easy. You're coming back to the cottage and *that* was the order. There's a room for you and my Grandparents won't hear of anything else, they're very fond of you.'

He groaned. 'But you'll be there as well. This is hard enough without you being under my nose *all* the time.'

'I'll be going back to Eden,' she said quietly. *If I know he's settled I can go back sooner.* 'I won't be around for five or six weeks and you've got the stumpery to do. Oh! Will you be able to do it with your hands like that?'

'Yeah, in about a week, I may have to wear gloves all the time for a bit, but I've got a very nice pair someone gave me for Christmas.'

She smiled. *What the Hell?* Leaning forward, she kissed him very gently and then moved back, to study his face. 'The green bits in your eyes are lovely, I can really see them up close like this.'

'It's no good, you being this close. Just this once and then I… can't.' He pulled her in and this time the kiss was longer, deeper and the glitter on his shirt swirled slightly in the spring breeze. 'I shan't come to you with nothing Lily, my life's just a tangled mess at the moment. I'm asking you to wait for me.'

'I'll wait,' she said, a little breathlessly.

Later, when they went for the bus together, something niggled at the back of her mind. Something about Murdoch's mother. Hadn't Grandma been going on about someone a while back, who ran away? She couldn't quite remember.

Chapter Nineteen

REPOTTING

Placing plants into a larger or smaller container
because they become pot or root-bound

Madge had made sure the room was all ready for their
guest and after a filling and tasty cottage pie, Murdoch
thanked her, then saying he was exhausted and if they
didn't mind, he needed to sleep. Merry had joined them
for the meal and glowed with pleasure, noticing the
glances going on between him and Lily. He had given
them all a brief explanation of what had happened,
saying it was a freak accident and that his father would
be alright at the end of the day. His protests about
staying in the cottage fell on deaf ears and he gave up
but was determined to make it up to them with work, if
they refused any payment. His hands were still sore and
he'd have to take a few days off, but he didn't take many
holidays, which would now be used to visit his dad.

Even though he was so tired, sleep eluded him for a
while as he thought about Lily, only a few doors away
and the kiss they'd shared earlier. She felt as if she'd
belonged in his arms, but he meant what he'd said, he
wouldn't go to her with nothing to his name. She now
owned the cottage that he was sleeping in, although, to
all intents and purposes, it was still Madge and Stuart's
domain. He could never be her equal, not in material
terms, so he had to offer something else. What that could
be, he wasn't quite sure yet.

The next morning, he insisted she go back to Eden assuring her he'd be alright. So, she called Roo and arranged the usual pick up, doing it all in front of Murdoch who looked a little sheepish, especially when he was given the message that Roo was very sorry to hear the news. Murdoch was pleased the guy hadn't come out with the usual platitudes of, anything he could do, please ask, because there was nothing *he* could do and most people said it without meaning it. Madge and Stuart were an exception, they were helping him in so many ways it was embarrassing.

Merry took him down to the patch with strict instructions that he was to touch nothing, but he could tell her what to do. Even with her special influence, she had been discreet and it didn't look too different, that would happen when she harvested the ones for delivery. He directed a few rows to be thinned and consulted the charts for sowing.

'All in hand,' she said. 'You mustn't fret about it at all.'

'At least I can supervise if nothing else. Can you help me check all the ferns and mosses for Foxmore?'

'Anything, just tell me what needs doing.'

Lily was having a last potter around the centre. She was more or less packed, now that Murdoch had insisted she go back. He'd also said he would drive her to Salisbury, his hands could cope with that. The subject of Murdoch's mother and what he'd been told, had temporarily been forgotten, she was more concerned with him.

There had been a letter for her on the mat which was hand-delivered during the night. One hundred pounds and a scribbled note. "*I won't have a daughter of mine short of money*". Lily decided to write her dad a letter once she was back in Cornwall.

She saw a man looking around and thought he'd taken a photo of her, but he seemed to be taking general pictures and studying the plants, so perhaps she was mistaken. 'Can I help you with anything?'

'Ah, you would be Lily, I think?'

'Yes, were you looking for me in particular?'

'I heard your name mentioned, err, by my neighbours who've been here. I didn't realise you were so young, I would have thought you were still at school?'

Martin was trying to look friendly and concerned, but with his wording, it made him come across in a rather unsavoury way. She backed off slightly.

Merry spotted and recognised him immediately. 'Murdoch, I think Lily might need some help. That man looks a bit odd.'

'What man?' he hurried off in her direction.

'I'm just wondering what a lovely young thing like yourself finds so appealing, grubbing around in the earth when you could be doing more, umm, ladylike things?' Martin stepped closer.

'Excuse me?' She was relieved when Murdoch appeared at her side and even more so when she felt his hand rest on the small of her back.

'Is there a problem here?' He glowered.

'No, not at all,' Martin spluttered. 'I was just saying, err, to this lovely lady how unusual this is as a career.'

'Is that right Lily?' Murdoch looked searchingly at her.

'Well, something like that. If you don't mind,' she said to Martin, 'I'll let this gentleman serve you.'

'I-I've seen what I need to, I'll be off.'

Murdoch was thinking he looked familiar and was sure he'd seen him before.

Merry wasn't going to let him get away with it so easily.

Having insect-proofed himself this time, Martin felt quite safe but as he left, he stepped on a rake, which pivoted upwards, smacking him right on the nose.

'Arggh, I've broken by dose!' he mumbled, 'I'll sue you.'

Stuart was coming down the path. 'What's the matter sir, are you alright?'

'Doe! I'm dot alright, look at by dose. It was da rake.'

'What rake? I don't see anything.'

'Right dere...' Martin pointed and then looked completely flabbergasted. There was nothing on the path at all. 'How did dis happen den?' he pointed angrily at his swelling nose, now an attractive shade of crimson.

'Maybe you burst a blood vessel?' Merry had also joined the group. 'Would you like me to put a bandage on it?'

'Doe! Don't touch me.' He'd had his phone all ready to take a photo of the rake and now there was nothing there. *I'll never set foot in this place again.* Marching up the path he kicked out at a watering can which promptly slipped onto his foot. Furious, he tried to shake it off and fell back into the raised bed of small gooseberry bushes. No leaves or fruit on them yet, but plenty of thorns.

Stuart and Murdoch, who were trying not to laugh, rushed to help him. Murdoch prised off the watering can while Stuart helped him up. Martin was squealing, his backside full of gooseberry thorns.

'Oh dear.' Merry said. 'What a very *unfortunate* man.'

Lily couldn't speak, she was doubled over. 'I thought I saw a rake as well,' she gasped. 'Can a nose just... explode like that?'

'It would appear so.'

Martin slapped Stuart's hand away as he was trying to brush off the thorns. Glitter danced in the sunlight and a few butterflies hovered in mid-air, enjoying the view. He hobbled out, once again cursing the place and Peter Simmons along with it. *I'm done with this.*

'Was he bothering you?' Murdoch asked Lily as he came back to her.

'He was a bit odd, saying how young I was and how strange it was I was working here. I didn't like him.'

'I don't think you'll be seeing him again. You all packed up for tomorrow?'

'Yes. I still don't think you should drive me.'

'I'll be fine and I want to see as much of you as possible. I'm going to visit my father now, we'll catch up later.' Nobody was around so he pulled her to him and kissed her. 'I'll be thinking about you all the time you're away.'

'Me too, thinking about *you* I mean. I hope your dad's doing okay.'

* * *

Corrine had popped into the supermarket on her way home. Robert wasn't in sight, but he wasn't generally on the shop floor, so she took her time in the aisles picking out things that were simple to cook, lots of ready-made sauces and casserole mixes she could stick in one pot and forget about. A nice selection of cheese, Robert did so love his cheese and perhaps a good bottle of wine. As she turned the corner onto the next aisle, she saw him with his back to her and just as she was about to call, a woman walked towards him. Corrine saw it was a member of staff, so not wanting to interrupt, looked at the shelves, choosing some cheesy biscuits.

When she glanced back, she noticed his hand on the woman's arm. Oh dear, was she upset about something? Two other members of staff pushed a trolley past her.

'He's at it again, can't keep his hands off his Polish princess.' The young man sniggered.

'It's disgusting,' retorted the young female operative, 'At his age, what a saddo.' They moved further up and started stacking the shelf, blocking Corrine's view.

She stood frozen to the spot in complete shock. Was it just store gossip or was it true? Hearing the clack of heels, she saw the object of Robert's attention walk, no, sashay, past her with a contented smile. Corrine felt like she'd been slapped in the face. Always having been proud of her figure, she now felt shapeless and unwomanly. But Robert had always said he loved her? How could he do this and, with a member of staff so that everybody knew and was gossiping about it? Leaving her trolley and her shopping, she walked out.

When Robert got home that evening, the house was in darkness. Wondering where Corrine was, he found a note propped up by the coffee machine.

I have gone away for a few days. When I come back I will have expected you to move out. Go to your 'Polish princess' as was described by your staff, when I overheard and saw you together, don't try any excuses.

Oh God, oh *God*. He broke out into a cold sweat. What had he done?

* * *

Murdoch drove carefully but steadily, pleased his hands were healing well. He didn't want to see Lily go but knew he'd have to encourage her to finish her course and she was now such a distraction when she was around. He'd only spent a couple of nights in the cottage and knowing she was so close, was the sweetest torture. Staying with her grandparents, it was the first time he'd really felt like part of a family, not being treated in any special way, he just fitted in. Madge and Stuart bickered and argued with each other in front of him, also being loving and affectionate with no self-consciousness. He felt humbled by how easily they'd accepted him, saying they enjoyed having him around and there was no rush at all for him to move out.

He owed them big time. He promised himself he would take no days off and as soon as he could work properly, he'd be up early and working until dark to make up for the hospital visiting time he was taking along with his bed and board. He also needed to go and see the Watkins, they had messaged him to find out the news and Jean said she had some things he was welcome to, for himself and clothes Ken had sorted for Brian. Some people were so kind, again, he felt humbled.

Lily had been quiet for a while, she too, knew how important her course was but in this seedling relationship, she felt every second together was precious, it needed care, bedding in and fertilising. Not literally she thought and giggled out loud.

'What's so funny?'

'Umm, nothing really, just thinking. Your hands okay?'

'Fine. We're here, I'll wait with you this time.'

'I'd like you to meet Roo.'

'You didn't tell him I thought you were a couple, did you?'

'He asked me if you thought that ages ago, oh, he's here.' She was a little disappointed, having hoped for some time to say a proper goodbye, but maybe it was for the best, as Murdoch didn't want to push things.

Seeing Rupert up close was disconcerting. He was tall, *very* good looking and getting out of a Rolls, thank God, he was gay, thought Murdoch. He'd have girls falling at his feet.

Roo and Lily hugged and then he looked Murdoch up and down. 'Well, heelloooo,' he said in an extremely camp voice.

Lily slapped him. 'Don't wind him up. Murdoch, meet Roo.'

They shook hands, carefully.

'Nice to meet you at long last.' Roo spoke in his normal way, 'I've heard a lot about you.'

'Likewise, but only recently.'

'How's your dad doing?'

'He'll get there, thanks for asking.' It was a little stilted, but Murdoch began to relax. The driver offered to take Lily's bags, but he carried them to the boot himself. 'Lily, I'd better get back.'

'Oh, umm, yes.'

'Come here.' Putting his arms around her, he kissed the top of her head. 'Look after yourself, message me when you get there.'

'I will and you look after *your*self.'

He watched as they drove away.

'He's nice,' Roo didn't mince his words.

'Yes, he is, he's not in the best place just at the moment, but he'll be okay.'

'It was probably quite traumatic, he seems to be coping well enough and you're happy about everything?'

'There's family fall out over the garden centre, I'll tell you on the way.'

* * *

Robert had called in sick for the first time in his memory. He lay in their bed, unshaven and having had a sleepless night. He looked miserably at the space where Corrine should be. What an utter and complete fool he'd been and how, if at all, could he put it right? He sent her a long message by email, hoping she would open it.

My dearest Corrine.

I cannot begin to say how sorry I am. I am not sure you would even believe me, but all I can say is, I am.

No excuses, I was the proverbial older man, flattered by a bit of attention, which went to my head. It has made me realise that I haven't flattered you for a long time and have slipped into the trap of a comfortable marriage, almost taken for granted.

Never think that I don't appreciate what I have now lost. I will see if I can stay with my parents for a while, but I beseech you to let us at least, talk this over. I don't want to throw away all we have had, or are yet to have, over my stupid mistake. I can only hope that you will, on reflection, feel the same.

I mean this sincerely, when I say, I am still your loving husband,

Robert.

In a nearby B&B, Corrine heard the ping on her phone indicating an email message. Seeing who it was from, she turned the phone off and tried again to get some sleep. Maybe later, if she felt strong enough, she *might* see what he had to say.

Robert had made himself a little more presentable and driven to Roots. Walking up the path to the cottage and changing direction, he walked around to the back. The garden was as he remembered with his, now replaced with Lily's, old rope swing on the oak tree. Also, the clump of bushes which had seemed so huge when he was a boy and where he had built dens and hidden from pirates or enemy soldiers. Butterflies were flitting from shrubs to spring blooms, their wings a myriad of colours in the light. It really had been a magical childhood, such happy, carefree days.

Madge stepped out with some washing and saw him. 'Robert? You look terrible, whatever's wrong?'

'Mother, I-I need a favour.' As he explained his fall from grace, Madge became furious.

'You great big fool! I'm not Corrine's biggest fan but you deserve everything you get.'

'You don't have to tell me. I'm well aware of what I've done. Lily's gone hasn't she, so might you have room for me?'

'You'll have to have the small room.'

'Why can't I have Lily's room?'

'Murdoch's going to use it while she's not here.'

'Who's *Murdoch* when he's at home?'

Madge sighed. '*If* you ever listened to what you were told, you'd know he's been working here for nearly a year. The poor lad's had a terrible family disaster and has nowhere to live. We're putting him up and he needs room to expand, so it's the small room for you or nothing.'

'Fine. I m-mean, thanks. It won't be for long I hope.'

While Robert went home to fetch some of his things, Madge quickly told the others what was happening. 'Merry, be a dear and help me move Murdoch's things into Lily's room. He won't be able to argue when it's all done and Robert doesn't deserve any favourable treatment.'

'I should say not,' Stuart said firmly. 'The man's an oaf, doesn't know what side his bread's buttered.'

Merry looked puzzled. 'Surely, he would see that, if it was upside-down, he'd just turn it over, wouldn't he?'

'Have you not heard that saying before? Really, you young people,' Madge tutted. 'I'll explain it while we re-arrange the rooms, come along.'

Merry tidied and dusted Lily's room, moving some of the soft toys to the window sill. Much as *she* liked them, Murdoch probably wouldn't appreciate these furry animals on his bed. His belongings at the moment were meagre and didn't take long to find a home for. She was frustrated that Lily hadn't remembered the story of the runaway, now it would be several more weeks before that could be sorted, or could it? Tidying one of the drawers she found Alexander Wavish's business card. Opening the window, she summoned one of the butterflies. 'I need you to take this to Cornwall and slip it inside one of Lily's books, can you do that? It will jog her memory.'

The creature trilled in excitement and taking the card, which changed to the size of a pin-head, she flew off.

Now to get this ridiculous building plan sorted. When she was finished, Merry asked if she could pop out for a short time.

* * *

Corrine had read the email several times. She was in no doubt whatsoever that he was sorry but could stew for a few days before she answered. Maybe, for old times' sake, she'd listen to what he had to say. For all his annoying habits, she missed him already but there would be no easy way back as she was *very* hurt and utterly humiliated. Lily had texted to say she was in Cornwall. Corrine thought there was no need to upset her daughter even further at the moment, so just texted back with a jolly message which in no way reflected her own state of mind.

* * *

Murdoch returned to the news that he'd been moved and Lily's father was staying for a short time.

'He's been putting it about and got caught, serve him right.' Stuart gave him the full story.

'He should have the bigger room,' said Murdoch. 'He's family, I should move out.'

'You'll do no such thing,' roared Stuart and had to sit down quickly. 'Now look what you've done, upsetting me like that. You'll stay put and I won't hear another word.'

Murdoch, knowing he was being manipulated, could do nothing. He re-assured Stuart that he wouldn't go anywhere but felt very awkward when introduced to Robert and said he'd leave them to eat their meal in peace. He'd have his a little later as he had a lot of work to catch up on.

Lily sent him a message late that night, saying they'd had a good trip down and was everything alright? Having been warned not to mention her dad, he just chatted about other stuff and how Madge had put him in her room while she was away. *Sharing my (ur) bed with these things!* Sending a photo of all her soft toys. To which she replied, *Lucky toys* and an emoji blowing a kiss, which made him glow inside.

Merry had flown to Peter Simmons house and had a good look through all the papers on his desk until she found what she wanted. Making sure the window was open so that they all flew across the room, some went outside and got stuck in bushes or wrapped around the garden furniture. A particular one was taken by an extremely strong gust, flying straight across town and tucking itself under a young spinach plant in Murdoch's garden, where he would find it in the morning.

* * *

After talking to Murdoch, Lily unpacked the rest of her things. As she pulled out her beloved sketchbook, now filled with designs, a card fell onto the floor. *Alexander Wavish, Barrister at law.* That was the man Grandma had told her the story of, about his daughter? And he was the friend of the Countess. She googled him and eventually found a reference to the story. Their daughter, Caroline who had run away and never been found. What was it Murdoch had said, the name on the birth certificate? She couldn't remember, it was Caroline, but a different surname. There was no way she would tell him yet, it might be nothing to do with him, but what if it was? She'd have to think about this and see what else she could find out. Maybe Roo could help? She drifted off to sleep thinking about Murdoch in the cottage, in her bed.

Chapter Twenty

SOWING SEEDS

Scatter for the purpose of growth
– ideas or plants

Up early, Murdoch wandered down to his beloved vegetable patch. It would be another day or two before he could do any serious work, but picking over it, he was surprised that every plant looked healthy, with none of the usual stragglers. Noticing some rubbish in amongst the spinach plants, he pulled away a sheet of paper and was about to ball it up for the bin when he saw the word, *Roots*. Maybe it needed to be kept? Taking it back up to the office come tea hut, he glanced at it and stopped in shock, reading more detail. Words swam in front of his eyes. Buying the Centre and cottage… houses… gated development… old folks… cut out Robert Overidge.

Cut out Robert Overidge? Was he trying to sell this place, if so, how could he do that? Had Stuart and Madge actually *seen* this? Or should he speak to Lily first? No, he shouldn't give her more to worry about, he had to make a decision as to what to do, it was very difficult with Robert actually staying here as well. Luckily, he had gone to work, one day off was enough for him while he waited to hear from Corrine. Murdoch found his employers finishing breakfast.

'Murdoch, sit yourself down and have some tea.' Madge poured him a cup.

'I need to speak to both of you. You may already know about this, but I found it in the garden.' Passing it over, he sipped his tea and wondered if he'd done the right thing, Stuart began to look agitated.

'I knew Robert wanted us to sell it, he said that on more than one occasion, but *this*... it more or less indicates he was in cahoots with these people and in line for a nice payout, thank you very much.' Stuart angrily stirred his tea, slopping it over the table.

'They wanted to cut him out, do you think it was anything to do with the leisure centre people? They did seem to make our lives very difficult.' Madge looked upset as well.

'Well if it was, they got their comeuppance, *their* lives became a disaster.' Stuart chuckled and began to relax. 'It's Lily's now anyway and we've put a covenant on it so that it can only be sold as a gardening site, they won't know about that of course.'

'It's very strange how this *particular* piece of paper ended up here of all places. In fact, quite a few strange things have happened lately.' Murdoch said thoughtfully. 'That man, the one with the rake, I could have sworn I saw it happen and there have been other things.'

'Maybe we've got a guardian angel looking out for us?' Madge smiled. 'Things always happen for a reason. If it was brought here on the wind, the wind knew which way to blow.'

'Don't be daft Duckie,' Stuart chuckled and added, for Murdoch's benefit, 'she's always been fanciful. We'll have to speak to Robert tonight, find out who he was dealing with and let them know we're onto them. That son of mine is a sad disappointment at times.'

'Don't be too hard on him,' Madge laid her hand over his. 'He's going through a bad time at the moment. Lily is the future of this place and it's safe in *her* hands now. Murdoch, where did you find this?'

'In my vegetable garden, wrapped around a spinach plant.'

'You were *meant* to find it, that's just what I was talking about. Anywhere else and it might have been missed.' Madge looked very pleased with herself. 'No need to bother Lily with any of this.'

'I know,' Murdoch smiled.

Merry arrived as they were coming out of the cottage and after wishing them a cheery, 'Good morning,' hummed happily to herself as she started the watering.

'Merry, was it windy last night?' Murdoch blocked her path. 'Another mini-tornado possibly?'

'Nothing like that, I did feel a few gusts though, why do you ask?'

'There are a lot of things I don't understand, things happening that aren't...'

'Aren't what?' Merry fluffed up her now, pale-gold hair with blue sparkles.

'I don't know, weird things, like the tornado and the rake and...' he had a vague recollection of some rats when he was in shock from Megan's abortion announcement. '*Dammit,* they're just strange. Anyway, in the real world can we sort the restaurant delivery?'

'Absolutely, you direct and I'll pick.'

There's something about her I don't understand. Frustrated, he followed her down the path.

When they had a boxful that met Murdoch's exacting requirements, he said he could take it himself.

'If you insist,' Merry handed it to him shaking a little glitter onto the slightly, too small, asparagus spears.

'I want to stay out of the way tonight when Lily's father gets back, Stuart and Madge want to talk to him.'

'That man, he does not know which side of the bread to put his butter on.'

'What? Oh, never mind, if you fancy a pizza or something, we could go into town?'

'That would be most acceptable, you deserve a treat.'

'It's *my* treat, I may have nothing, but I still have some pride, okay?'

'Indeed, your treat.' She smiled.

* * *

Lily had told Roo as much of the story that Murdoch had recounted to her and then, told him about Mr Wavish and what Grandma had said.

'Wouldn't that be a fairy tale ending if it turned out to be his family?' Roo said thoughtfully. 'Let's get on the case, Watson.'

'Why do I have to be Watson? I can be Sherlock Holmes.'

'Don't be silly, a deerstalker hat would *so* suit me. We'll start tonight after tea, you may come to my room.' He grinned.

'Only because you've got a better computer.'

That evening they began the search by putting in Alexander's name. It was surprisingly easy, coming up right away with his law credentials and showing he had covered some high-profile cases. There was a picture of him which had been taken a few years ago.'

'Does it look like Murdoch? I only met him quickly, I can't tell.' Roo asked her.

'It doesn't jump out at me, his hair's greying so I can't even tell if that's the same. Maybe, the jawline? Or is it just wishful thinking? Does it mention his wife? I can't remember her name, maybe Murdoch looks like *her*, she died early this year, I think it was. Of course, he could look like his dad, I've never seen him so I don't know.'

Roo continued scrolling, 'Can't find the wife at the moment, but there's a story here with the name, a missing girl, let's see.'

There it was, some of which Lily had already seen. Local coverage and nothing really made of it because she was eighteen and had left a note. Caroline Wavish, her parents were pleading for information as to her whereabouts. There was some speculation that she had gone travelling, as she had disappeared at the same time as a group that had been camping on some nearby waste ground.

'Oh, that's her name, Rosemary, I remember now. Doesn't she look sad?' Lily peered at the grainy newspaper photo.

'They both do, wouldn't you, in those circumstances? You said Wavish wasn't his mother's name on the birth certificate?'

'No, it was C-Carruthers, yes, I'm sure that's what he said.'

'Look, I can't promise it'll help, but I'll send all this info to Dad. He might know people who can do some digging, you know what reporters can be like.'

'I shan't say anything, it may all come to nothing and he may not like me poking around like this. If it did turn out to be them, he'd be pleased, wouldn't he?'

'You understand him better than I do Lily. If it was me, I'd want the truth. I might be a bit put out that you'd done it without telling me, but as you say, if it comes to nothing and he doesn't know, then there's no harm done.'

'Thank you Roo, you're a marvel, you know that?'

'What would you do without me?' he grinned again. 'How do you fancy making two hot chocolates, while I do this email?'

'With marshmallows?'
'Is there any other way?'

* * *

Robert had received a terse reply from Corrine saying that she was returning to the house seeing as he was not there but, he could come around tomorrow evening as they obviously had things to sort out, she would set aside an hour. *An hour!* At least she was going to speak to him, but it was a frosty invitation. He had cooled towards Szarlota and had not allowed her to change her day off the next week. The rota had been done, he said and also, he didn't think they should continue their liaison, as nice as it had been. Her eyes had narrowed and before she could say anything, he informed her that his wife already knew what had gone on and it would not be in her best interests to stir things up any further. He busied himself with his paperwork before she turned, presumably swearing at him in Polish, and slammed the door.

He prayed the number of nights in the small room at the cottage would be numbered as he went back there for tea. Once inside, he was met by his grim-faced parents sitting at the table, with some paperwork in front of them.

'Sit down Robert,' his father said. 'We need to have a chat.'

He paled as he scanned the paper in front of him. 'Where did this come from?' he blustered.

'It doesn't matter where it came from.' Stuart banged his fist on the table. 'You wanted us to sell, you made that very clear several times but, how do you explain your involvement with these people and a house that you wanted? What gave you the right to try and do such a thing?'

'I-I was only trying to look out for the family, now they want to cut me out of the deal!'

'I think you're missing the point. As I said, what right did you have anyway and I'm glad they've double-crossed you, serves you right. I want to know who it is and you had better tell us.' Stuart felt a pain in his chest. *Calm down.* He took some deep breaths and regretfully, in front of his son, reached for his angina spray.

'Dad, what is it?'

'Now look what you've done,' Madge shouted. 'Are you trying to kill your father? He's got angina, he didn't want you to know and you're *not* to tell Lily while she's doing her course.'

'I d-didn't mean... Dad, I'm sorry, I'm so sorry.' Robert was in shock. He never meant for anything like this to happen. 'Do you need to go to the hospital?'

'No, I'm alright now, I didn't want anybody in the family worrying about me. Let's all start again and talk this over calmly. Roots is not for sale.'

Robert slumped in the chair. 'No, I accept that and please, forgive me. My greed got the better of me, family comes first, I've learnt that to my cost and now I've lost all of them.'

'You haven't lost us, Robert, you're our son.' Madge said quietly. 'What you've lost, is your way, and you need to find it again.'

'The developer is Peter Simmons, but you're not going to speak to him, Father, not in your condition. *I* will do it. I have to put this right.'

'Only if you take young Murdoch along with you. He's the one who found this piece of paper and gave it to us. He'll be back up for you and, I think you ought to get to know him a bit better.' Stuart said firmly.

'What, why? It's not his business.'

'Lily's his business and that's all you need to know. He's the manager here now until she's back and decides how she wants things to be done. You have to accept he's probably going to be an important part of her life. He may not have much but, he has integrity.' Father and son stared at each other and the son was the one who looked away, shame-faced.

'As you wish. It might help me build bridges with her I suppose.'

* * *

Peter Simmons sat with a large glass of brandy and a snapped pen which he had broken earlier when confronted by Martin. The man had ranted and raved and washed his hands of the garden centre development, the place had a curse on it, he'd said. His nose was the victim this time, practically broken by a non-existent rake, then he'd babbled on about a watering can and his arse full of thorns! Good riddance to him, the man was a liability and a walking disaster. "*Find out about Lily*", that had been the directive, but no, the fool had blundered in and ruined everything, leaving Peter with the problem. Not only that, his office at home had been a complete mess with half of his papers strewn around the garden. He gulped his brandy and felt his neck swell alarmingly, what was the matter with his throat?

His secretary buzzed him, 'Mr Simmons, there are two gentlemen to see you, a Mr Overidge and a Mr Lawton.'

Overidge? What did he want, he'd already been dismissed from Peter's mind and who was this other one? Perhaps, he just may have some positive news. 'Very well, give me five minutes and I'll see them.' Stepping into his office shower room, he looked in the mirror and staring back at him was a frog-like face! He shut his eyes, shook his head and looked again. No, it was a figment of his imagination, it was his own face, too much brandy, that was it. Good God! That had been unreal. It must have been that nature programme Natalie had been watching last night. Thousands of frogs all croaking and she kept looking at him and laughing. The woman irritated him beyond measure at times.

Composed and sat at his desk, he waited. Robert and some... boy were shown in. A butterfly had obviously come through the open window and was trapped in the room but it settled quietly so he'd sort that out after they'd gone. 'Overidge, good to see you and err... Mr Lawton was it? Sit down, what can I do for you?'

Robert silently pushed the piece of paper across the table. He'd been quietly impressed by how Murdoch had conducted himself in the short time he'd known him. He was polite and apart from wearing some rather odd combinations of clothing, which had been explained, he was an improvement on some of the young people that came into the store. He noticed him watching Peter Simmons carefully.

'Where the devil did you find this rubbish?' Peter's face was a mottled green and his eyes started to bulge.

'Rather strangely, it appeared in my vegetable patch yesterday morning,' said Murdoch. 'It made for interesting reading.'

'It's nothing, just some rambling notes.'

'Very particular notes,' Robert glared at him. 'Two old fogeys, I think the description was. A *common* supermarket manager with ideas above his station and obviously, once the idea had been put to you, you pushed me aside to try and get it yourself. Well, that's not going to happen. My daughter isn't selling and it now has a twenty-year covenant on it.' The way Robert puffed himself up, one would have thought it was all *his* idea.

'You jumped up shop-worker, it was all your idea in the first place, how dare you come in here accusing me?'

Peter's fist was stopped by an iron hand belong to Murdoch.

'I don't think that's a good idea, do you?' he said quietly and wondered how he suddenly seemed much stronger than he thought he was and where had that butterfly come from? He was vaguely aware of pale gold wings and glittery blue spots.

Peter's voice was a croak. 'Your silly little garden centre can go to hell and you with it!' He tore the paper into pieces and threw it on the floor.

'That was a copy,' said Murdoch. 'The local paper might find it all very interesting, when's your next planning application going in?'

Robert looked approvingly at him, the boy, as he thought of him, had plenty between his ears.

Peter was incensed. 'You little upstart,' then, remembering how immovable the hand had been, took a step back. Furiously, he scrabbled in his drawer, pulling out a chequebook. 'How much is it going to cost me to get rid of you?'

For a minute or two, Robert was sorely tempted and then remembered he was trying to be a better person. 'What do you think Murdoch?'

The butterfly danced around his head. 'I think... you sort out the road that you left in a mess, I know it was you so don't come any crap and, as a concerned citizen, you offer to refurbish the old Park Homes on the edge of town which are a fire hazard.'

'Yours has to be rebuilt,' Robert pointed out.

'I don't want anything for myself.'

'*I* insist on your behalf.' Robert smirked at Peter.

The man felt ill, in fact, his face was now an even more vivid green colour. 'That's going to cost a fortune.' The croak was getting worse and he heard a faint sound of laughter which Robert was unaware of, but Murdoch looked around to see where it was coming from.

'Think of the publicity you'll get from *that,* you should count yourself lucky. Come on Murdoch, there's a nasty smell in this room, we'll say goodbye, Peter.'

The secretary, when she came back in, was very concerned. Her employer was a sickly colour, with his eyes bulging and his throat looking as if he had a tennis ball lodged in it. Quickly getting him a glass of water, she threw the window wide open for more air and the butterfly flew out. He waved the woman away, and said, in a croaky voice, he would be alright in a while and didn't want to be disturbed. When he was on his own, he sat in a daze wondering how his life had come to this and knowing they had him by the balls, although at that moment, he didn't feel as if he had any.

* * *

That evening, Robert presented himself at the house. No flowers, or wine and definitely no chocolate. Just him and his apologies and his request for forgiveness.

Corrine let him in, said nothing and let him follow her to the dining room where she sat, forcing him to take the opposite chair with the table between them.

'Corrine, I...'

'You hurt me very much you know. Hurt and humiliated me. To hear it like that, from the mouths of your staff.'

He flushed with shame. 'It was unforgivable, I am so sorry.'

'I'm sure you are. Why wasn't I enough for you? You always indicated that you loved me.'

'I did, I *do,* truly Corrine, I was a fool, a silly old fool. I would spend the rest of my life making it up to you if you could find a way to try and make it work again. Please…'

'I've been thinking. I don't really want to start again, at forty-one. But things will change here.'

Robert saw a glimmer of light in the darkness. 'Anything, I'll do anything.'

'If, *if* you move back in, it will be to the spare room, for however long it takes for us to be a couple again. You will make it up with Lily and admit to her what you did. You will change your job even if it means a pay-cut. Those are my terms.'

'Ch-change my job?'

'If your job's more important than me?'

'No, it-it's not that. I have to give three months' notice and find another one, they don't grow on trees you know.'

'That's fine, you can go off with stress, tell the doctor what's happened. You're threatened with divorce, no wonder you're stressed. Take it or leave it.' She was being hard but inside she was falling apart. She did love Robert and didn't want to lose him, but this would be his only chance. If it *ever* happened again there would not be another.

'I agree, to everything. May I… may I please move back in?'

'Tomorrow and then we'll lay down an agreement about meals and more housework sharing.'

'Of course.' Robert gulped.

* * *

Three weeks passed before Roo had anything to tell Lily. 'Listen to this, Alexander Wavish married Rosemary Carruthers, that was her maiden name. Caroline obviously used that and that's not all, a Caroline Wavish was on a flight to Cyprus with a man almost a year ago.

They were upgraded because they were flying out to get married. She must have taken her original passport when she left home, she may still be there?'

'Oh my God, that's fantastic. The man *has* to be Murdoch's Grandfather. I still don't know what to do though, should I tell him?'

'I have a better idea, where's his card. This is what you should do.'

Alexander answered the phone. 'Alexander Wavish speaking.'

'Mr Wavish, my name is Lily Overidge. We met at Roots garden centre?'

'Lily, I remember. My friend Elizabeth, Lady Foxmore told me you're helping her with a project. How are you?'

'I'm very well thank you. Lady Foxmore told us about your wife. I'm so very sorry.'

'Thank you,' he said quietly. 'It was not unexpected as you probably realised. You said... us?'

'That's what I need to talk to you about, but I'd like to do it in person. I'm down in Cornwall at the moment but I'll be coming back for a week at the end of the month. Would it be possible for me to come and see you?'

'Of course, is it a legal problem I can help you with?'

'Not exactly, I'd rather not say over the phone. Can I see you at your office?'

'I'm most intrigued, Lily, certainly. Ring me nearer the time and we'll arrange it.'

'Thank you, Mr Wavish. You won't regret it I'm sure.'

She put the phone down and smiled at Roo.

Chapter Twenty-One

GRAFTING

*Two plants combined to give the best
qualities of both*

The stumpery was coming on well. Now that Murdoch's hands had healed he was able to get on with it and his collection of ferns and mosses had been planted in crevices and grafted onto the surfaces of the tree stumps, odd bits of interesting wood and Lily's prized piece of driftwood. The rustic seats had been delivered and placed and by the summer it would look a little more established but would take a few years to bask in its full glory. He'd constantly taken photos to send and told her about it in their chats every few days. During the last one, he sensed something on her mind and had asked what it was. The course was getting a bit intense, she said and was working hard, studying plant use in landscape. One night, on facetime, she was quite upset and he could see she'd been crying. She told him that her father had phoned and explained the situation and that he and her mother were trying to sort it out and he hoped they would get there, but it would take a while.

'Actually Lily, I'm really sorry, but I knew.'

'You *knew*? You should have told me.'

'He stayed here at the cottage, for a couple of nights. He and your Grandparents didn't want you upset. It put me in a difficult position.'

She sighed. 'I *do* get that, but there shouldn't be secrets between us.'

He saw her flush red and turn away from the camera slightly. 'Lily? What aren't you telling me?'

'I-I may have a surprise for you but I don't want to spoil it.'

'A surprise? O... kay, it better be a nice one.'

'I hope it will be. How's everything else?'

He told her all about the piece of paper, she was furious with her father once again but laughed as he told her how the events unfolded. 'Your dad and I got on quite well that day, I haven't seen him since.'

'I spoke to Mum after and she said it's difficult, but hard to stop loving somebody. I don't think I could be so forgiving.'

His mind fleetingly went to Megan and how he'd felt at the time. 'You'd never have to forgive me,' he said so softly she hardly heard him.

It was the first time he'd indicated any sort of long-term relationship possibility and a rush of feelings came all at once, warmth, excitement and arousal amongst others. 'T-that's good to know.' *What a lame thing to say, that's good to know.*

It had given him a bit of a jolt as well, having envisaged them being together long term but, it was a nice jolt. All he had to do was to get back on his feet so he had something to offer.

Merry had carried on helping Murdoch with the vegetables and because he was often at the stumpery, he was grateful for the extra pair of hands. It was a beautiful May late Spring day and they ate the sandwiches that Madge had prepared, out in the sunshine. The lane had been re-tarmacked and the hedge thinned, so the road to the centre was more visible encouraging extra traffic with the new sign they'd had put up. More people were coming in and after discussions with Stuart and Madge, it was decided they could take on another member of staff. As Mr Taylor had finally retired, they took on another man, Reg, who loved gardening and had been out of work for a while. He was very pleased to have found something and worked well with the team. It also took pressure off Stuart which was a relief to everyone.

Murdoch offered Merry a ham sandwich and she looked horrified.

'Oh no, I don't eat any animal flesh, eggs, cheese and milk is okay, but no flesh, thank you.'

'Oh, sorry I forgot, I'll leave the cheese ones for you. Didn't you eat a burger when we went out?'

'A *veggie* burger. Madge knows, when she makes something with meat, she always does an alternative for me, have you never noticed I had a separate dish? My people have never eaten animals.'

'Your people?'

'I mean, my family.'

'Who exactly *are* your family, Merry? And you have an unusual name, Merry... what was it?'

'Merry Faith Good, what is strange about that?'

'I'm not quite sure, it's like it means something.'

'All names mean something, I'm a good person, that's what mine means. You think too much.'

'Do I? I think there's something... strange about you, I don't mean that to sound rude, but things have happened and I just sort of feel you have a connection to them. I sound daft, don't I?'

'Most assuredly. Come on, eat up, we've got a hanging basket class coming in this afternoon, remember?'

He groaned. The hanging basket tutorials had proved most popular and nearly everyone went away happy, with a basket or two to hang for the town competitions. 'Another of Lily's wonderful ideas which we have to put into operation.'

'That's what managers do, Murdoch.' Merry's tinkling laugh made him think again that there was something unusual about her.

* * *

The paper had run a front-page spread. *Local Developer to upgrade Park Homes*. There followed a piece about Simmons Developments, who, after hearing of a terrible fire, which had completely destroyed a home, offering to completely renovate and fire-proof all the original homes on the site. In addition to that, they would immediately replace the burnt out one. A picture of the Mayor shaking hands with Peter Simmons took up a lot of page space as well. Simmons had taken to wearing a cravat which looked quite out of place and rather affected. His wife had insisted on it when she saw his throat. A visit to the doctor had shown nothing wrong and it didn't appear to diminish his appetite. His voice had also become croaky and her remedy was, not to talk so much.

Inside, he was seething, but there was nothing he could do. However, he was very much in public favour and he saw no reason why his next projects, well away from that damned centre, would not get full approval. He spent every morning and evening gargling different concoctions trying to get rid of the blasted croak in his voice. The throat swelling was bad enough, but at least Natalie's suggestion kept it hidden. He did worry that it looked a little effeminate and yesterday, one of the builders on his site had *whistled* at him! Nobody pointed the finger, so he didn't know who the culprit was, another fact that annoyed him. It wasn't often people got the better of him and he didn't like it, it made him feel insignificant.

* * *

Robert loaded the washing machine and tried to remember the instructions. Everything at forty degrees was usually safe, that's what Corrine had said. It was also his turn for tea. After the first week, they started to sit at the table together for a meal. Conversation was non-existent or at best, stilted, but it was progress. He'd been told takeaways were not an option, he had to put some effort in. Ready meals seemed to be acceptable as long as he put a few lettuce leaves, a tomato and a few other bits in a dish to go with it. He'd been to see the doctor who had, as Corrine had predicted, signed him off. A quick shop this morning and a fish pie was in the microwave with the obligatory salad prepared. He had some wine chilling and if Corrine was a little less chilled than *that*, they may take a step forward.

Finding another job was not easy. He was over-qualified for many of them and surely even Corrine wouldn't want him to take a major decrease in salary. He had an interview lined up at an out of town Home Centre as a deputy manager. It was a bit of a drop in money and would mean an extra half hour commute each end of the day. Hopefully, she wouldn't mind that and would realise he was prepared to put himself out. He would mention the interview tonight which may also smooth the way a little.

Corrine was wavering. It was hard to relax around Robert, but she wanted to move on. Three weeks they had been in separate rooms and she couldn't sleep properly knowing there was a wall between them, mentally and physically. He *was* trying. He'd taken on his share of the chores without too much fuss, the only thing she'd seen him struggling with was the ironing and took pity on him after seeing him wrestle with a shirt for twenty minutes.

It still hurt, the memory of the curvaceous woman in the supermarket haunted her. Robert had been complimentary every day but did he mean it? She had to know that he still... wanted her. Putting on a dress, knowing it was one he liked, she wondered whether they would share a bottle of wine tonight?

* * *

Murdoch waited at the station for Lily. Roo wasn't bothering to come back this week, his partner Sam, was going to have a break in Cornwall, so she was catching the train, spending the night at the cottage, then she said she needed to catch up with her parents and her friend Amy, so would be gone for the day. He was working anyway, so as long as he saw her later, he didn't mind. Six weeks had seemed forever and he'd really missed her being around.

The train was pulling in. Lily was excited at the thought of seeing him and also, about her meeting with Mr Wavish. She *was* going to see her parents tomorrow and a quick check-in with Amy but her time was mostly going to be spent getting to the next town and meeting, possibly, Murdoch's Grandfather.

She stepped onto the platform and all his good intentions of not rushing things, disappeared as he pulled her into his arms. 'I missed you.'

'I missed you too,' she whispered and they both ignored the tutting of people pushing past in a hurry.

On the drive back, she told him she and her father had had a chat the night before. Her mother had said that things were settling down and she'd appreciate Lily's support and not condemnation of her father's behaviour. That was for the two of *them* to sort out. Robert had said they were stronger together and she also believed that so please, could Lily just treat them both as normal? 'Dad said as much when we talked last night, so I'm going around to see them, pick up a few of my bits and go back to the cottage. That's my home now.'

'Still mine as well, at the moment,' he said. 'My new residence won't be ready for a couple of weeks.'

'That was a fantastic gesture, whatever made them do that?'

'Don't know,' Murdoch brushed over the subject. 'Just good citizenship I suppose. At least Dad can stay there while he's convalescing.'

'He still wants to go off then?'

'He says so, but *I* said he needs time and *no* drinking.' Murdoch looked angry. 'Until he realises and accepts that he's got a problem, I don't know what to do.'

'Just be there for him, try and make him see.'

They had tea with Stuart and Madge and could hardly take their eyes off each other.

'It's a lovely evening, why don't you two go for a walk along the river, there are still some bluebells around and the wild garlic is in flower.' Madge suggested innocently.

'Sounds good to me,' Murdoch jumped up. Leave the dishes, I *mean* it, we'll do them when we get back.'

'Away with the pair of you, it's Lily's first night back.' Stuart grinned.

It *was* lovely on the path. The Spring rain had swollen the river and it swooped and tumbled over the rocks, the late sunshine reflecting on the surface like water diamonds. They walked hand in hand until there was a log where they could sit and watch.

'When I used to walk down here with Grandad, we sometimes saw a kingfisher. I wonder if there're any still around?'

'There are lots of butterflies, look at them out over the water.'

'They're so colourful, I don't recognise the variety.'

Murdoch's eyes went back to her as she turned to him. The butterflies' wings thrummed as the two of them kissed, one butterfly, in particular diving over them, leaving a trail of glitter.

Lily was breathless. 'Murdoch, I...'

'Shush, let's not rush, it's got to be right, I don't want this spoilt. Here, I got you something.' He pulled out a small pouch and tipped the contents onto her hand. It was another charm, a tiny silver hand trowel. 'I thought you could put it on the same chain as the watering can, I noticed you wear it all the time.'

'I do, thank you, it's lovely, but if you buy me any more I'm going to have to put them on a bracelet and I can't wear that when I'm gardening.'

'Okay, no more charms. I'll have to think of something else,' he added at her crestfallen look. He kissed her again before they walked back.

The next morning Lily went to see her parents. Speaking to them on the phone was not the same as seeing them in person. Her father seemed embarrassed, but her mother was slightly more upbeat, although Lily felt she was a bit tense. By the time she left, it was a little easier and she was pleased, if surprised, that her dad was changing his job and going to the big Home Centre on the outskirts of town. He was starting in three weeks, the supermarket relieved not to be paying any more money while he was off sick. His new employers had been sympathetic when he explained how he and his wife had been working through a difficult time but were on the right road now. They appreciated his honesty.

She left them, had a quick catch up with Amy and promised to see her later in the week and fill her in on all the gossip. Amy herself had a new boyfriend and wanted to talk about *him,* but once she pinned Lily down, said she could wait.

Finally, she stepped off the bus and found her way to Mr Wavish's office. They weren't normally open on a Saturday, but he'd made arrangements to be there. She was now very nervous. She had all the paperwork that Roo had printed off for her, along with prints of photos she had on her phone of Murdoch, one, a really nice close-up.

'Lily, how nice to see you, please come in, can I make you some tea?'

Hello Mr Wavish, not just at the moment thank you.'

'Well, then, what is it I can do for you?'

'I think it's something I might be able to do for you. My boyfriend, well he wasn't my boyfriend, he was just a friend, but he is now, he works with me at Roots and told me his mother had left him when he was eight.' She knew she was babbling a bit, but once she started, couldn't stop. 'He was brought up in the park homes, where some travellers had settled?' She didn't notice Alexander's face harden as he listened to her. 'He got a copy of her birth certificate,' she started spreading the papers over the table, 'and my friend, another friend, who doesn't work with me, but we're at Eden, has newspaper connections and Grandma told me she remembered your name after you'd seen me in the garden centre. She told me about your daughter...'

'Stop!' he shouted and Lily jumped in shock. 'I'm very disappointed in you, Lily, I never expected this.'

'Oh, but please, I haven't finished.'

'Yes, you most certainly have. Do you know how many people over the years have come to us claiming to know where Caroline was or what had happened to her? It broke my wife's heart, *both* of our hearts. I had to put a stop to it. Is it money that you want? I'll give you some if it makes you go away.'

Lily was struck dumb with shock. She'd never expected this reaction. She stood, shaking now with a mixture of anguish and anger. 'I don't want your *money*, Mr Wavish, I was only trying to help. Murdoch's mother's name on his birth certificate was Caroline Carruthers, your late wife's maiden name I believe. Here are some photos of what I hoped you would see was your grandson. He's a wonderful person, you don't deserve him! Thank God I didn't tell him I was coming here.' She turned and fighting back tears, ran.

Alexander sat, remembering all the times their hopes had been raised. Caroline *Carruthers*, it meant nothing, there must be hundreds of people with that name. He leant forward, scooping the papers up in a fury, to put in the bin. Staring up at him was a photo of a young man, about Lily's age probably. Brown hair and eyes, nothing unusual about that. A butterfly in the room, which had entered when he opened the window fluttered above him. A cloud moved away from the sun and a bright light illuminated the photo for a second, just long enough to see the hint of green specks in the brown eyes.

With trembling fingers, he picked up the picture and looked at it again. The face reminded him of Caroline... no! he just wanted it to. He threw it down on to the table, but he couldn't stop looking at it. There were other photos, he picked those up and sat there, for a long time.

* * *

Lily rushed into a public toilet and was violently sick. She was so upset, she sat and sobbed, she'd messed it all up and now they'd never know if he had a family or not. Some girls came in, took one look at her and hurried out again, not wanting to get involved.

After a while, she splashed cold water on her face and used soaked paper towels to press over her eyes. When she thought she looked half respectable, she headed back.

'Lily love, whatever is the matter? Come here.' Grandma opened her arms.

'I just got a bit upset, after I'd seen Mum and Dad,' she hated lying but there was no help for it. 'I'll go and have a shower, freshen up a bit before I see the others.'

'Merry's on a day off, so it's just Murdoch and Reg, he's settled in nicely. You go on up, I'll make you a nice cup of tea.'

Murdoch put her slightly reddened eyes down to her visit home and didn't press her on anything but kept up a tirade of cheerful banter about everything that had happened that day.

She felt like screaming and resorted to an excuse as old as time, feeling a complete fraud, on top of everything else. 'I'm sorry I'm not good company, time of the month, you know? I feel shitty so I'm going to bed. I'll be fine tomorrow.'

'You poor thing, do you need anything?'

She felt terrible, that wasn't a lie and she could hardly look at him, knowing what he could have had.

'No, thanks, I'm not fit company when I'm like this.' Managing a weak smile, she squeezed his hand and wished today had never happened.

Sunday she was still subdued but had to try and put everything behind her. Merry was back at work, singing happily and smiling at everybody. She kept saying that she felt this Bank Holiday Monday was going to be the best day ever. It was very busy and kept Lily's mind occupied which at least she was pleased about. It hadn't helped that she'd had a text from Roo asking how the visit had gone. She sent a reply saying, not as she'd hoped, but didn't want to talk now, he sent back, *Luv & hugs xx.*

She shook off her mood by the end of the day. Murdoch was going to visit his father and Merry stayed on for a bit to help prepare some more baskets for what she kept saying, was going to be a special day. She'd had to pop out for a while earlier, so was making up the time.

* * *

Alexander had gone to the woodland burial site where he always found it peaceful to walk the paths, remember Rosemary and mull anything over that was on his mind. He didn't find it peaceful today. He had hardly slept, staying up most of the night reading the smoothed-out pieces of paper that he'd almost destroyed. Making his way towards the plot where his wife had, given herself back to the earth, as she had put it when requesting this type of burial, he saw a carpet of wood anemones adorning the area and two last bluebells, intertwined, holding onto their life for as long as possible. He liked to think that signified them both, their lives together. After Caroline had left, it had always been just them, their grief making them stronger. What would she have believed?

The airline report had given the name of Caroline Wavish, so maybe she was still in Cyprus? Well, she knew where her parents were, just her father now of course. How could she have left an eight-year-old boy? He couldn't imagine any mother doing that. In many ways that pushed her further from his mind than ever. But the boy? Now nearly nineteen, a grandson, as Lily had said? He was terrified at being disappointed again, but the photos...

He stood for a while and watched the most beautiful butterfly skipping over the wood anemones and alighting on the stalks of the bluebells. Then he noticed a piece of newsprint tangled in the roots. He couldn't abide litter, especially in a place like this, as he retrieved it, the creature flew right past him and for a second, he could have sworn it had a face. *Don't be daft, that's the sort of thing Rosemary would have said.*

Holding the paper and walking towards the nearest bin, a photo and headline caught his eye. It was from a while ago when he'd taken all those pots, for the bulb competition. He'd seen it before but not really paid attention.

It was some of the staff at Roots and there was the boy again, looking self-conscious, Alex thought with a wry smile. He had found it on Rosemary's burial site, like a sign. Was it telling him something, should he give it one more try? The two bluebells sank to the ground, their job done and the butterfly nodded its thanks as she flew away.

*   *   *

Murdoch groaned as he switched off his alarm, another Bank Holiday, which meant a lot of people not really knowing what they wanted. He hoped Lily would perk up a bit today, obviously, she suffered during her time but he'd never seen her quite so down. She'd had a bath and gone to bed early again last night, just as he got back from the hospital.

Brian was feeling quite upbeat about the prospect of a new home. 'I promise you,' he'd said, 'I won't mess this one up. Until I move on, it'll be like a little palace all nice for you when you're on your own. *If* you're on your own, that is.'

Lily, living there? He didn't want that, especially with Megan on the same site. She'd probably feel her grandparents would need her as they got older and want to stay with them.

He thought about that as he tried to wake himself up. How were they ever going to make this work, he wouldn't live off her, that was for sure. He was earning a bit more now, with the profits from the vegetables and a few garden designs that he'd helped customers with. Stuart said, anything he did outside of work was fine, it all helped to promote the centre anyway.

Lily wasn't down for breakfast.

'She'll be out in an hour or so,' Madge said. 'We won't be busy to start with and she's helping me with all the bedding first.'

'I've told you I'll do my own bedding.' Murdoch argued once again.

'And I told *you*, that it's easier to do it all together, I'm making pasties for lunch as well, you'll be glad of those later.'

'I guess I will,' he knew when he was beaten. 'I'll just have another coffee to fortify myself. Tomorrow, I'm going to fix those loose slates on the back porch, I have to do something for you.'

Madge smiled.

It was a very busy day with all the usual serious and not so serious customers. Murdoch's heart sank when he recognised the clematis woman and... Hugh, trailing behind her.

'You, young man, I want a word.'

'Yes, is there a problem?'

She *beamed* at him. 'Far from it. Those Montana *Rubens* are magnificent this year, masses of flowers. Wonderful aren't they Hugh?'

'Yes, dear.'

'Anyway, here's my card. I want you to come and landscape me a proper rockery, can you do that?'

'Err, yes, are you sure...'

'I have some pictures of the sort of thing I want, but of course, I will be open to your... suggestions, you obviously know what you're talking about. Give me a ring next week. Come along Hugh, there are far too many people here today.'

Murdoch tucked the card into his pocket. It was more work and money. He'd do a rockery for the Devil if he got paid for it.

Merry laughed when he told her and said she'd known it was going to be a good day and it wasn't over yet.

He saw Lily a few times but had no chance to talk much. It was getting towards the end of the day and he was looking forward to another pasty, Madge always made plenty.

Lily was bringing in some of the display plants from outside of the gates when she saw a large car pulling up. *Oh no, not another customer, it's nearly time to close.*

Mr Wavish got out. 'Lily, I err, think I may have been a bit hasty, would you accept my sincere apologies for what I said?'

Her heart leapt. 'I rushed in, not explaining myself properly and you were upset, that was the last thing I wanted.'

'Is he here and have you said anything to him?'

'He *is* here and I've not said a word. He doesn't know anything about what I've done. Umm, shall I send him out?'

'Maybe that would be best. I-I'm very nervous, will you stay, while I talk to him?'

'Only if you want me to.'

'I do.'

'Well, hello stranger, I've hardly seen you all day.' Murdoch was putting his gloves away and Merry hovered in the background.

'Yeah, I'm sorry about that. Listen, do you remember I said I might have a surprise for you? Well, come out to the car park, there's somebody who wants to meet you and please, don't be cross with me.'

'Why would I be cross with you, what's all this about?'

Murdoch saw a man he guessed was in his sixties, kind looking but who seemed quite on edge. The man walked towards him and stared.

'You wanted to talk to me, sir?'

'Murdoch, my name is Alexander Wavish.'

'Lady Foxmore's friend?'

'Yes, I am, but more important than that, I believe I may be your Grandfather.'

* * *

Much later, in the cottage, after a lot of tea had been drunk and a lot of words spoken, Murdoch still felt as if he was dreaming. His mother was Caroline Wavish, this man's daughter. He was told the whole story and shown photographs. The last ones of her before she disappeared, he found hard to recognise from his memory of her coloured blonde hair but there was no mistaking the eyes.

As soon as Alex saw them for real he knew. They could have all the tests in the world, but he *knew*. This young man was his flesh and blood. He'd even brought a photo out of his wallet, of his mother. Caroline, with different hair, but he could see it was her holding the young Murdoch.

'Lily, why didn't you tell me?' Murdoch sounded hurt.

'I had to know it was a possibility before you knew anything. It may all have been a dead end.'

'Perhaps Murdoch and I might have some time together now?' Alex asked kindly.

'Of course, I'll leave you to it.' She worried that Murdoch didn't appreciate how she'd gone about this and whether it would put any strain on their relationship.

Alex waited until the door closed. 'This is a shock for both of us, but a nice one, I hope. She thinks the world of you, you do realise that? To go through all this to try and bring us together.'

'Yeah, I guess so.'

'This isn't going to be an instant thing. We need to get to know each other but I really hope that's what you want. Why don't you bring Lily for tea at the weekend and you can look through some more photos, see your mother when she was young and... your Grandmother. She'd have been so proud of you.'

'I-I'm sorry I won't get the chance to know her. There's no doubt about this is there, you really are my Grandfather?'

'If you want a blood test or whatever, we can do that, but I can see it. You're my *only* Grandchild and I don't want to let you out of my life now.' Once the boy was fully accepting and they had built a relationship, then Alex would tell him about his inheritance. He hoped it would go to him *and* Lily, he owed her so much.

'Tea would be good, thanks, umm, I don't quite know what to call you, it's a bit odd at the moment.'

'Call me Alex. Shall we go and find Lily?'

* * *

Merry sat in her cottage, which wouldn't be hers for much longer. Her job was done, there was no need to move on immediately, she liked the garden centre and she'd give them time to find a replacement. A letter had been left that Murdoch would find a few years from now, along with a special planting of bulbs, lying dormant until the right time.

Epilogue

POLLINATION

The transfer of pollen to allow fertilization

FIVE YEARS LATER

Two-year-old Poppy watched her father putting seeds into the holes he'd made in the earth. Murdoch guided her hand which held the small watering can, amused at his daughter's tongue, poking out in concentration.

'We've finished now Poppy, let's get cleaned up for tea, Mummy has invited all the family tonight.' Mummy, Lily, his wife and soulmate. He'd proposed at her twenty-first birthday party with all their family and her friends, now his friends as well. Poppy had been a surprise bonus to the many future plans he and Lily had discussed on numerous occasions and if things hadn't happened quite in the order they'd expected, so what? Arriving a week after their first wedding anniversary, she was the most cherished and wanted addition he could have ever hoped for.

This was just a family tea tonight. Robert and Corrine, settled and happy together, Stuart and Madge, Stuart frail now after two small heart attacks and an operation and Murdoch's grandfather, Alex.

It had been a long road discovering each other but they had walked it together and were now close. Closer than he'd ever been to his own father, who was a traveller again. Brian checked in with his son from time to time and was delighted with his little granddaughter.

Alex had explained what decisions he and Rosemary had made and put into place. Murdoch's future was assured and money had already been made available to him, despite his protests. He justified it by investing in the centre and making sure both he and Lily had a decent vehicle to drive and her Grandparents wanted for nothing. An extension had been built onto the cottage, almost self-contained so that Stuart didn't have to negotiate stairs anymore. He liked to say it made Duckie's life easier and everybody agreed with him to keep the peace.

Murdoch was beginning to be a success in his own right. The stumpery at Foxmore had been featured in a high-class magazine and then picked up by a TV gardening programme. Lily insisted he be the one interviewed as he'd done nearly all the work. Some of the gardens he had designed, now with Lily as well, were regularly mentioned and opened to the public for charity days. His life had turned around and he couldn't be happier.

Lily was arranging her vase of flowers for the centre of the table when she felt his arms around her. 'You two took your time.'

'You know what Poppy's like when she's with me, can't tear her away from the flowers, I don't know where she gets it from.' He kissed the back of her neck and moved his hand down to her stomach. 'How's the little one?'

'I felt a flutter today, I think we should tell them all tonight. Roo's been pestering and asking when he's going to be a Godfather again.'

'Tell the family first, then you can call him. Is he back with Sam yet?'

'I expect so, I wish they would just accept they're meant to be and settle down. Oh, by the way, I was clearing out a bit more stuff for the new bedroom and there's a box of what looks like some of your old papers and sketches, can you sort it?'

'I'm going to have a shower, Poppy's in with Madge at the moment. I'll have a quick look when I've changed.'

The box was dusty and there were some faded drawings on the top of the pile. All rubbish, he thought as he pulled them out. An envelope fell on the bed, with his name on. As he opened it, wondering if it was an old birthday card he'd missed, a load of glitter fell out. *Christmas card maybe?* It was a letter.

Dear Murdoch,

**I hope you think of me sometimes,
your 'strange' friend, Merry.
I am sure you are now having the life you
deserved and are happy beyond measure. *I*
always knew things would turn out well for you.**

Your friend,

Merry Faith Good

PS Check the crocus patch

The crocus patch? What was she going on about? She'd never given a forwarding address when she left and was greatly missed. He wandered out to the garden and looked towards the crocuses, all in flower now. They'd been planted in drifts, as Rosemary had done, to look natural. Now, they seemed to be more in a line.

Her name was buzzing about in his head. Merry Faith Good and as he was thinking about her, the flowers seemed to spell out another name...

FAIRY GODMOTHER

The End

Carmella McKenzie

HABERDASHERY

A little twist of magic has this story all sewn up

Also by this author

HABERDASHERY

Hannah has always been a bit of a dreamer. She loves nothing more than escaping into the pages of a bodice ripper, where the men are a darn sight more impressive than her husband, Michael. It would be fair to say her 5-year marriage was not living up to her romantic expectations.

She channels her frustrations and creativity into her sewing and crafts some beautiful pieces. It started with her own wedding dress, which had a strangely magical look after she discovered a mysterious haberdashery shop and its even more mysterious owner, the quirky Fae Dorothy Grim.

A chance encounter with a tall, dark stranger sets a chain of events in motion, which turn her life around. Still spinning, she hurtles from one big life change to another. Can Hannah make, cut, sew and put a special finish on her own life?

This heart-warming tale will have you rooting for Hannah as she stitches together her new life.

Follow Carmella on Facebook
www.facebook.com/carmellamckenzieauthor/

Or visit her website
www.mckenziesisters.com

Carmella would love to hear from you if you have
enjoyed this story. Please also leave her a
review on Amazon.